How to Steal a Piano

and other stories

John Hughes

Matador
9 Priory Business Park,
Wistow Road, Kibworth Beauchamp,
Leicestershire. LE8 0RX
Tel: (+44) 116 279 2299
Fax: (+44) 116 279 2277
Email: books@troubador.co.uk
Web: www.troubador.co.uk/matador

ISBN 9781788039765

British Library Cataloguing in Publication Data.
A catalogue record for this book is available from the British Library.

Printed and bound in the UK by 4edge limited
Typeset in 10.5pt Minion Pro by Troubador Publishing Ltd, Leicester, UK

Matador is an imprint of Troubador Publishing Ltd

For my sister Wendy

... and also for Jenny
with lots of love from
Uncle Author

John Hughes

X

ACKNOWLEDGMENTS

Thanks to Sebastian Wormell, *Harrods* Archivist, for allowing me to see again the piano sales ledgers, including my own entries as a salesman, after thirty-five years.

Thanks to Vera Peiffer for advice on correct and incorrect use of the German language.

Thanks to *Brighton and Hove Stuff* for permission to reproduce the photograph at the end of *Rude Words.*

Thanks to Nicola Holt of the *Metropolitan Police Dog Training Establishment* for information about the naming of police dogs.

AUTHOR'S NOTE

Although some of these stories are written in the first person, it should not automatically be assumed that I am the narrator. On the other hand, nor should it necessarily be assumed I am not – with the obvious exception of *Woof Justiss*.

CONTENTS

HOW TO STEAL A PIANO

I sat on the toilet with my trousers and underpants round my ankles and for the next quarter of an hour let nature gradually take its strained, painful course. It took me even longer sometimes, constipation having been a lifelong companion. My first wife was a nurse and one of the abiding legacies from our twenty-year marriage was a familiarity with the Bristol Stool Form Scale. She gave me a little laminated summary sheet, the size of a credit card, with all seven types of stool illustrated on one side, and concise, imaginative descriptions of each on the reverse… or backside might be more appropriate. I have it in my wallet to this day. Typically, mine will be Type 1 (*separate hard lumps, like nuts – hard to pass*) or at best Type 2 (*sausage-shaped but lumpy*). The perfect Type 4 (*like a sausage or snake – smooth and soft*) has generally eluded me over the years.

As I struggled with my scatological ordeal, I mulled over the morning's events in court, wondering at the strangeness and irony of the situation. I was fairly certain the defendant had no idea who I was; he certainly gave no hint of recognition of any kind. We hadn't seen each other for thirty-five years and I'd aged and changed in appearance as you would expect. I was sixty now with barely any hair, and what I did have was pure white. I wore glasses and my skin was wrinkled. Of course he too had changed, yet curiously I recognised him instantly. He was older than me by almost a decade and looked frail and wizened. Yet the distinctive voice was the same, so too were a few giveaway mannerisms. He was using a different name, but there was no doubt in my mind. The man in the dock was Martin Allwright.

Thirty-five years, two marriages, a divorce and two children had passed since then. Nevertheless, a steady and successful career had underpinning it all for me. And the irony was that it may never have happened were it not for Martin and the rewards of an adventure we'd shared as young men.

When I had eventually finished on the toilet, I had lunch alone in my chambers and deliberated over how to deal with this man. As I did so, rightly or wrongly, I allowed memories to flood back into my consciousness in a fine detail that had been suppressed for a long time, and for good reason.

It happened in the summer of 1981, during the weeks building up to the royal wedding.

★ ★ ★

I can't remember why I was over in the piano workshop that morning. In the three years I worked at *Harrods* I probably only ever went there a handful of times. I spent almost all of my working day on the shop floor trying to sell the things. There must have been a query of some sort.

It was a large, light and airy space on the third floor of the building, tucked away in Trevor Square on the other side of the Brompton Road from the store itself. This was where deliveries were made and departments had stock rooms; I seem to remember that turkeys were plucked there in December. It was connected to the store by a tunnel under the Brompton Road.

The workshop manager was an Irishman called Aiden; he was pleasant enough, quietly spoken, easygoing and seemed to keep the schedule of repair and restoration jobs flowing nicely. It was something of an open secret that he brought pianos of his own in to do private work from time to time; no one seemed to mind, and no harm done so long as the *Harrods* work took priority. It surprised many people to learn that *Harrods* sold second-hand as well as new pianos; the store often purchased back instruments originally sold there as new, usually in part-exchange. But the heyday was over, and by the time my story takes place the second-hand trade was on the decline; once a thriving business, now merely a tag on to the sale of new instruments.

Even so, the workshop was crammed with pianos of all shapes, sizes and makes. On the floor were the instruments being worked on in varying states of repair or restoration. Along one wall was a storage unit where grand pianos, devoid of legs and wearing padded covers, were parked in a long line. Along another wall were all the legs. Some instruments were waiting to be repaired, others had been restored and were awaiting delivery. I wandered along them, reading the labels.

At the very end was a piano that seemed slightly different from the rest but I couldn't immediately discern why. I could tell from the size that it wasn't a full concert grand – a medium I guessed, under six feet in length. Then I realised. The cover looked older and had a neglected air about it. It was thick with dust. I looked at the once bright, now faded yellow label:

SOLD Jane V. Walker – Shropshire. H71529.

All *Harrods* pianos had a unique identifier – an H followed by a series of numbers. They were logged in a set of ledgers dating back to the very first instrument sold when *Harrods* opened their piano department in 1895. The ledgers were stored in a rack in the buyer's office in the corner of the department.

"What's this one, Aiden?" I asked.

Aiden came over and took a look. "Haven't a clue," he said. "It was here when I came and that's four years next month. I keep meaning to look it up when I'm over in the boss's office but I never remember. You don't fancy checking do you, James?"

"That's a job for Brown-nose." I mimicked the accent of a supercilious upper-class twit. "*I am the department manager, you know.*"

Aiden smiled. "He's a useless piece of gobshite, that one. You do it or it won't get done properly."

"I will." From my jacket pocket I took out my scoring notebook in which I marked down each contact and circled it if it was a sale – to work out my contact to sale ratio – and scribbled down the H number on the last page.

I promptly forgot about it.

★ ★ ★

A week or so later, having made a sale and feeling rather smug, I was flicking through my notebook to update my ratio. In truth, I had nothing to be smug about; my sales volume was abysmal and it was my first success in ages. I'd picked up the notebook idea from a friend – Martin Allwright no less. It was motivating to see your conversion rate improve, though disheartening when it slipped in the other direction. Martin worked at a piano showroom in New Oxford Street called Curetons, long since gone. They were doing well in those days, conveniently situated just around the corner from Denmark Street, London's answer to Tin Pan Alley, with its plethora of music shops and recording studios.

I noticed the H number on the back page, and puzzled over it for a moment. Ah yes, the dust-covered grand at the end of the storage rack in the piano workshop. I'd promised Aiden I'd look it up for him. The department was quiet. Raymond, the other piano salesman, was sitting at a Knight upright playing some Chopin, oblivious to everything around him, unaware of his surroundings; he rarely sold anything. The department manager, Clarence Brownlow, was sitting at his desk talking quietly on the phone – probably to his weird girlfriend Debra. So I wandered over to the buyer's office. The door was ajar. The buyer's desk was empty but our clerk, Laura, was at her desk, reading a magazine and sucking her thumb.

"Is Mr Huxley around?" I asked.

"At lunch. Probably in the pub. Why?"

"Oh nothing, just a query about a piano." I looked across to the row of leather-bound tomes that filled a whole shelf along the office wall. "Mind if I take a look?"

"Do anything you like. I'm easy."

"So I've heard."

"Shove off!"

"How's that limp boyfriend of yours?"

"None of your business!"

"Why do you suck your thumb, Laura?"

"Piss off!"

"Fancy a bit of nookie?"

Laura hesitated, then in a matter-of-fact tone said: "Yes I do." She turned and stared at me, a look of withering disdain. "But not with you."

Rejected yet again by our insanely gorgeous, busty, leggy, blonde clerk, I had no answer to that so I checked the H number again and pulled out the ledgers until I found the one containing H71529. I lugged it over to Mr Huxley's desk and sat down in his chair.

"You'll be for it if he catches you sitting there," said Laura.

"I'll take that chance." I flicked through the heavy-duty, almost cardboard-like pages of the ledger. Pianos were entered in numerical order by H number as they were purchased by the store. The numbers were printed in a column towards the middle of each row, and the rows spread across each double-page spread of the ledger. All other entries were made by hand in ink. Pianos were added into stock in one hand, details of sales in another – a division of labour between buyer and clerk.

It took no time at all to find the piano in question. The entry read as follows:

Date of Purchase:	*26th March 1971*
Name of Piano:	*Bechstein*
From Whom Purchased:	*New*
Description:	*Model L ("Lilliput") 5' 6"*
	Maker's No. 16205
Stock Number:	*71529*
Date Sold:	*4th June 71*
Cost:	*£2,495*
Selling:	*£4,495*
Price Sold:	*£4,495*
Customer's Name:	*Miss Jane V. Walker*
Address:	*Rose Cottage, Plough Lane,*
	Much Wenlock, Shropshire.
Salesman:	*08049 (Thomas Morgan)*
Terms:	*Cheque*
Delivery:	*Store until delivery instructions*
	received. Customer abroad for
	summer season.

I wrote it all down in my notebook. Sold ten years ago, almost to the day. Must have been sitting in storage ever since. No wonder it was covered in dust. "What are you doing anyway?" asked Laura between thumb sucks.

"Checking a query."

"Anything I can help you with?"

"I just offered and you turned me down."

"Piss off!"

"Tell me, Laura, how can someone who looks as gorgeous as you be so potty-mouthed?"

"Same way you're good on the piano. Lots of practice."

"You're only nineteen."

"I started young."

The office door opened and our beloved department manager, Clarence Brownlow, popped his head in. "Mr Huxley about?"

"At lunch," replied Laura, "as you very well know because I heard him telling you as he went."

"Ah yes, many thanks." He looked across at me sitting at the buyer's desk with the sales ledger open in front of me. "What are you up to, umm...?" The tone was disapproving.

"My name is James."

"I know. You ought to be out on the floor. What are you up to?"

"About 1971."

"I'm sorry?" Blank expression from Brown-nose whose sense of humour was non-existent. "If you have any queries they ought to come to me... I am the department manager, you know."

I supressed a snigger. "Just a bit of personal research."

"Yes, well get back onto the shop floor as soon as you can, would you?" The door closed.

I caught Laura's eye. "Such a knob." I placed the ledger back on the shelf. So, I ruminated, that was one hell of a long summer season. Ten years! Why did she never make contact to arrange delivery? What happened? Did she die? Did she forget? She was a *Miss*. Perhaps she met someone on holiday and got married and her husband hated music. Perhaps she was very old and died. She must have been worth a few bob to let nearly five thousand quid slip by without a second thought. I closed the sales ledger deep in thought. I glanced through my notes. Out loud I said: "Miss Jane V. Walker… I wonder what the V stands for."

"I've got a suggestion," said Laura, helpfully.

"I bet you have."

"I was going to say Virginia."

"Hmm, in terms of your vulgar vocabulary that's neither one thing nor the other."

"Anyway, who's Miss Jane V. Walker when she's at home?"

"Just a customer."

"Has she made a complaint about you?"

"Nothing like that."

"You'd better get back on the floor then, otherwise tosser will be back any minute."

As if on cue, Clarence Brownlow appeared and opened his mouth to speak. I beat him to it.

"I know… you're the department manager."

I barged past him onto the floor. It was still a large department in those days and a sea of pianos stretched out in front of me. There were few people about, but my eagle eye quickly honed in on an elderly gentleman towards the far end looking at an upright Yamaha. He was giving out strong buying signals; gently playing a chord, touching the sides, inspecting the edges checking for scuffs and scrapes. Clarence Brownlow, who was extremely competitive and hated losing a sale to anyone else, had followed me out of the office and seen him too. I sensed rather than saw him flitting between pianos at speed to try and reach the man first. Suddenly there was a loud crash and he disappeared behind a Bösendorfer concert grand. He'd collided with a piano stool.

I strolled nonchalantly up to the man. "I wouldn't recommend this one, sir. Cheap Japanese rubbish."

He made eye contact, a puzzled, almost anxious look on his face. Then he saw I was smiling, and smiled back. "I know that's not true, young man. Yamaha is a good make."

"It is indeed. Would you care to try it?"

"Well, I'm not sure." He glanced around shyly.

"Or would you like me to play it while you listen… so you can hear the tone?"

"Would you mind?"

"I'd be delighted. Are you thinking about a piano for yourself?"

"My wife actually. A surprise anniversary gift. We've had an old upright for years but it's past its best."

"Very thoughtful. What music does she like?"

He thought for a moment. "Ooh all sorts. Well now, let's think… the good old tunes I suppose. We met during the war and she's fond of the songs from that era."

I played *The White Cliffs of Dover*. Ten minutes later he was sitting next to me at my desk writing out a cheque.

Clarence Brownlow looked on from the middle distance, rubbing his knee. His face was puce and his entire being seethed with frustration at having missed out on a sale. I smiled across at him and mouthed a single word that reflected my feelings towards him.

★ ★ ★

Martin Allwright took a sip from his pint of *Guinness*, a draw on his *Dunhill* cigarette, and sat back in his chair with the air of a man whose contentment level is nigh on complete. He was slightly built with lean features; good looking and a snappy dresser. Today he was in a pinstripe suit with a paisley tie and highly polished shoes. He was attracted to, as well as attractive towards, women and to remain friends with him you had to get used to the fact that his eye contact was rarely on you, but any half decent woman within view. Nothing personal; it's just the way he was.

We were in *The Bunch of Grapes*, a pub on the Brompton Road a couple of hundred yards down from *Harrods*, almost opposite the Oratory. A quick one after work, Martin had suggested on the phone earlier; he could be over from Curetons by six. Quick ones after work with him were rarely that. But I didn't care. He was a good mate and great company; and I had no other plans.

"So," I said. "Did you score today?"

"I did indeed. A Kemble upright and a Yamaha grand – C3. You?"

"Well done. Yes, a Yamaha too – upright."

11

"U1?"

"Larger – U3."

"I bet that put Brown-nose's hooter out of joint."

"Just slightly. He belted across the showroom to try and beat me to the customer. Tripped over a piano stool and fell on his arse."

Martin guffawed. He too had worked at *Harrods* – in fact he got me the job there – and he knew first-hand what Brownlow was like.

"Still a tosser then."

"Bigger than ever."

"He was the reason I left. Plopped in as a showroom manager over my head with no relevant experience other than being a failed concert pianist and a Class A knob. The job should have been mine. And to have your line manager in direct competition with his own salesmen – on commission. Outrageous!"

"Yep, sometimes it's a hard cross to bear. He gets to see the post first, sits by the phone and takes the calls. All the incoming leads go to him. He gets all the good leads."

"It's tough being a salesman."

"If only I could get the good leads."

"It's not like that at Curetons. They're a good company to work for."

"Perhaps I should jump ship like you did."

Martin gave me a quizzical look. "Would you be interested?"

"Are they looking to recruit?"

"Not at the moment, but they may be at some stage in the future. If you're serious I might be able to put a word in for you."

"I'd appreciate it." I smiled. "Funny, you got me this job – now you're hinting at getting me another."

"It would be good to work with you again." He took another sip and another drag. "You know, you could have a good career in piano retail, or in the piano manufacturing business. There are still some fine British companies around – Knight, Danemann, Broadwood, Kemble."

"I'd definitely be interested in moving on, Martin. I'm maybe not the most ambitious man in the world, but I want to progress."

He leaned forward and glanced to either side to make sure we weren't being overhead. When he was sure, he spoke in a hushed tone, as if imparting a secret of enormous worth. "I may be able to help you – more than you think. You see, there's something that all the main men in the piano industry have in common. If you're prepared to embrace it then you're halfway there, and pretty much ensured a career for life."

"And that is?"

"They're all Masons."

"Oh!"

"You sound surprised."

"I wasn't expecting that. I don't know much about it."

"It's like a big private club. There are local groups, called lodges, and we meet up once a week. Mostly social, but the members are all useful to know and I've made some really good contacts."

"Have you been in it long?"

"A couple of years."

"Was that how you made the move to Curetons?"

13

"It helped."

"Is there a joining fee?"

"No, but there are certain… there's an induction process, shall we say. To be honest, James, a lot of members join purely to get on in the world – to make contacts in their business. That's how I got involved. I was approached by someone who told me pretty much what I've just told you, so I asked if I could become a member."

I thought about this but said nothing. The notion of a secret club didn't appeal; in fact it sounded rather childish. My somewhat embryonic political views veered towards left rather than right and this had a whiff of privilege and elitism about it that left me cold. Years later, I realised that that was the moment when I should have shown more interest, more enthusiasm, asked to join even. I didn't. I sat there expecting Martin to take the initiative. He didn't. So the moment passed. Martin never mentioned it again. Nor did I.

"Still, being honest," Martin continued, "I don't go to every meeting. About one in three. Chrissie thinks I do but it's a good opportunity to see Imogen.

Chrissie was his wife, Imogen was his bit on the side. I knew the whole saga. He lived with Chrissie in a flat in Acton, and he'd been seeing Imogen for a couple of years. They'd met during his *Harrods* days; she was a buyer in Perfumery. At that time, in my early twenties, single and eager to find someone to love and cherish and devote myself to for the rest of my life, I found it all rather sordid. I never said so, but that's how I felt at the time.

We moved on to talk about other things. The next round was mine and I went to the bar; a *Guinness* for Martin, a pint of *Directors* for me. I fumbled picking up the change and stuffed it into my jacket pocket to sort out back at the table. As I did, my notebook fell out and landed open at the back page.

"What's this?" said Martin, picking it up and reading my scribble. "*Bechstein L. Sold 1971, Salesman, Thomas Morgan* – good heavens I know Tom, he's in our lodge. *Miss Jane V. Walker, Much Wenlock.* What's that all about?"

"Oh, it's a piano in storage over at Trevor Square. I noticed it and looked it up out of curiosity. It's still there, awaiting delivery."

"After ten years? You're joking!" I nodded. Martin was staring at the details. "Just under five grand. They've gone up since then."

"Doubled. And yes, it's still there."

"Ten years. She's either forgotten about it or died, this Miss Walker."

"That's what I thought."

"Does Aiden know anything about it?"

I shook my head. "Nothing. It was before his time."

"Before everyone's time."

"Except Harry. How long has he worked there?"

"A lifetime. I wouldn't be surprised if he's been there since he was demobbed. You should ask him about the piano."

"I think I will."

Martin ran his finger across the purchaser's name. "I wonder what the V stands for."

"Yes, I was wondering that too."

★ ★ ★

Wilfred Huxley was a charming man. He'd been a professional tap dancer in his younger days and his claim to fame was to have performed with a very well-known American singer when she came to London in the early sixties; the one who sang of a land over the rainbow... somewhere. There were just two dancers on stage, one on either side of her, and their prime role, according to Mr Huxley, was not to dance so much as to keep her upright. She liked a drink. So did he. When he retired from dancing he'd come to work in *Harrods* and had been there ever since, mainly in the linen department. He adored the place. The opportunity to become a buyer had come after more than twenty years of service; it meant a move into Pianos which he had made reluctantly. He played a little and was a good organiser but he knew nothing of the piano industry and had to learn it from scratch. I can't be sure but I don't think he was a Freemason.

I was making myself busy lifting up piano lids and dusting before the store opened, feeling fuzzy headed, as you often were after a *quick drink* with Martin Allwright. Wilfred appeared from the direction of the buyer's office and came and stood next to me. His eyes were bloodshot. So were mine.

"Good morning, James," he said in his gentle, soporific voice.

"Morning, Mr Huxley."

"James, Clarence tells me that you were impolite towards him yesterday. You mouthed a rude word at him across the showroom when you were with a customer."

16

"Did I?" I said, sounding mystified.

"Yes you did. A word beginning with *w* that rhymes with *anchor*."

"Oh that. He must have misread my lips, Mr Huxley. I said *rancour*."

"I beg your pardon?"

"I mouthed the word *rancour*. It means bitterness or resentfulness. It must look very similar to *wanker* when mouthed. He was staring at me as if I had stolen his customer. He was full of rancour, so I wanted him to appreciate that I was aware of it."

Mr Huxley pulled a face of absolute disbelief. "I know what *rancour* means." He pondered for a moment, then grinned. "You're a bad boy, young Holloway, I don't believe you for a moment. All I ask is that you don't do it again. He is a *w* that rhymes with *anchor*, we all know that, but please, don't express your opinion across the shop floor."

"I promise."

He began to walk away, then turned. "And for Christ's sake don't ever mouth that he's a runt."

★ ★ ★

I had wanted to escape the shop floor early to nip over to the workshop before we became too busy. Harry Smith was based there and I needed to pick his brains. But I was hindered by some excitement which could not be ignored. Lady Diana Spencer chose that morning to pop in and do a bit of shopping.

She came in early and word spread amongst the staff like wildfire. Before I knew it, she appeared in our

17

department, flanked by a couple of burly bodyguards and with a divisional manager leading the way. Apart from the entourage she appeared very non-descript, wearing blue jeans, a white blouse and pink cardigan. But if you caught a glimpse of her face, she really was stunningly beautiful, even at the tender age of nineteen. Clarence Brownlow, at his obsequious worst, verily flung himself across the room to the piano closest to them and sat down ready to play. Lady Diana, however, had no interest whatsoever in purchasing a piano; she hugged the edge of the department and disappeared into Records.

There then followed a surreal fifteen minutes. The windows into Records from Pianos were one-way. From Pianos you could see into Records but from inside Records all you saw was your own reflection; a mirror effectively. The store detectives often stood outside looking in, trying to catch record thieves red-handed. (I used to annoy them by sitting down at the nearest piano and playing the theme from *Dixon of Dock Green*.) Today, they would have had to queue up; staff appeared in droves from all directions to take a peep at the princess in waiting, as she browsed obliviously. Brownlow tried to move them on but was ignored. Eventually, red-cheeked, he gave up, went back to his desk and pretended to make a phone call.

I took my turn at the window and saw her pick up an Elton John LP, then put it down again, as I would have done. A discerning lady of taste, I thought. Then she picked it up again and handed it to one of her bodyguards to add to her other purchases. I instantly changed my mind about her. Moments later she appeared at the entrance and, with bodyguards and divisional manager in tow, headed off in the direction of Garden Furniture. Miraculously the crowd of gawpers had evaporated.

As Lady Diana Spencer exited, she all but barrelled into Raymond who had been standing in the middle of the department in a daze. She passed within feet of him and smiled her beautiful smile as they made eye contact.

When she had disappeared, he looked towards me. "Who was that?"

"Shirley Bassey," I replied.

"Oh," he said. "I thought she'd be older than that."

* * *

Fortunately for me, Harry came over to the department that afternoon.

Harry Smith was a French polisher who had learned his trade as an apprentice just before the war. A Dunkirk veteran with a limp as a permanent reminder, he spoke with a strong Cockney accent and suffered from chronic wind. On Christmas department outings he curiously adopted a posh voice not unlike the actor Edward Fox, though devoid of his usual profanities and peppered with 'old chaps' in the manner of Joe Gargery talking to Pip; it was strange, eccentric, downright weird even. The glory days of French polishing were over by then and Harry had had to adapt and learn the skills of repairing lacquer and polyester. Inevitably in a department containing nigh on a hundred pianos, accidents happened. Porters bashed trollies into them, customers knocked bags against them, or they collided with each other during rearrangements of the display. Harry was good at his job; a craftsman. When he'd finished a repair job you could barely see where the damage had been done.

The down side about Harry was that if he collared you and there was no way out, he would bore the tits off you on his given subject.

"Generally there's two types of finishes on pyanners nowadays – lacquer and polyester. Polyester's usually the mirror finish on grands and uprights. Though lacquer can achieve the sheen, polyester resin is better to obtain that look due on account of its intrinsic properties. While lacquer is somewhat hard, it's also thin and brittle. Poly, as we say in the business, is thick and durable. I usually tell people that it's got similar properties to glass – looks beautiful for a very long while. Chip it and you're fucked. It don't repair well. Lacquer on the other hand can be easily touched up but don't have the same long term durability, more's the pity. I've seen twenty and thirty-year-old poly pyanners looking in showroom condition but I can't honestly say that about lacquer."

Harry could talk for England but fortunately had a weak bladder and there was mutual relief at hand whenever he started to jog around a bit and uttered those magical words: "Scuse me, sir, I need a drain off."

On this occasion, however, I was the one doing the collaring. Harry was repairing a dent on the corner of an upright.

"Harry…" I began.

"Wish they'd be more careful with them fuckin' trolleys."

"Me too. Harry…"

"Look at this. I'll do me best but it'll never be the same again."

"That's unfortunate. I'm sure you'll make it look like new. Umm, Harry…"

"Yes, sir."

"There's a piano in storage over in the workshop. I wondered if you knew anything about it."

"I don't know nothin' about it."

"I haven't told you which one yet."

"I just repair and polish 'em. Don't know nothin' about storage."

"I just wondered as it's been over there for a long time. Ten years."

"You'd best ask the guvnor… ask Mr Aiden."

"I did and he doesn't know anything either. It's been there since before he came to *Harrods*. I just wondered if you know anything as you're the only person who was here then."

"What make?"

"A Bechstein grand. L model."

"Black? The one on the very end?"

"That's it."

"I know the one you mean but I don't know nothin' about it. I never worked on it coz it's never been out of its covers. What's it still there for? Waste of fuckin' money, buying somethin' like that then leavin' it. Some people got more money than brains. Who's the customer?"

"A lady from Shropshire. Miss Jane V. Walker."

"Maybe she snuffed it."

"That's what I thought."

"I wonder what the V stands for."

21

"Me too, Harry, me too. Vertiginous would be my first guess."

"Do what?"

★ ★ ★

I mentioned that Martin got me the job in *Harrods*. We were in a band together; he played guitar and sang, I played electronic piano. We were called *Melody and Harmony* and performed in social clubs and at functions around and about South West London, where the band was based. I lived in East Sheen in those days, renting a room in a house owned by a barrister. He sowed the seeds in my mind that later grew into a career change.

Rehearsals were on a Thursday evening. We were sitting in a pub in Tolworth having a pre-rehearsal drink one evening when Martin asked if anyone knew anyone who wanted a job selling pianos in *Harrods*. One of his colleagues was leaving, or rather had been invited to leave; late for work too often, or not turning up at all, due to a preference for whisky rather than milk on his Corn Flakes. I was working in a mundane office at the time – first job out of college – and told Martin I'd be very interested. He mentioned me to Mr Huxley who called me in for an interview which consisted of a friendly chat. He had a thing about Deanna Durbin, the Canadian singer and film star. I got the job because not only had I heard of her but I could name one of her films and hum one of her songs. An honours degree in music and years of piano lessons counted for nothing.

Sitting again in that same pub enjoying another pre-rehearsal drink, Martin said to me in a low voice so that no one else could hear: "Did you ask Harry about that piano... you know, the Bechstein grand that's been in storage forever?"

"I did. He's aware of it but wasn't able to tell me anything I didn't know already."

"So it's just sitting there, unclaimed by the woman who bought it ten years ago, off everyone's radar at *Harrods*, and basically forgotten about."

"That's about the sum of it. Such a waste. I wouldn't mind a Bechstein grand to play of an evening. I wonder if they'd let me borrow it."

"I've got a better idea," said Martin blandly. "Why don't we relieve *Harrods* of it altogether?"

I loved a pint of *Directors* in those days, but in a glass or in my mouth and not all over the table top. I had sprayed it everywhere. After I'd mopped up and the moans and groans from other band members had waned and their attention was elsewhere, I eventually replied.

"What, steal it?"

"That's one way of putting it."

"But how?"

"Easy. Phone up, pretend to be Miss whatever her name was..."

"Jane V. Walker."

"That's her. We pretend to be her and phone up and ask for her piano to be delivered."

I stared at him. "You're not serious!"

"Why not?"

"It sounds so simple."

"That's because it *is* simple."

"But how on earth…"

"I've been thinking about it. All we need to do is make a fake call to the department asking for delivery, get Mr Huxley to sign a despatch docket and have it away."

"But surely they'll need some sort of assurance, need to make checks to be sure it's genuine."

"Not necessarily, not if we give all the right details and they match what's on the paperwork – invoice number, date of sale, sale price. Who else would know all that other than the customer who bought the piano?"

"And to what end?"

"Sell it and pocket some cash. Won't get anywhere near the full value of course, but a nice little wedge each."

"Sell it where, who to?"

"Leave that to me. I have contacts."

I was speechless. No words would come. It was time to head off for the rehearsal. As we finished our drinks, Martin said: "Have a think. Let's talk about it another time."

I was rubbish in the rehearsal; my mind was elsewhere. I kept missing cues, playing duff notes, and generally being useless. Martin knew why, but the rest of the band didn't. I apologised at the end; said I wasn't feeling too great. As we were saying our goodnights in the car park, I collared Martin: "Are you serious?"

"About Miss Walker's piano? Deadly serious."

"It's criminal. It's stealing."

"Well, you know, that's one way of looking at it… but only if you get caught. No real harm done. If you can afford to buy a grand worth five grand and forget about

24

it then clearly it's a drop in the ocean. No loss to her whatsoever. Besides, we're only talking about it."

"Are we only talking about it, or are we actually talking about it?"

"We're talking about it."

"Holy cow, we're actually talking about it!"

Martin put his arm round my shoulder. "James, my friend, calm down, we are only talking about it. It's an idea. A thought. That's all. Go home and mull it over. Come over for Sunday lunch. Chrissie's away visiting her mother – we can have a roast down at my local. I'd like to give it some more thought too."

★ ★ ★

On Sunday the conversation continued and in between I had thought about very little else. I was going out with a girl called Jill at the time. We'd spent Saturday together and it had been a disaster. I was preoccupied and quiet and she interpreted it as waning interest in her. She confronted me about it as we said goodnight. I tried to reassure her that it was nothing to do with my feelings for her and that I was genuinely keen to carry on seeing each other. She didn't believe it and dumped me. I barely registered any emotional fallout.

Seated in the corner of Martin's local with plates empty and stomachs full, I pulled out my notebook and put to my would-be partner in crime the points that had occurred to me. As I confronted him with each one it was apparent from his replies that he had thought the whole thing through in detail.

I looked at my notebook. "*One*. Who's going to phone the department and what are they going to say? It could be anyone who answers."

"I'll phone. I'll ask switchboard to put me through to the extension in the showroom, so only one of three could possibly answer – Brown-nose, Raymond or yourself. It must be you who answers of course, so we do it when Brownlow is at lunch and at a precise time so you can make sure you're nearer the phone than Raymond. Brown-nose usually goes at the same time most days as I recall."

"Twelve-thirty, for half an hour."

"Okay, I'll call at quarter to one."

"What if someone else answers?"

"I put the phone down immediately and we try again the next day."

I drew a tick next to the word *One*.

"*Two*. What if Mr Huxley or Brown-nose want to take charge and arrange the delivery? What if they phone the number on the sales invoice and it's still that of Miss Jane V. Walker? What then?"

"If you offer to organise the delivery, Wilfred will be delighted, anything for a quiet life. Brown-nose might try but there's nothing in it for him, no commission, so my guess is he won't want to get involved, especially if he's bombarded with some hot leads on the phone to keep him occupied." He winked. "I can arrange that. After all it's just arranging a delivery. Regarding trying to contact Miss Walker, she has changed address and I shall be giving you the new details for the delivery, fictitious of course – plus a new phone number."

"What if they try calling the new number?"

"It won't work – it'll be false. If push comes to shove you can say you probably wrote it down wrongly when you took the details over the phone."

"What if they try calling her old number? They might end up speaking to the real Miss Walker."

Martin shook his head. "I tried phoning it yesterday."

"And?"

"Disconnected. It no longer exists. So she really has moved or popped her clogs."

I drew a tick next to the word *Two*.

"*Three*. Completing the despatch docket is straightforward, I'm sure Mr Huxley will sign it without any questions. But what about delivery? *Harrods* men will be picking it up and delivering, presumably to the new address. If it's not a real one… how are we going to get round that one?"

"I've thought about this and have a solution. Miss Walker has recently bought some other pieces of furniture for her new home, and she's arranged for it all to be delivered together. They're coming from various stores around London and she's got a delivery firm coordinating it. Everything is arranged and paid for. She is proposing that her delivery men stop off at *Harrods* and pick up her piano en route."

"Sounds a bit weak to me. They'll never buy it."

"Oh I don't know. It'll save *Harrods* a considerable amount of time and money, especially a trip to Shropshire, or even further afield if we decide she's now living in Northumberland – Scotland even! *Harrods* don't charge their customers for deliveries like this, as you know, so it'll be a hefty saving. I think they'll jump at the chance."

"And who will your delivery men be? I hope they know what they're doing."

"Who they are is my concern and it's better that you don't know. They'll know what they're doing."

My pencil hovered over the word *Three* but I didn't draw a tick. Instead I added a question mark.

"*Four*. How the hell do you sell a dodgy grand piano discreetly and what will we get for it?"

"As I've said before, I have contacts – let's leave it like that, shall we? The people who will be in on this know their stuff. Within forty-eight hours it will be on a container ship on its way to… let's just say abroad."

"And the price?"

"Nowhere near the full value. I reckon nearer the cost price back in 1971… a bit more maybe. I'll be happy to get two and a half for it. Broken down, that would mean three hundred for my main contact, and a hundred a piece for two delivery man. That leaves two grand split between us – one each. Not bad for taking a phone call and filling out a despatch docket eh?"

"A thousand pounds! Not bad indeed." My basic weekly take home pay then, not including commission, was £64.

I looked down at my notepad and gave number *Four* a solid tick.

"So what do you think?" said Martin.

Still peering at my notebook, and after a lengthy pause as I struggled to come out with the words, I said: "I don't think I can do it. I'm scared shitless."

"Well, it's up to you, James. We're only talking about

28

it. If you're not comfortable then we can forget the whole idea." The disappointment was apparent in his voice. "It would be a shame though."

"It would indeed."

"Think of the money. What would you do with a thousand quid?"

"I know exactly."

"What?"

I didn't reply.

"Okay," Martin continued. "Look at it this way. Consider the risks. What are they to you personally? You answer the phone in the department and take a message. You check through the records and find the piano is there in the workshop. The customer who owns it wants it delivered, at last. So you inform Mr Huxley, offer to arrange the delivery, get him to sign the despatch docket and liaise with an external delivery firm to come and collect. Where in all that, should anything go tits up at any point in the proceedings, are you culpable? All you did was take a phone call and act accordingly. You'll simply be doing your job. When you think about it there's no risk to you whatsoever. Others are taking the chances, and if anything did go wrong there are no comebacks to you of any sort."

"You and I are friends. There is a connection between us."

"And do you think for one moment that I would betray that friendship and drop you in it if the worst happened?"

"Of course not."

"Thank you. Besides, it would be virtually impossible

to link me with this either. I shall be covering my arse, take my word."

"A thousand quid," I mused.

"Cash." He put on his Orson Welles as Harry Lime voice. "Free of income tax, old boy. Free of income tax."

"How long would it take to set up?"

"Not long at all. A few days. All I need from you is the number off the despatch docket and away we go. You'll need to forewarn security at Trevor Square, give them the docket details, and tell them when to expect. How about the end of next week?"

"So soon? Jesus!"

"Why not? Strike while the iron's hot… and before you change your mind."

"I haven't agreed yet."

"That's right, you haven't. And I'm not going to press you."

"I'd like some more time to think it over."

"Of course."

"Something occurs to me that might be a problem. I have only recently been looking into the background to this piano. I asked about it in the workshop and checked the details in the buyer's office. Then I asked Harry about it as well. It's going to be fresh in the minds of anyone I've mentioned it to. It's a bit of a rich coincidence if the piano that's been sitting there for ten years is suddenly wanted so soon after I took an interest in it."

"Coincidences do happen, but I take your point. Who in the department knows?"

"Aiden in the workshop. I asked him about the piano initially."

"Don't worry about him."

"How do you mean?"

Martin touched the side of his nose. "Never mind. Who else?"

"Laura, the clerk. You don't know her, she's one of the management trainees – they circulate them every six months."

"I know. I've been out with a couple of them."

I frowned. "Very creditable. Laura was in the office when I looked up the details. We had a joke about the name Miss Jane V. Walker… what the V stands for."

"She sounds like a dirty girl."

"She is, and as sexy as hell."

"I'd like to meet her."

"You steer clear," I said emphatically. "How's Chrissie by the way – how's your wife?"

He ignored my jibe. "'Do you think Laura will remember, if she hears about the delivery, which is quite likely as the buyer's clerk?"

"Probably. She's a bright girl."

"Is she honest?"

"If you mean enough to shop me if she puts two and two together, I'm not sure. I don't think so. I don't know."

"Hmmm… and Harry?"

"I asked him about the piano, as you know. He probably won't remember and even if he does it's unlikely he'll say anything."

"And the others?"

"Raymond knows nothing, nor have I mentioned it to Mr Huxley or Brown-nose."

'Good, so Laura is the person to worry about. Why don't you wow her with your male charisma and personal charm?"

"Because she's got a boyfriend and she's not interested in me in the least."

"Right," said Martin. "Business concluded for now I believe. I must go. I've been invited for tea and crumpet with my neighbour."

"You mean you're off to be unfaithful to your wife with Imogen?"

"James! That's a bit harsh. But I am indeed. You mull over what we've talked about and let me know if you'd like to earn an easy thousand quid, or let a great opportunity slip through your grasp. Quite probably for someone else less deserving to pick up on it and reap the benefits."

"What's that supposed to mean?"

He patted me on the shoulder as he stood up to leave. "Only kidding," he said. "No pressure."

I drove home with our conversation swimming around in my head. I had to admit that Martin seemed to have thought of everything. And what he had said about the lack of risk to me personally had made an impression. I pulled up outside the house in East Sheen and sat in my car for a good hour, going over every detail of the plan, imagining what could go wrong, and if it did what the consequences might be. The more I thought about it, and the more I pondered Martin's responses to my questions, the more I was convinced it was workable and watertight. Most importantly, the more I felt confident that we'd get away with it.

I took out my notebook. I scribbled over the question mark next to the word *Three* and added a huge tick. That evening I phoned Martin and announced dramatically: "Let's steal a piano!"

★ ★ ★

P-Day, as we christened it, was the following Tuesday, this being the day when I took the phone call about the piano. The plan was to arrange for its collection two days later. Martin thought it might be slack over in Trevor Square on a Thursday with most deliveries arriving for the weekend on the Friday; there might be fewer Security on duty and so less chance they would bother about a routine piano collection.

That morning I stood on the escalator as it brought me up from platform to ground level at Knightsbridge Underground Station, my legs shaking with nerves and my mouth as dry as a bone. Ordinarily I walked the few yards along Hans Crescent straight to the *Harrods* staff entrance; but today I felt the need to take time out, so I detoured into the *Arco Bar* café next door and ordered a black coffee. I sat and stared out of the window, across the street at the department store that employed me, put money in my pocket, paid my bills, bought me pints and late-night kebabs, enabled me to fly away to the hot sun and white-sanded beaches.

And I was about to rob them.

I drank my coffee quickly so as not to be late for work, then made my way into the store and up onto the second floor. Clarence Brownlow was there already, opening

33

the lids of the grands and mincing around with a feather duster. He nodded when he saw me which was the most you ever got from him by way of a greeting. I took my jacket off and hung it on the back of the chair behind my desk, took out a duster and started to do my bit towards brightening up the instruments. I could feel my stomach churning. Moments later I was rushing through Books to the gents to throw up my Rice Krispies. Within the hour I was back there parting company with a Type 7 (*watery, no solid pieces – ENTIRELY LIQUID*); although I couldn't have identified it as such at the time.

The morning seemed to drag on forever. Strangely, as each hour passed I became calmer and more in control. I even sold a piano. Just a tiddler – a cheap Zimmerman upright – but enough to help keep my mind off what was looming. By the time I had finished the paperwork, exchanged the price ticket for a yellow *SOLD* label, and taken pleasure from seeing Brown-nose's look of envy, it was midday. I felt inexplicably relaxed. When twelve-thirty came, I watched Brown-nose as he sat at his desk, talking on the phone. It didn't look as though he was in a hurry to finish his conversation and head off for lunch. Raymond was sitting at a piano in a world of his own, playing some Bach.

The relaxed feeling began to vanish. I could feel my heart beginning to race. Brown-nose wasn't sticking to the script. He should be gone by now. Jesus, the first time in weeks – months even – that he hadn't left on the dot. What would happen if he was still there at twelve forty-five, and he took the phone call! I knew the answer. If anyone other than James Holloway answered, Martin would put the phone down immediately as planned and we'd default to the next day. That *was* in the script.

For Christ's sake go to lunch, I begged of him. My palms were sweating now and my emotions had swung from calm to panic stations in the space of a few minutes.

Mr Huxley came to the rescue. I saw his head peeping out from the office and frowning. Ah yes! He couldn't go to lunch until Brown-nose came back – and he always went at one sharp to meet up with his old Linen colleagues. He saw me looking at him looking at Brown-nose; he raised his eyebrows, rolled his eyes and mouthed something that looked suspiciously like *rancour*. The next thing I knew he was marching across the floor towards Brown-nose and cut right across his conversation.

"Mr Brownlow, please go to lunch."

In a voice that oozed smarm, Brown-nose replied: "One moment, Mr Huxley, I won't be long."

But Mr Huxley's dander was up. "Will you go to lunch?" He leaned forward, face purple, and said: "I am ordering you to go to lunch!"

Brown-nose looked stunned. "Call you back," he said into the phone and had the hand piece back in its cradle in seconds. "I really don't think there's any need…"

"NOW!" Mr Huxley marched back into his office. Brown-nose meandered away towards Televisions and Hi-fi, his tail between his legs, sulking.

The telephone rang.

Brown-nose stopped and glanced back. I was standing right next to the phone and picked up the receiver. He started to walk back towards me, so I shook my head and waved my arm at him as dismissively as I could manage. I may have had my middle finger slightly more raised than the others; I can't be sure after all these years. Brownlow got the message and wandered off for good this time.

"Piano department. Good afternoon, James Holloway speaking, how may I help?"

At the other end I heard Martin Allwright doing an extremely accurate impression of Dame Edith Evans as Lady Bracknell.

"Is that the pyaarno department? Splendid! Now listen to me, young man, my names is Walker – Miss Jane V. Walker… that's V for vagina. I bought a pyaarno from your establishment ten years ago and now I'd like it delivered as soon as possible, preferably this afternoon. I live in Scotland now."

I hadn't expected this and was momentarily stunned. "I…"

"Are you there?"

"Yes… yes I'm here."

"You sound rather – what's the word those dreadful Americans use all the time – ah yes, cute! You sound cute. Perhaps you could deliver it yourself, in person."

"I don't think…"

"Are you married?"

"No."

"Are you well hung?"

"No! I mean… not bad."

I could hear Martin giggling. I decided to play him at his own game. "I'm sorry, madam, but I think you need to speak to our Security Manager. I'll put you through."

"No, wait!" Martin reverted to his normal voice.

"Just trying to break the ice, Jimmy boy. I'm phoning on behalf of Miss Walker…" He went on to give me all the information I needed in our well-rehearsed script. He told me the piano number, the invoice number, the sale price, Miss Walker's old address and her new one – a nice long way away in Kirkintillock, East Dunbartonshire, to the north-east of Glasgow. He also explained that they would make their own arrangements to collect the piano on Thursday, if convenient. I wrote everything down, thanked him and said I would check the details and get back to him to confirm. I asked for his contact number and wrote that down too, knowing it did not exist and that I'd be confirming from home that evening.

I went into the office with my notepad and told Mr Huxley about the phone conversation. Fortunately, Laura was at lunch and not around to hear the customer's name, which was a piece of luck.

"Shall I deal with it for you?" I asked.

"Would you mind?" replied Mr Huxley, relieved at the thought of not having to get involved. "Don't let Brownlow interfere… he'll only screw it up. If he tries, tell him to speak to me."

"I'd be pleased to help. It's lucky the customer is arranging collection herself."

"Unusual. Does that seem a bit odd to you?"

"No I don't think so. If she's having a load of other items shipped it makes sense to have someone coordinate them all."

"I suppose so. Do we know who's coming to collect? I assume they'll know how to handle a piano."

"Not yet. I'll find out."

"Thank you."

I said: "If it's going to Scotland that will save us a fair amount."

"That's true, so it won't cut into our margin. Ten years ago, did you say? I presume we still have the thing."

"I'll go over to the workshop after lunch and find out."

"Thank you, James."

That evening I phoned Martin and told him he was the biggest twat on the planet.

"Calm down," he said. "I was just lightening the mood – bringing a bit of levity to the proceedings. You sounded so uptight."

"I was! Brown-nose was late going to lunch. A minute earlier and he'd have answered the phone."

"So how did it go with the arrangements?"

"Smoothly. Mr Huxley is happy for me to deal with everything. I went over to the workshop to confirm we still have the piano, just for show. Then I completed the despatch docket and got Mr Huxley to sign it. All your delivery blokes need to do is quote the docket number to security when they turn up on Thursday and Bob's your uncle."

"No further problems with Brown-nose?"

"He tried to interfere and say it was his job to deal with queries, but I referred him to Mr Huxley and didn't hear any more after that. Anyway, he got tied up dealing with a phone lead for a Bösendorfer grand for delivery to a Greek island of all things!"

"I know."

"Was that you?"

"Indirectly."

"You sly one! Presumably it will go pear-shaped?"

"Eventually, but we'll milk it until the end of the week to keep his focus elsewhere."

"Okay, you've redeemed yourself. You're now the second biggest twat on the planet."

"And what about Laura?"

"She wasn't in the office when I told Wilfred, so she doesn't know anything about it."

"Let's hope it stays that way."

"Is everything arranged with your delivery people?"

"Everything."

"You'll need to let me know the company name so I can inform security." He gave me a name. "Will they have ID?"

"Of course."

"What can possibly go wrong?"

"What indeed."

★ ★ ★

Thursday. P-Day plus 2. Collection day. A day I had to go in to work and behave as normally as I could possibly manage knowing that a bogus delivery team would be turning up at Trevor Square to steal five thousand quid's worth of Bechstein grand piano… and I was responsible.

I had spoken to Martin the night before. I was anxious, and it showed. He assured me that everything was arranged and that all I had to do was go into work as usual, try and sell some pianos and go home. He would phone me in the evening at home to let me know how it had gone. He told me again to consider the risks, or rather the lack of any. Others were taking chances, but for me there would be no comebacks. All I'd done was my job by taking a phone call and acting upon it. His words were comforting and I felt better for hearing them. Nevertheless, I could tell Martin was nervous too.

By morning his assurances had disappeared from my thoughts entirely. So many things *could* go wrong. My head was swimming with *what-ifs*. What if the delivery team gave themselves away by behaving nervously. What if Security became suspicious and started to make enquiries. What if they phoned the department for clarification and spoke to someone other than me who tried phoning the contact number and discovered it didn't exist.

There were answers to them all of course. They delivery men wouldn't behave suspiciously because they were professionals – this was what they did all day long, every day. There would probably only be two of them, three at the most, and quite likely just one who knew what was really going on. If Security phoned the department I could make sure they were put through to me.

I wondered what time they would arrive at Trevor Square. Shit, I never thought to ask! I should have insisted Martin gave me a rough idea; morning or afternoon would have been good to know. Now I'd be worrying all day and wouldn't have a clue how it had gone until that evening. Only if there was a cock up would I be aware sooner. Oh God, what a day lay ahead!

This time I didn't manage to get to work before

throwing up. I was still on the District Line when I felt my stomach complaining to the point of no return. I got off at the next stop, rushed out of the station and said farewell to my meagre breakfast in a rubbish bin across the road. When I had retched until it hurt because there was nothing more to bring up, I wiped my mouth on a tissue and stood for a moment looking across at the station. How appropriate, I thought. I was at Turnham Green.

On the tube again, I wondered if it was too late to back out of this whole sordid caper. I'd never done anything dishonest in my life. And here I was wrapped up in a criminal act; theft. Not just a minor bit of shop lifting… an enormous one! Five thousand pounds' worth! I would phone Martin as soon as I got to Knightsbridge and tell him the whole thing was off. I'd changed my mind.

Instead of my usual routine change onto the Piccadilly line, which took me to Knightsbridge, I got off at South Kensington and walked the rest of the way to get some fresh air and to mull over my predicament. I was frightened. What had I done! I stepped into a phone booth on the Brompton Road, ironically right opposite *The Bunch of Grapes*, where I'd first mentioned Miss Jane V. Walker's Bechstein to Martin. I dialled his home number. Chrissie answered. Martin had already left for work, she told me. No message, I said, I'd phone him later.

In the department I tried very hard to behave as normally as possible. I opened up some piano lids, did some dusting and then sat at my desk flicking through my order book, pretending to check something or another. Clarence Brownlow and Raymond had desks next to each other and were both sitting at them. Mine was further down the department. I stood up and walked purposefully in their direction.

"That piano – the one that's been in storage for all those years," I said. "It's being collected today. If there are any queries about it will you please refer them to me?"

Raymond nodded.

Clarence gave me his stare and responded predictably. "All queries ought to be dealt with by me. I am the department manager."

"Mr Huxley asked me to deal with this one." In my head I added, *because he didn't want you to screw it up, you knob.* Then out loud: "Besides, aren't you tied up organising the sale of a Bösendorfer grand?"

"How did you know about that?"

Oops, good question.

"Laura must have mentioned it. Terrific commission if it comes off. Special order I assume, as we don't have one in stock. How's it going?"

"Complicated. I need to arrange for it to be shipped directly from the factory in Austria to the delivery address."

"And where is that?"

He consulted his order book. "Mykonos."

"Where the hell is that?"

"In the Aegean Sea. It's a Greek island."

Despite my anxious state, I found it hard to supress a giggle. Martin Allwright at his mischievous best! That would keep Brown-nose busy.

"They want it by next weekend."

In a lightened mood, though determined not to go through with the theft, I made my excuses and headed towards the gents, but instead kept going until I was downstairs, outside and in a public phone box. I dialled the number for Curetons in New Oxford Street. A female voice answered and in a rough attempt at an American accent I asked to speak to Mr Allwright. She asked who's calling. I replied: "Burt Bacharach."

When he picked up the phone, Martin had clearly been briefed. "Mr Bacharach... Burt Bacharach? What an unexpected pleasure – and an honour too, sir. How can I help you?"

"Martin," I said in my normal voice.

"Oh." The disappointment in his voice was palpable. "It's you."

"I'm phoning about the delivery," I said, trying to keep the call generic and any sense of panic hidden. "I've changed my mind and want to cancel the order."

There was silence at the other end of the line. A long silence.

"I'm sorry to hear that," Martin replied eventually. "May I ask why?"

"It's no longer required. I don't want to go through with it."

Another silence, shorter than the first. "Unfortunately, that won't be possible. The ship has sailed, so to speak... or rather the van has left and is on its way."

"Can it be stopped?"

"I have no way of making contact, I'm afraid." There followed a painfully awkward silence. "Has anything happened I ought to know about? Anything that might be cause for concern?"

"I just changed my mind."

"Don't worry," said Martin reassuringly. "I'm sure everything will be fine and you'll be delighted once the day is over and the collection has taken place."

I suddenly felt foolish, and weak, and a coward. I needed to get off the phone quickly. "When will they be here?"

"Difficult to say precisely. Some time this afternoon I imagine."

"Okay, thanks anyway."

"You're welcome, Burt."

"Mister Bacharach to you!" I slammed the phone down.

★ ★ ★

For the rest of the day... nothing happened.

Raymond played the piano, then went to lunch, then came back and played the piano some more. Brownlow spent most of the time on the phone sorting out his Bösendorfer order, punctuated with occasional leaps across the showroom if anyone so much as glanced at an instrument. Then he'd adopt his smarmy salesman persona, pontificating about the design, the action, the touch, the mechanism, the history of the manufacturer, culminating in an inordinately self-indulgent performance of Chopin's Minute Waltz by which time the potential customer had either glazed over or vanished.

44

Or rather… nothing happened until just a few minutes before closing time, which in those days was five o'clock. I was praying that absolutely nothing at all would happen because that meant everything had gone to plan, the piano had been collected without any hiccups, Security hadn't intervened, the delivery van was on its way to a port somewhere with Miss Jane V. Walker's Bechstein on board, we'd got away with it, and a thousand quid would soon be in my bank, or more accurately in an envelope stuffed at the back of my pants drawer.

Then, at four fifty-five, Laura appeared from the office, looking like sex on legs, spotted me and shimmied her way across the showroom in her very tight skirt. "Mr Holloway," she announced using her public voice. "Trevor Square on the phone for you – in the office."

My heart sank. "Really?" The office, not the showroom phone. Bad sign. "Why in the office?"

Laura was standing right next to me now and adopted her quieter, non-public voice. "Because Brown-nose has been monopolising the showroom extension all afternoon and no one can get through to you out here."

My public voice: "Thank you, Miss Davies." My non-public voice: "If it's good news there's a shag in it for you."

Miss Davies, non-public voice: "Piss off."

"Is Mr Huxley in there?"

"He disappeared off home half an hour ago."

I made my way to the office with my stomach churning and the veins around my temples throbbing. This was horribly ominous. I closed the office door behind me, took a deep breath and picked up the telephone hand set.

"James Holloway speaking." It was a croak, barely audible.

"Mr Holloway? Err 'ello, sir, it's 'Arry speaking to you, from the workshop, by telephone. 'Arry Smith."

I sighed a huge sigh of relief. Not Security wanting to quiz me about the attempted theft of a piano. Just Harry Smith. But hang on! Harry never phoned anyone – ever. This itself was unusual. My blood pressure remained cautiously high.

"Yes, Harry."

"French polisher."

"I know who you are, Harry. What can I do for you?"

"Mr Aiden's gone home, he's left for the day."

"Thank you for the update. How can I help, is anything the matter?"

"Only these blokes come to collect a pyanner just now, that Bechstein grand you was asking me about the other week. Remember?"

"Yes, I remember." So did he. Shit! "Is anything wrong?"

"They came after Mr Aiden had left, so I 'elped find it for them. Lucky you was asking about it recently, otherwise I wouldn't have put two and two together."

"Have they taken it?"

"Yes, sir. They had a despatch docket with the H number and everythin' so it was all above board. Get what I mean?"

"I get what you mean, Harry."

"I didn't recognise 'em. I know most of the pyanner

46

shifters but I'd never seen this lot before. 'Ope they was kosher."

"I'm sure they were. Have they gone now?"

"Yes, they're gawn."

I felt a wave of relief gently flow over me. Just a small one. A ripple. "When was this?"

"Ooh now then, let me see… about an arf hour ago I'd reckon. Yes, sir, about arf and hour ago."

"No need to call me sir, Harry. James is fine."

"Right you are, sir… Mr Holloway."

"James."

"I apologise, Mr James. I don't use the phone very often. I ain't used to it."

"Not to worry. So is everything alright? Are you just letting us know?"

"Yes, Sir James. A coincidence you asking about it, after ten years sittin' there, then just a couple of days later they come an' collect it."

I winced. This was not what I wanted to hear. "Life's full of coincidences," I said reassuringly. "Now tell me, is there anything wrong?"

"No. Yes. Well sort of."

"What is it, Harry? There's something isn't there…"

I heard a thumping sound and there was a pause. He'd dropped the phone.

"Ello?"

"Yes Harry, I'm here. What on earth is the matter?'

"Them blokes… I don't think they're used to dealin' with pyanners."

"What makes you say that, Harry?"

He sniffed incredibly loudly down the phone and

I heard what sounded suspiciously like a fart. Then he cleared his throat. "They left the fuckin' legs behind."

My knees buckled and I slumped into Mr Huxley's chair. I placed the handset gently onto the cradle, and as I did I could hear the faint, tinny sound of Harry's voice saying "Ello... 'ello? Sir James?" Presently I stood up again and made my way back into the showroom. Laura and Raymond were hovering around Brown-nose's desk. They were giggling and looked as if they were about to wet themselves. I went back to my desk, locked the drawer and in a robotic state made my way out of the department. As I did so I overhead Brown-nose's telephone conversation and understood what was funny. He was struggling to get through to a non-English speaker at the Bösendorfer factory in Austria.

"Mykonos! My... ko... nos. *Ja*, Mykonos. *Es ist ein* island off Greece. *Können Sie* deliver there from Vienna direct – *direkt aus Wien? Direkt! Es muss* next week *sein* without fail *oder nicht gut... kaputt! Verstehen sie?* Very good. *Das ist gut.* Now, *bitte*, please listen carefully. *Mein* customer hast just gephoned again... *wieder angerufen... mit ein* additional – oh Lord what's German for additional?"

"*Teigrolle?*" volunteered Raymond.

"Many thanks! *Ein Teigrolle* requirement. *Teigrolle.* Why are you laughing... is that the wrong word?"

"What does Teigrolle mean?" I asked Raymond.

"Rolling pin, I think," he grinned.

"New," persisted Brown-nose. "Extra! *Er möchte...* he wants, insists, *dass das Klavier muss rosa sein.* Do you understand... *werstehen sie? Der Klavier must rosa sein.* The piano has to be pink!"

Laura rushed off in the direction of the ladies, clutching herself between the legs. Raymond had stuffed a handkerchief into his mouth and was turning purple.

Martin Allwright, I thought… you, evil, resourceful, hilarious, clever bastard!

★ ★ ★

"Martin's upper lip had developed a Mr Pastry moustache, as *Guinness* drinkers often do after their first mouthful. He licked it away and smacked his lips.

We were in a pub somewhere; the *Princess Louise* in Holborn I think. I'd made my way over to Curetons so it was somewhere around there. Looking back, that evening was a complete blur to me. All I can recall is Martin's attempts at comforting words.

"It's going to be fine. Don't worry. They're going back in the morning to fetch them."

"Why did they forget them?"

"One of those things. They just did. No harm done."

"No harm done! Apart from ageing me twenty years and bringing me within a hair's breadth of heart failure."

"You'll get over it. Everything will be fine."

"You said they were in the piano business. How then could they make such a basic mistake as to leave the legs behind!"

"I had trouble booking any of the usual piano removers, so I had to use what I could get. They were nervous, being a *Harrods* pick up. Also…"

"Also what?"

"They were a bit pissed."

"WHAT!"

"Apparently they nipped into the *Tattershalls* for a couple to calm their nerves. I was furious when I found out."

"I'm furious now!"

"Keep calm, Jimmy boy. Be assured, they will go back to Trevor Square first thing in the morning, collect the legs and be away. No one will be any the wiser."

"What about the lyre?"

"How do you mean?"

"The pedal lyre… did they forget that too?"

"Of course not, pedals are an essential part of a grand piano."

"So are the legs!"

Martin looked sheepish. "Everything will be fine."

"Harry seemed to think they hadn't a clue what they were doing."

"Sure they did… what does Harry know, he's a French polisher. Why did he say that?"

"Because they forgot the legs."

"Ah, there is that. But tomorrow they'll collect them and…"

"I know, and everything will be fine."

I wasn't in a sociable mood so didn't hang around for long. I went home to more alcohol and a sleepless night.

★ ★ ★

There isn't much more to tell. The delivery team did return the next morning and collected the piano legs. During Brown-nose's lunch hour I got a phone call from Lady Bracknell telling me that the legs had landed and that I was a very naughty boy for not having every faith in her.

It was a Friday. That night I went out after work with some colleagues in Kitchenware and got very pissed indeed. On the way home I tried sliding down the metal divide between escalators at a tube station – Oxford Circus I'm fairly certain. Lord knows why! Unfortunately, I made no consideration for the ribs that held the metal sheets together; they had sharp edges and ripped through my trousers and cut my buttocks. I didn't feel much pain at the time but woke up the next morning with bloodstained sheets and a really sore backside. Most of Saturday I spent in A&E. Not pleasant, but it took my mind off pianos and piano legs and pedal lyres and Lady Martin Allwright Bracknell.

The following week no one came to arrest me. I didn't hear from Martin until I saw him at the Thursday evening rehearsal. Predictably he assured me everything was fine and said he hoped to have some good news by the weekend. True to his word he invited me to join him on the Sunday afternoon for a stroll in Richmond Park, roughly halfway between our respective homes. There, sitting on a bench, high up with a stunning view across the snaking Thames and Eel Pie Island towards Twickenham, he handed over a brown envelope with an elastic band wrapped around it. I opened it. Inside were wads and wads of ten and twenty pound notes.

"Count it if you like," said Martin, "but I just did before I came out. One thousand pounds exactly, I promise you."

I peered into the envelope hardly believing my own eyes. I'd never seen that much cash before. It was surreal. Instead of speaking, I stretched out my hand and we shook.

"What are you going to spend yours on?" I asked.

"Oh, same as George Best," replied Martin. "Mostly wine and women, and I'll probably waste the rest. What about you?"

I knew precisely what I would do with it, but I wasn't going to tell him. I was going to use it to finance a change in career; to study what I had always wanted to but had been side-tracked into thinking music was for me. "The same," I replied and left it at that.

★ ★ ★

I resigned from *Harrods* soon afterwards and parted company with the piano business altogether. Not long after that I left *Melody and Harmony* too, for a bigger, better band. I never saw Martin again; not until he appeared in the dock in my courtroom more than three decades later.

I did however see Laura – about four years afterwards. I'd completed my Graduate Diploma in Law by then and had landed a pupillage with a City law firm. I was well on my way to becoming a barrister. I bumped into her in *Foyles* bookshop in Charing Cross Road and we had lunch together. She too had left *Harrods* and was now married and expecting her first child. In the full bloom of pregnancy she looked even more gorgeous than before, if that were possible.

She told me that Mr Huxley had taken early

retirement and Clarence Brownlow had left to set up his own music shop somewhere; in Reading possibly. The piano department had moved to a different floor and was half the size now; more electronic organs and keyboards than pianos. Poor Harry Smith was dead! Collapsed one morning on his way to work and died in A&E.

Most interesting of all, she told me that Aidan, the piano workshop manager, had been sacked for dishonesty. Apparently he had severely overstepped the mark in terms of doing private work in *Harrods'* time. A chance inspection and audit by a divisional manager had revealed that almost every instrument Aiden worked on in Trevor Square was being sent out to a shop in North London owned by his cousin. Mr Huxley hadn't known a thing about it, but was greatly embarrassed that it had gone on during his tenure; hence the early retirement.

"They didn't prosecute Aiden," said Laura. "They just wanted him gone. I believe the workshop has closed down now completely." She sipped her sparkling mineral water and looked at me intently. "About three months after Aidan left we had a phone call from a woman asking for her piano to be delivered. It had been in storage for years because she had gone to live abroad and was now back in England. We couldn't find it over in Trevor Square, and when we looked into it we discovered it had already been delivered... to a fictitious address in Scotland."

"Really," I said as blandly as I could manage. "How extraordinary."

"Very. Naturally it was put down as Aidan's doing.

He got the blame, although he had gone by then and they had no proof whatsoever to pin it on him."

"Makes sense," I said, nodding in agreement. "What did they do?"

"Ordered another one."

"What was it?"

"You know very well, James Holloway."

"It could have been a number of makes."

"Take a wild guess."

"A black Bechstein grand... model L?"

Laura smacked my arm. "I knew it! You sly old fox. I can't remember her name now but her middle initial was..."

"V for Virginia?"

"How much did you get for it?" she asked boldly.

"I don't know what you're talking about, Laura," I declared. "And I would be most grateful if you never asked me that again. However, à propos nothing we have discussed in the slightest, lunch is on me."

★ ★ ★

As I walked back into the court room and sat down, I glanced across at the defendant to confirm my suspicions. Adrian Steele it said in my notes. But it was Martin Allwright for certain.

The jury had found him guilty; all twelve unanimously, and in less than an hour of deliberation. I was sure they had reached the correct verdict. The evidence was compelling and very well presented by the prosecuting barrister. The defence, on the other hand, had focused primarily on planting doubts in the jurors' minds and stressing to them in the summing up that they had to be absolutely one hundred percent certain in their minds of the defendant's guilt in order to convict him. In other words, steer them away from the factual evidence which was watertight. I'd heard it dozens of times before; I'd done it myself when I was a barrister. As it turned out, the members of the jury were one hundred percent certain.

According to the documents in front of me he was previously of good character and this was his first offence. I knew differently... although the scale of the crime was somewhat different, albeit not dissimilar in nature. Stealing a piano from *Harrods* is chicken feed compared with attempting to embezzle half a million pounds in an online banking scam. He had fallen on hard times, the defence emphasized; his judgment had been fogged by his desperate circumstances.

Be that as it may, and speaking as myself and not in my professional capacity, he was clearly as guilty as hell.

Adrian Steele was ordered to stand in the dock. (Steele! Of all the pseudonyms for a thief to choose!) I spoke for a while as a preamble, emphasising his previously unblemished record, before announcing the sentence. Two years' custody suspended for two years. According to official guidelines, it was the lowest possible I could award. He looked at me curiously, as if I had made a mistake. There was a gasp from the public gallery where some of the people he'd tried to embezzle sat, expecting him to be sent down. They were clearly appalled.

"Mr Steele, do you have anything to say?" I asked.

"No, my Lord. Nothing, thank you." He seemed confused and bemused. He too had expected to be going to prison.

"Are you alright?" I asked.

"I think so."

"Did you hear me correctly?"

"I did."

"Not quite I think. Let me ask you again, and please listen carefully… are you *Allwright*?"

He made eye contact with me for possibly the first time during the whole trial. A veil seemed to lift from his eyes and a spark of recognition appeared followed by half a smile. "Yes," he said. "I am Allwright."

"I thought as much. The court is now adjourned."

As I removed my robes and prepared to go home, I was fully aware that I might be criticised for having been so lenient. Nevertheless, that was that, what was done was done and could not be undone. I decided upon a light supper before heading on to the lodge meeting. At least that was where my wife Imogen thought I was going.

But first, another visit to the toilet, hoping, praying, for a Type 4; only to be disappointed yet again.

GRASSHOPPER

Hester arrived at 7.45pm and parked carefully, and thoughtfully, close to the pub entrance where the car park was well lit. She reversed in, to be on the safe side, just in case a quick getaway was required… like the last time. They weren't due to meet until eight, but she liked to be early, always, for everything.

It was February and dark. She switched on the dashboard light, pulled a lipstick from her bag and using the rear-view mirror touched up what she had done half an hour earlier before leaving home. This was followed by a gentle brushing and patting down of her hair. She was a brunette; the recent highlights looked good, she thought. Then she took her mobile phone out of her bag, checked for messages (there weren't any) and opened the *Plenty of Fish* app to take another look at her date.

TrimJim – she liked his username. It suited him, she thought, implying a sense of fun and originality as well as a neat appearance. She really liked his main profile photo. He was good looking, fiftyish like herself, with dark wavy hair, lightly tanned skin and a smile to die for. She was very attracted towards him.

Looks aren't everything; she knew that, and her friend Caroline was always at pains to remind her. Divorced and a veteran of the dating circuit like Hester, Caroline was additionally a complete hypocrite who didn't practise what she preached. She fell in love at first sight routinely – every few months or so – with no real insight into the person behind the looks, and every few months she had her heart broken. Hester liked to think she was shrewder than that. Reading a profile was as important as looking at the photo, or photos. You could tell a good deal about someone from how they expressed themselves. On the other hand, there was no getting away from it, she had to concede, the chemistry had to be there. If it wasn't you were wasting your time. He had to be snoggable.

She had a good feeling about *TrimJim*. He had a gorgeous voice. She had melted the first time he phoned her, when was it… last Thursday. Less than a week ago but it seemed like much longer. Such a deep, manly tone. She could have listened to him for hours. In fact she had. The conversation had gone on for ages with him taking the lead. They had spoken twice since. Even though they hadn't actually met yet, she felt she knew him well already.

He was a company director; divorced, like her, with two grown up boys, also like her. He lived in Bromley, she in Horley, so *The Grasshopper* just outside Westerham was a convenient place to meet… roughly half way. It was his suggestion; she had been there before a couple of times to dances and knew it had a reputation as a serious pick-up joint, but *TrimJim* had assured her he meant the pub, not the dancehall. Besides, this was a Monday evening, so no dance. She looked across at the entrance to the pub. She hadn't noticed it before. It looked nice.

Hester checked her phone again. Five to eight… no messages. She hoped he'd be on time. Punctuality was important to her, and being late was a form of rudeness in her opinion. It was how she had been brought up. As this was going through her head, a car pulled into the car park, the bright headlights panning across her briefly and making her squint. It came to a halt a few bays along from her. It looked quite a nice car with, she was relieved to see, no logos or other signage; always a relief. Her mind flashed back to the previous summer and a date she had had with the sales manager for a chain of Japanese restaurants. He'd turned up in a van with **YO! Sushi** plastered across both sides and a huge plastic spicy tuna roll clamped to the roof. There had been no second date.

She sat and watched as the man got out of his car and walked over to the pub entrance. He peered inside, then checked his watch and stood rubbing his hands together. It was cold, and his breath made clouds of condensation.

Oh dear, he looked older than his photos. *Why did men lie about their age*, she wondered, not for the first time, and conveniently forgetting that on her profile she had shaved a few years off her own, to keep her on the

59

dateable side of fifty. He looked older, and very different, though not unpleasant.

Here we go again. She picked up her handbag from the passenger seat, got out of her car, locked it and walked across to the pub entrance. "Hello," she said. "Are you waiting for your date? Here I am."

"Hello back." The voice wasn't as deep and manly as it had been on the phone.

"Shall we go in?" suggested Hester. "It's freezing out here."

"Yeh, alright."

It would have been nice if he had held the door open for her, but alas no. He went in first and she followed. The room was virtually empty. It had a strong feel of mock Tudor about it, with fake oak beams, a rich burgundy carpet and dark mahogany tables and chairs.

"What do you want to drink?"

"I'll have a glass of merlot, please," said Hester.

"Go Dutch?"

"If you'd prefer." Oh dear again. Was it really too much to expect to be bought a drink? She would always offer to buy a second round on a date, but nice to be bought one first. The gentlemanly thing to do. It looked as if *TrimJim* might be turning into *GrimJim*. She fumbled in her bag and pulled out her purse, placing a five pound note on the counter. He took it.

He said to the barman: "A glass of merlot and a pint of *Guinness* with a whisky chaser."

She could have sworn he'd said on the phone that he only drank wine. Or was that someone else? She couldn't be sure now.

60

He handed her a glass of wine, but no change, and walked over to a table in the corner. Hester followed. As she sat down, he took a large swig of *Guinness*. "You don't look much like your photo," he said bluntly, wiping his mouth with the back of his hand.

"Neither do you."

"Mine was all taken recent."

"So was mine… were, I mean. You look different."

"So do you. And older."

"Thanks for the compliment!"

There followed an awkward silence. She took a good look at him. He had a pleasant enough face but was bulky, bordering on overweight. Certainly not trim. And she didn't like the look of the tattoo peeping out from underneath one of his sleeves. She couldn't see what it was but it looked rather unsavoury.

Snoggable? No.

"Oh well," said Hester eventually. "Let's not get off on the wrong foot. How was your day?"

"Alright."

How enlightening, she thought. Perhaps an open question might draw him out. "What did you do today?"

"Got up, went to work, came home, ate, drove over here."

"You were much chattier when we spoke on the phone. Is everything alright?"

"Fine."

"Am I a disappointment?"

"You ain't really what I was expecting."

"Oh dear, I'm sorry about that. I must say you're not quite what I was anticipating either."

He had his back to the entrance but Hester was sitting facing it. As they sat in silence again, the door opened and in walked an attractive woman with auburn hair, heavily made up, wearing bright red lipstick and showing a surfeit of cleavage, despite the cold. In her mid-forties, Hester estimated. Her dear departed mum would have described her as *blousy*. Behind her was a smartly dressed man, holding the door open for her. When he came into view Hester recognised him instantly. She gazed across at him. There was no mistake – it was *TrimJim*.

She looked at the man sitting opposite her drinking *Guinness*. No resemblance whatsoever to the man in the profile photos, nor in personality. How could she have been so stupid, she had met up with the wrong person! So had *TrimJim* it would seem. They must have all arranged to meet at eight outside *The Grasshopper*, and she and *Guinness* Man had been first to arrive.

In the mix up, *TrimJim* had clearly fared better than Hester. They seemed to be getting on well, both smiling and chatting as they crossed over to the bar. He asked her what she would like and ordered two glasses of wine. When she pulled out her purse he held his hands up in mock horror at the thought of her paying. Then he was inviting her to choose where to sit. She crossed the room to a table in another corner of the room; he followed. As soon as they were seated there was non-stop eye contact and an easy flow of conversation.

Hester sat back. Well of all things! What to do? Should she go over and explain what had happened – or would that be impolite?

"You're very quiet" said *Guinness* Man.

"So are you."

"Who do you support?"

"I'm sorry?"

"Football. I'm Spurs, me."

"Oh I see. I prefer tennis." This was painful. She really ought to put the situation right. But how? She looked across at *TrimJim* and the woman. She noticed the tips of their fingers touch across the table – accidentally on purpose. She couldn't interfere now. What was done was done.

"I'm chattier when you get to know me," said *Guinness* Man.

"I thought that's what we were here to do." He grunted. "Are you really a company director?"

"No, what made you think that? I'm a plasterer."

"What's your name?"

"Dave."

"You said it was Jim on the phone."

"What's yours?"

"Hester."

"You told me it was Sally."

The auburn-haired woman got up and made her way across the room to the Ladies. *TrimJim* sat back in his chair and sipped some wine, an air of contentment emanating from him. He casually looked around him, eyeing up his surroundings. As he did so, he pulled out his mobile phone and tapped in a pass code to check for messages, his attention flitting between the room and the screen. Hester watched his progress until eventually he looked in her direction. Their eyes met. She smiled.

He smiled back. Then recognition hit him. His eyes widened as the penny dropped.

The woman returned. As she sat down *TrimJim* shrugged towards Hester and held his arms out as if to say, "What can I do!"

She took her phone from her lap, tapped out *Save me!* and pressed *Send.* She heard it ping from across the room. *TrimJim* glanced down at his phone, tapped in a reply, closed it down, put it in his pocket and absorbed himself in getting to know Sally.

When his message arrived, it said: *That's the way the cookie crumbles.*

Hester felt her cheeks reddening. She knocked back her drink and said: "Dave, I have no doubt you're a very nice man, but I'm afraid you're not the one for me."

"Uh? Are you leaving?"

"I am. No need for you to as well, stay if you want." She stood up, put her coat on and picked up her bag. "And for your information, if you hadn't worked it out for yourself, I am not the woman you expected to meet tonight."

"Uh?"

Hester pointed. "She's over there."

Dave's head turned obediently until he noticed the auburn-haired woman sitting with *TrimJim*. "Sally!" he exclaimed.

Hester walked across the room, her attention focused firmly on the door, passing unnecessarily close to *TrimJim* and brushing against him. Out of the corner of her eye she saw him glance up at her, a look of momentary anxiety on his face, as if worried she was going to make a scene. Hester reached the door and as she closed it behind her, she saw Dave approaching their table and heard him say, with a hint of *hard done by* in his voice: "Sally, it's me… *I'm* Dave!"

Standing just outside, Hester took a packet of cigarettes and a lighter from her bag and lit up. The smoke felt good; reassuring and comforting the way only a few drags of a *B & H* can be. It was still cold and she shivered.

She turned around and looked through the pub door. In clear view, Dave could be seen leaning provocatively over *TrimJim*, making a point forcefully. Sally sat impassively, sipping wine and glancing from one to the other, saying nothing. Hester could only imagine what was being said.

TrimJim stood up and pointed a finger at Dave, remonstrating with him. Dave looked at Sally and back at *TrimJim*. Hester could lip read Dave's words which were slow and monosyllabic: "SHE'S… MY… DATE!" *TrimJim* shook his head. Whatever his reply, Dave did not take to it kindly in the slightest. He pulled back an arm and aimed a fist at his dating rival.

As it turned out, *TrimJim* was indeed very trim. He raised a forearm to parry the blow, hooked a foot behind Dave's leg and pushed his body weight into his attacker. To Hester's astonishment, Dave, bulky as he was, went down like a nine pin and sprawled across the floor. But he wasn't down for long and, once back on his feet, made a lunge at *TrimJim*, sending them both flying and crashing into a table that toppled sideways.

65

Hester had seen all she wanted to see. The last thing that stuck in her memory as she turned away was Sally, still seated calmly, checking her phone, as if this sort of thing happened to her all the time.

Two hours later, Hester was snuggled up cosily on her sofa with her feet up, a mug of cocoa in her hands, watching *Strictly* on catch up. She was wearing the onesy that no other living person had ever seen her in and probably never would.

Her mobile pinged. A text from *TrimJim*.

Hester, my love, so sorry about the mix up. I'm in A & E. Broken nose.

She looked at the message for a while, impassively, and wondered if Sally and Dave had ended up together after all. She had no feelings either way.

Hester casually tapped out a one-word reply – *Good* – pressed *Send* then blocked his number.

ROAD RAGE

Mary bleated: "I think my waters have broken," her voiced loaded with anxiety. There was some relief too. If they'd broken it wasn't a false alarm this time, and there had been several.

Len glanced across at his wife in the passenger seat. "Are you sure you ain't just pissed yourself, princess?" He grinned. "Don't you go making a mess on that seat. Get a towel or something under you."

She attempted a smile. Tugging a towel from her grab bag she tried to lift herself up off the seat. "I can't do it," she said pathetically. "There's no room."

"Undo your belt then."

Mary tried but even without the restrictions of a seat belt it was no good. "I can't!" She started to cry.

Len pulled over at the side of the lane, put the hazards on, walked round to the passenger side and opened the door. "It's okay, my darling, let me help. Jeez, you've made a right mess. Put your arm round my shoulder." He took her weight, lifted her off the seat and slid the towel underneath her. "There, that'll have to do until we get to the hospital. Now put your belt back on as best you can with that lump." He kissed her on the forehead and got back into the driver's seat.

Mary tried to relax. She grimaced. Pain was beginning to kick in.

"Don't worry, angel, I'll have you there in no time."

Poor Len, thought Mary. He was tired, and hungry. She'd had him halfway to the hospital during the night before realising it wasn't anything, and he was short of sleep. Now here they were again, off before breakfast. At least this time it was the real thing. He could get something to eat when they arrived.

They were driving out of Charlwood, once a sleepy Surrey village until the equally sleepy hamlet of Gatwick next door took on a whole new life after the war. Miraculously Charlwood had managed to retain some of its rural charm, although a whole lot noisier these days, whereas Gatwick village had ceased to exist. They were on a lane that snaked its way past long-term car parks towards a large roundabout at Hookwood where the A217 and A23 converged. A right turn took you towards the M23 and the airport; straight on was Horley and a couple of miles further along their destination – East Surrey Hospital.

Len was speeding. He always did. Sticking to the speed limit was for wimps. Mind you, speeding wasn't difficult in a Mitsubishi Barbarian 4x4 with its 2.5

litre engine. His *White Beast* Len called it. He believed if they didn't mean you to speed they wouldn't build cars that went so fast. He reached the roundabout and barely slowed down. The lights had just turned green and he thrust forward into the flow of traffic that was still making its way round from the right. A motorbike was last in line. Len cut in front of it forcing the rider to brake heavily. The bike skidded and lost control for a second. The rider hooted and shook his head.

Len wound his window down. "Fuck off!" he shouted and stuck a finger up to the rear-view mirror.

Mary winced. She hated it when Len got behind the wheel and turned into Mr Hyde. He was so loving and kind and thoughtful at all other times; nor did he use foul language, apart from when there was football on the telly. But driving brought out the worst in him, all his aggression seemed to boil over, and he felt he really did own the road. The law didn't apply to him. Every other road user was a moron. She had learned to grin and bear it, and not to comment, because if she did his hostility would be directed at her too.

They took the exit off the roundabout onto the A23 towards Horley. Len's eyes were now as much on his rear-view mirror as the road ahead. The motorcyclist was right behind him, close, and looking to overtake. Len had other ideas. He slammed on his brakes and took great pleasure in seeing the rider struggle to keep control again as he braked hard to avoid a collision.

"Serve yer right," shouted Len. "Observe stopping distance, bastard!" He drove off again at speed to catch up with the line of traffic ahead. The road was wide enough now for the bike rider to overtake. As he did so, he pulled up level with Len and shouted something. Even with the window wound down it was impossible to hear what he was saying through the helmet and visor. He sounded angry, but from the passenger seat Mary couldn't make out any swear words.

"Fuck off and die!" yelled Len. The motorbike sped up and pulled in front of them. Len hooted; his horn was considerably louder than the bike's. The rider's head turned and he shrugged. "Shithead," Len added.

Mary moaned from her passenger seat as a reminder that there were more important things to worry about, but Len was oblivious to her. The red mist was upon him; she was forgotten. All that mattered was getting one over on the man on the bike. They were approaching some traffic lights, the Wacky Warehouse on one side of the road, the Air Balloon pub on the other. The bike was immediately in front of them and as it reached the lights they turned from green to amber. The bike slowed to a halt.

Len hooted again. "Yer could of got through easy. Wanker!" He pulled up behind the bike and stopped for a few seconds, then edged forwards until he nudged the rear wheel.

The rider climbed off his bike and inspected the back. He looked at Len. "What did you do that for?"

"I've done nothing. You rolled back into me."

"I did nothing of the sort."

"Bloody did… you calling me a liar?"

The rider shook his head again and remounted his bike. A pedestrian waiting to cross at the lights said something to him, then looked back at Len and made a wanking gesture towards him. The rider shrugged.

"Bastards are laughing at me!"

"No they're not, Len," said Mary, against her better judgement.

"So you're siding with them are you?"

"No, I'm not. I'm just saying."

"Well keep out of it!"

Mary was close to tears again. Her husband's rebuke on top of the pain was too much.

The lights had changed and the bike pulled away, the four-by-four right behind it. But the bike wasn't going fast enough for Len's liking; deliberately, provocatively slow in his mind. "Now what's the shithead doing!"

"Observing the speed limit." Mary bit her lip. That too was a mistake.

"Shut your mouth!" screamed Len. "Speed limit? A fucking motorbike observing the speed limit? Don't make me laugh. He's doing it on purpose to piss me off." Mary burst out crying, deep sobs that welled up from her core. "See, he's upset my wife now. I'll sort the fucker out once and for all."

Len drove up as close as he could to the bike without hitting it and sat on the horn. It was really loud. Pedestrians turned to stare, other motorists slowed to work out where it was coming from. The bike rider didn't react at all and continued along the centre of the road at exactly thirty miles per hour. By now Len was incandescent with rage. The blood was pounding through him and his face had turned purple.

They were approaching a *Tesco Express*, in front of

which was a short-stay pull-in area for customers. Len saw it was empty. He sped up until he was parallel with the bike and twisted the steering wheel sharply to the left. The rider had no time to take evasive action and the *White Beast* ploughed into his side, sending him and his bike toppling sideways into the pull-in area. The rider was spread-eagled on the ground next to his machine.

Len pulled to a halt in front of them, and left the engine running. He opened his door. As he did he fumbled in the side pocket and pulled out something long and thin and metallic.

"Len!" cried Mary. "What are you doing?"

"Getting even." He shut the door and walked out of Mary's sight. She tried to turn around to see where he was going but was too restricted. Moments later he returned. He got in the car, put the metallic object back in the door pocket, selected first gear and drove off.

"All sorted, princess," he said. "Now let's get you to the hospital, shall we?"

Mary's sobs had subsided into sniffles; gradually they died away too. For a while she sat in silence, wanting to say something but scared to speak. Eventually she plucked up the courage. "What have you done?"

Len seemed calm and composed. Hyde had gone and Jekyll had taken his place. In a measured tone, he said: "Taught him a lesson."

"Have you hurt him?"

"That was the general idea."

"Did you kill him?" No reply. "Did you kill him?"

Len shrugged. "Look, we've just passed McDonald's

which means we ain't far from the hospital now… be there in a couple of minutes. How's the pain?"

In truth, the pain had been pushed onto the back burner by events with the motorcyclist. With its mention, a tsunami of pain seemed to return on cue and envelop Mary. She was close to fainting from a combination of anxiety and agony. She put her hand down between her legs and felt more wetness. When she brought it back up it was covered in blood.

"I'm bleeding."

"Not long now."

Len had phoned ahead to say they were on their way and as they pulled up outside A & E, next to an ambulance, a midwife and a porter with a wheelchair were waiting for them. Len opened the passenger door and between them they helped Mary out and eased her gently into the wheelchair. The porter wheeled her through the entrance. Len got back in the *White Beast* and drove off to park, moaning to himself about having to pay to park when the NHS was supposed to be free. As he did so, he noticed the ambulance setting off towards the main road, lights flashing, siren blaring.

When he returned, he was directed towards maternity reception and invited to sit down in the waiting area.

"I want to see my wife," he demanded.

"She's being assessed," replied the receptionist. "If you'd like to wait over there it shouldn't be long."

"Where is she? I want to see her now."

"That's not possible just at the moment." The receptionist pointed towards the sleeve of his jacket. "You have blood on you. Is that from your wife?"

"Must be," replied Len, taken aback. He took out a tissue and dabbed at the blood.

"There are some toilets over there," said the receptionist. "Why don't you go and wash it off?"

Len thought for a moment. "Alright, but when I come back I'm seeing my wife." He went into the gents. There was quite a lot of blood. He filled the sink with warm water and washed off as much as he could, then dried his jacket under the hand dryer. A stain remained, but the jacket was dark blue, almost black, so was barely visible. As he approached the reception desk again, there was a young man standing next to the receptionist. They were looking at her computer screen together and talking.

"I want to see my wife," interrupted Len.

"I'll be with you in a moment," said the receptionist calmly.

"I want to see her now."

The young man said: "Kindly give us a moment."

"NOW!"

The man turned and looked at Len. "And your name is?"

"Len."

"Do you have a surname?"

"Philpott. Who's asking?"

"I'm Jason Parker. You must be Mary's husband. I'm afraid you can't see her just at the moment. She's still being assessed and we're a bit worried about her. There are complications."

"Are you a doctor?"

"I'm a junior doctor."

"That's like a trainee ain't it? You're no bloody good. I want to see a consultant, that's what you call them? Where's the consultant?"

"He's isn't available at the moment."

"I'm not talking with you. I want my wife to be looked after by a grown up. Someone who knows what they're doing."

"I can assure you I…"

"Where's the consultant?"

"We're waiting for him to come on duty. He's late."

"Oh that's fucking wonderful. Having trouble getting his arse out of bed I suppose. Is there only one?"

"Only one on shift. We're short staffed."

"So who's in charge here?"

"At the moment I am."

"You've still got pimples."

"Mr Philpott, I am perfectly capable of running this department and I would ask you to calm down and remain civil. Your wife is being cared for by a team and is with the midwife. She is bleeding rather heavily and we have given her something to help with the pain."

"Listen, boy, my wife is in here giving birth to our child, and I want the best for her. Get it sorted will you, and I want to see her."

"You can see her soon. Meanwhile, please sit down and let us get on with our job which is to look after Mary."

Reluctantly, Len backed off and sat down in the waiting area. The junior doctor lowered his voice when he spoke to the receptionist, but Len still heard what was said. "Try his mobile again – we really need him with this one. It's not like him to be late." He disappeared through some double swing doors. Len watched her dial a number and wait patiently. It must have gone to answerphone as she spoke briefly then put the phone down.

Ten minutes later, Len was back at the counter. "What's going on? I want to see my wife."

"There is nothing to report, Mr Philpott," said the receptionist. "Please sit down."

"Where's that boy?"

"If you mean Dr Parker, he is in with your wife."

"Where's the consultant?"

"Dr Agrawal is not here yet."

"Agrawal?"

"Yes, Agrawal."

"Is he a...?"

"Is he a what, Mr Philpott?"

Len's mouth opened as if to speak, then closed again. "Never mind." He returned to his seat.

Moments later the door from the main corridor opened and a nurse came in and spoke to the receptionist. Len couldn't hear what was said, but the receptionist was visibly upset by it. She pointed through the double doors and the nurse went through. The receptionist pulled out a tissue and wiped a tear from her eye.

"What's up?" called out Len.

The receptionist shook her head by way of reply and focused on her computer screen.

Len waited another ten minutes then went across to the counter again. "Right that's it, I've had it waiting. Show me where my wife is right now. And where's that boy Parker… and has that lazy consultant turned up yet?"

"Please be patient, Mr Philpott, we're doing everything we can. Just wait there and we'll give you an update as soon as we can."

Len moved towards the swing doors. "She's in here isn't she?"

"Please sit down."

"I'm going to find her."

"No, Mr Philpott, you can't go in there, it's a restricted area."

"Restricted my arse. I'm going in."

"If you do I shall have to call Security."

"Call them. I don't give a fuck."

As he reached the swing doors, they opened towards him and Dr Parker appeared. He blocked the way and found himself face to face with Len.

"Mr Philpott, please come and sit down."

"I want to see my wife."

"Sit over here and I'll bring you up to date." He took Len's arm and led him to the seats.

"What's going on?"

"Mr Philpott, your wife is not well at all. As you know she started to bleed before she even arrived here and since then it has deteriorated. Any chance of an ordinary vaginal delivery was clearly impossible so we rushed Mary into surgery and performed a C section."

"What does that mean?"

"A Caesarean section. It means we made an incision into her womb and delivered the baby that way."

"What, you cut into her?"

"That's right."

"Without my permission? You had no right."

"We had every right. Your wife's life was at risk, so too was that of your baby. You have a beautiful healthy baby girl."

"You had no right."

"Did you hear me, Mr Philpott? You have a daughter."

"I want to see my wife."

"I'm afraid you can't at the moment. You see, Mary has lost a great deal of blood. She's stable but unconscious. She's awaiting specialist treatment."

"From that Agrawal bloke?"

"Not any more."

"Is he here yet?"

"Yes and no."

"What's that supposed to mean? Where is the lazy bastard?"

"He is anything but, I can assure you, and please do not swear like that. It's unacceptable."

"Listen, boy, I tell you what's unacceptable…"

"We have an urgent call out for a locum consultant obstetrician."

"I'll tell you what's unacceptable. Lazy bollocks like your Dr Agra-something that's what."

"Agrawal."

"Whatever! It's lazy fuckers like him putting my wife at risk. That's what's unacceptable. If anything happens to her I'm going to…"

"What are you going to do, Mr Philpott?"

Len lowered his voice. "I'm going to kill him."

"That may not be necessary."

"What do you mean?"

"Dr Agrawal did not turn up for his shift this morning because on his way he was involved in what is commonly referred to as a *road rage* incident. He rides to work on a motorbike. Apparently, someone knocked him off deliberately and attacked him with a knife."

Len went silent for a moment. "Is he dead?"

"No, but he is currently in our ICU – Intensive Care Unit – with multiple stab wounds. He's fighting for his life."

"Oh." Len mulled this over for a while. "A daughter you said."

"Yes, a daughter." Dr Parker was struggling to keep his true feelings about this man under control and out of the tone of his voice. "Now, if you will bear with us, I'd appreciate it if you would sit down again. Perhaps someone can bring you a cup of coffee?" He looked across at the receptionist who nodded and asked Len if he took sugar.

She was a while getting him a drink and when she returned she seemed on edge. Nervous. She handed over the coffee and hurried back to her work station, fixing her gaze onto her computer screen.

A few moments later, the door to the corridor opened and a policemen wearing a high viz jacket entered. The receptionist did not seem surprised. The policeman glanced across at Len, then back at the receptionist with a quizzical look as if to say: "Is that him?" She nodded.

The policeman walked across to Len and said: "Mr Philpott?"

Len nodded. 'Who's asking?"

"Excuse me sir, are you the owner of a white Mitsubishi Barbarian, registration number HG10 FUY?"

"Yeh, what business is it of yours?"

The policeman pulled out a set of handcuffs. "I am arresting you on suspicion of attempted murder. You do not have to say anything, but it may harm your defence if..."

The door to the corridor opened again and another policeman appeared. He crossed the room and whispered in his colleague's ear. The arresting officer nodded and turned his attention back to Len.

"Correction, I am arresting you on suspicion of murder. You do not have to say anything, but it may harm your defence if you do not mention when questioned something which you later rely on in court. Anything you do say may be given in evidence. Do you understand?"

Len looked at him vacantly. "I want to see my wife... and daughter."

BENCH

I have my own bench in the grounds of Chartwell. It's very ordinary; a metal two-seater, modest and not especially comfortable. But, located on high ground on the top edge of a sloping field, it enjoys stunning views across Winston Churchill's beloved home territory, with the roof of the house peeping out from behind a clump of trees to the right, and an unbroken panorama across the weald towards... who knows where. Tunbridge Wells perhaps?

Not *mine* in terms of ownership of course. However, I've been sitting on the bench for years now and in all that time no one has ever been there when I've arrived and no one has joined me to share it. So I feel a strong sense of its being my own. My sanctuary.

I usually park in Westerham, don walking boots and rucksack and set off from the green through a funny little alleyway called Water Lane on to high ground. Half an hour later I reach a bridle path that slopes gently down along the edge of the grounds of Chartwell, following a high and dense hedgerow. There's a gap through which you can squeeze quite easily, then across a track, through a kissing gate, and the bench is immediately on your left under the protective branches of an imposing oak tree.

The content of my rucksack varies slightly depending on the season, and I walk there all year round. In autumn, winter and early spring I have coffee in a flask, nuts and brandy. In late spring and summer, the same, only bottled water instead of coffee. I have sat there and contemplated all manner of events in my life – marriage, divorce, career moves, redundancy – in emotional states ranging from intense happiness to crippling self-doubt.

My visits vary in length from a brief pit stop to an entire morning or afternoon, the latter with a book, or more recently my Kindle. Occasionally I'm there with a female companion; mostly I'm on my own, which I prefer.

If ever you would expect my sanctuary to be compromised or intruded upon you would imagine it to be in the height of summer, when visitors are so prolific that the bottom half of the field, which is flat and level, is opened up as an overflow car park. You can watch the cars come and go and people meander their way towards the shop, the tearooms and the entrance into the grounds proper that lead you to the holy of holies for Churchill admirers (as I am) – the house itself. As it happens, the one and only time my space was invaded was a cold and raw January afternoon.

I was huddled on my bench with the lid of the vacuum flask between my hands acting as a cup. I took occasional sips of the rich and marginally metallic blend of coffee and brandy. My thoughts were elsewhere; precisely where I have no idea. As I sat staring into oblivion my attention was drawn to an elderly couple and a dog entering the field from the main car park and making their way gingerly along the far edge. He was slightly bowed and walked with a stick. He wore a full-length coat and a peculiar hat with ear muffs that seemed to be part of the whole and bore some resemblance to a Sherlock Holmes deerstalker. His hands were protected by thick sheepskin gloves. She wore what appeared from a distance to be a Barbour – green, waxed, very county – and a long tweed skirt and wellies (also green). On her head was a thick scarf knotted below her chin. She was in charge of the dog which pulled constantly at the lead to the extent that the poor thing was choking itself. I'm not very good with identifying breeds of dog; it was medium-sized and black.

A black dog at Chartwell. Churchill would have appreciated the irony. We have a familiarity with that particular beast in common.

When they reached the corner of the field where two stout fences form a perfect forty-five degree angle, the couple turned to the left and continued their circuit. At the next corner they turned again, bringing my bench directly into their pathway, barely fifty yards ahead of them. The old man was flagging. I sensed rather than saw them out of the corner of my eye as I concentrated my focus on Tunbridge Wells, or where I imagined it to be.

"Here's a nice bench for you, Roger." A plummy voice with, it seemed to me, a hint of superciliousness mixed with indifference. "You rest here while I take the pooch for a bit of a stretch along the bridle path."

Fuck it, I could hear myself saying inside my head in a mountainous internal groan.

"No, I'll be alright, Rosie. I can keep up with you. I'm fine."

Good man, I willed encouragingly. *Keep going. Keep up with her. You can do it.*

"Nonsense, I insist. You stay here, it's too much for you. You have to pace yourself. Now sit next to this gentleman and I'll be no longer than half an hour." Roger sat down as he was bid and argued no more. Rosie entered the kissing gate and encouraged the black dog through with the tip of her boot. "Come along, Ludwig!"

Half an hour!

An eerie silence descended. I took a sip of coffee and stifled a belch. I hated the thought of sharing my bench; absolutely hated it. He wasn't welcome. I just wanted him to go away and leave me with my own, precious space. I felt tense. *Please don't talk,* I begged of him silently. *Please don't make polite conversation. If you must be there, be there in silence then bugger off with posh Rosie and your black dog. And don't ever come back!* Then as an addendum: *Ludwig? Jesus! Really?*

Alas, that golden silence lasted barely a minute. It was inevitable I suppose. I thought I might get a greeting of some kind, or a very English comment about the weather. When it came, it was at least unusual and original, if not downright bizarre.

"You've heard of Shorty Longbottom."

Not a question; a statement. The voice was rather high-pitched, plummy too, though not so much as his wife's. I kept staring ahead of me, blocking him, imagining I could just make out that rather nice coffee shop I knew in the distant Pantiles.

"Shorty Longbottom," he repeated. "You know, and his pink Spitfire."

Spitfires interest me. My ears pricked up, though my face gave away nothing.

"Have you heard of him?"

Against my better judgment I answered. "No I haven't."

"Not surprised. Nobody has these days. But he was a hero in his time."

"And what time was that?" I probably sounded a tad sarcastic.

"Almost the entire length of the war. From thirty-nine to forty-five… until just a few months before it was all over."

"And he flew a pink Spitfire?"

"Reconnaissance. In thirty-nine he flew over Germany taking aerial photographs. Apparently in clear skies pink is a better camouflage colour than blue. So they painted his Spitfire pink."

"Well I never."

"Later on, in forty-three, he was the first pilot to drop Barnes Wallis's bouncing bomb successfully in trials, at Reculver."

The Dambusters; something else that interests me.

"I never knew that."

"He wasn't anything to do with 617 Squadron… he didn't go on the raid. He was a test pilot." The old man paused and clapped his hands together gently to help keep them warm. He sat fairly upright and with his knees together. "Of course the war was pitted with heroes and heroic deeds."

"Were you a pilot?"

"Good heavens no, nothing like that at all. I was only a child during the war. What do you do, young man?"

"I'm a teacher."

"What do you teach?"

"Music."

"Well that we have in common. I've done quite a bit of teaching myself over the years. Still do, privately."

Lord preserve us, another bloody teacher! My enthusiasm for my new bench partner took an immediate nose dive. Out of politeness rather than genuine curiosity I asked him what he taught.

"Piano. Though I'm a performer mainly… or rather used to be."

Potentially interesting again. For the first time I stole a sideways glance at the old man. There wasn't much to see of his head beneath the deerstalker affair, but I could make out the profile. A sizeable aquiline nose was his most prominent feature, followed by a protruding chin; he was beetle-browed with dark bushy eyebrows beneath a wisp or two of white hair. His skin had a bloodless pallor. I couldn't see his eyes. I was getting parts of a jigsaw but not the entire picture. I kept looking and, very gradually, the missing bits began to fill themselves in in my mind until, quite suddenly, there came a point when I could see the whole.

A pianist called Roger. Oh my God – Roger Andrews!

My interest level instantly shot off the end of the scale. I was sitting next to one of the finest concert pianists of his generation. I'd seen him perform numerous times; at Prom concerts, Wigmore Hall recitals, and the Royal Festival Hall more than once. I had quite a few of his recordings. He hadn't played in public for years. To be honest I thought he was dead. I suddenly felt nervous.

"Mr Andrews?" I said, tentatively.

"Correct. And you are?" I told him my name. "Delighted to meet you."

I had absolutely no idea what to say next. Fortunately, he did, and apparently he'd been reading my mind.

"I bet you thought I was dead."

"Not at all," I lied.

"If you did you'd be halfway to the truth. I haven't got long to go."

"I'm sure that's not the case," I said, presuming he was making a general reference to the inevitability of old age. I presumed wrongly.

He tapped his chest. "Cancer. Slowly eating its way through my insides."

What do you say to that? I said: "Oh dear."

"I've got months rather than years. Won't see the summer out."

"I'm sorry."

"I'm not. I've had a good innings, a wonderful innings actually. It will be a relief. Cancer is extremely unpleasant and extremely painful at times. I don't do pain."

Without being prompted, Roger Andrews proceeded

to tell me all about his life. The touring, the concerts, the orchestras he had performed with worldwide, the highs and the lows. He'd studied at the Royal College on a piano scholarship under Cyril Smith. I learned that he had really struggled in his early career. Gradually he had battled his way onto the circuit of concert recitals, often travelling to far flung parts of the country; a bit like being in rep is how he described it. Eventually the big break; a last minute replacement for Clifford Curzon in a Prom concert. He'd played Rachmaninov's 2nd Piano Concerto in C minor, which in the fifties was still enjoying huge popularity off the back of *Brief Encounter*. It had been a huge success. After that the floodgates opened wide and his career flourished: recitals worldwide; televised concerts; tours with Previn, Solti and Haitink; several film appearances; lecture tours talking about the composer he specialised in interpreting most of all – Beethoven. He was in his eighties now and had retired from performing a decade ago, though still active as a teacher. He'd been battling cancer for two years, and was losing.

In return, and only when prompted, I told him about myself; a meagre, mundane, prosaic existence. It didn't take long. Left university with a degree in music, slid into teaching because I hadn't had the imagination to think of anything else; been there ever since. I didn't tell him how much I hated it. Nor did I mention the divorce, or estrangement from my children, or my battle against depression, or being sectioned a few years back. I didn't tell him because I was ashamed, and because I didn't want to remember any of it.

In more general chat it transpired that we were both Midlanders; he from Lichfield, I from Cannock.

"Roger! Helloooo, Roger!" His wife appeared at the gate next to the bench.

The black dog came up to his master, wagging his tail furiously by way of a greeting. He got a pat in return. "Hello Ludwig, old chap. Good boy. Rosie, I've had a wonderful time chatting with this gentleman. Such an interesting and charming man. The time has flown by. We're both music teachers... *and* Midlanders!"

"That's nice. Come along now, we should be getting a move on."

Roger Andrews stood up cautiously and held out a hand. "Goodbye," he said as we shook. "It's been a pleasure chatting with you."

"The pleasure was all mine," I replied. "I hardly said a word."

"Oh dear, did I go on? I have that tendency. Hope I didn't bore you or interfere with your peace and quiet."

"Not at all!"

He leaned forward towards me and lowered his voice conspiratorially. "When I came along and sat next to you, I bet you thought *Oh fuck it*."

"Of course not!" I said, lying again.

"I very much doubt we'll meet again, so I shall say goodbye rather than cheerio." He turned to walk away.

"Before you go," I called. "There's something I'd like you to explain, if you wouldn't mind."

"By all means. What is it?"

"Shorty Longbottom. You mentioned him when you first arrived. May I ask why?"

He chuckled. "Ah, the things that come into your head at random! Especially at my advanced age, you'll discover that yourself one day. It was being here that did it, in Winston's back yard, so to speak. Took me back to my childhood during the war. I saw Shorty Longbottom die."

"Goodness, how?"

"He was testing a new plane, out of Brooklands – a Vickers Warwick. I used to have an uncle who lived in Walton-on-Thames. I was staying there with my parents at New Year in forty-five, just down the road from Brooklands. I saw the crash, at Haines Bridge. I heard the plane before I saw it, then watched it spin into the ground. Didn't know who was in it at the time of course, but I found out later and read all about Shorty Longbottom. It wasn't his fault, some sort of technical failure apparently. I was only twelve at the time and it had a profound effect on me. Such a hero, and he achieved so much with one thing and another... then dead at twenty-nine. Makes me wonder what my life achievement in almost three times as long represents. Paltry by comparison."

He turned and started to walk away. I watched him make his way across the field, in the wake of Rosie. I felt almost tearful. There was he, questioning his life's work in music against that of a man whose life had been honed and cut short by war. There was I, devoid of talent as a musician; a teacher by default because I didn't have what it took to do anything better in music – the thing he had spent his life doing. He had lived the life I had only dreamed of. I would have swapped places in a flash, exchanging one year of his for twenty of mine, gladly.

And he had enjoyed *my* company, and *I* was an interesting man! In return I had lied to him, twice. I felt an overwhelming sense of guilt. Raw emotions were beginning to well up inside me. He'd touched upon a nerve and exposed it, and the pain was rapidly becoming acute. Self-doubt; anxiety; a feeling of worthlessness. Depression. My black dog. I even felt bad about selfishly claiming ownership of a crude metal bench.

He had reached the far side of the field. He waved without looking back. The dog was all around his legs. Ludwig. Of course, what else would a Beethoven aficionado call his pooch!

In a pleading, almost pathetic tone, I yelled out to him: "You can share my bench anytime you want, maestro!"

He didn't hear a word.

HALITOSIS HENRY

PC Madeley cleared his throat. "Sarge, don't look now, but look who just walked in…" At a table in a corner behind the reception desk, Sergeant Andy Rudge was tapping away at his computer, struggling to top and tail a report for Superintendent Doyle that should have pinged into the boss's inbox days ago. His brow furrowed with frustration at being advised to look and *not* to look at something at the same time. But that was young Madeley for you; illogical, inconsistent and at times downright contrary. The boy would go far.

He looked up, towards the entrance of the police station. Standing in the doorway was an all too familiar figure; a man in his late fifties who would have been the epitome of ordinariness – medium height, medium build, plain features, grey hair – were it not for the extraordinary clothes he was wearing. A battered trilby hat, a plaid jacket on top of a turquoise waistcoat, bright red corduroy trousers (several sizes too big so they sagged embarrassingly despite the best efforts of a well-worn belt), and round, thick lensed glasses that sported wide red rims. On his feet were scruffy Jesus sandals over badly worn socks, not a matching pair. Topping it all, around his neck was wrapped a yellow Rupert Bear scarf, one end of which dangled on the floor and was black with engrained dirt. It was an appallingly tasteless combination of styles and colours; a sartorial shambles. The overall appearance was of someone who had pulled items at random from racks and shelves in a poorly managed charity shop, which was almost certainly the truth.

In his left hand, he held a dark grey briefcase with chrome edging and a number lock. A Samsonite.

Andy Rudge's heart sank. Halitosis Henry – Hastings' greatest police timewaster. If he became embroiled in a conversation, that would be an hour gone at least, just when he desperately needed space to catch up with his expanding backlog of paperwork.

"Madeley," he muttered. "Get rid of him. Head him off at the pass." He looked back at his computer screen and said a prayer to himself, hoping the profanities contained within would not automatically rule it as inadmissible by the Almighty.

He could not fail to overhear the conversation that ensued at the reception desk.

"Good morning," said PC Madeley from behind the reception counter. "What can we do for you?"

"I want to speak to a sergeant or higher rank if available."

"In connection with what?"

"A crime."

"Is it something I can help with, sir?"

"No."

"Do you wish to report a crime?"

"Yes."

"Are the victim of a crime?'

"No, I have committed one."

PC Madeley leaned forward and lowered his voice. "This wouldn't by any chance be the same crime you came in about last week… shoplifting from *W H Smith* as I recall?"

"*Waterstone's*. No."

"Another crime then."

"Yes."

"What this time?'

"I can't discuss it with you. I want to speak to a sergeant or higher."

"I'm afraid there is no one available."

Halitosis Henry pointed accusingly towards the man at the computer. "There's one."

"Sergeant Rudge is occupied at the moment."

"No he's not, he's sitting at a computer."

"That's right, sir, he's occupied on the computer."

"Probably chatting on Facelift, or Twittle."

"I can assure you he is not," stated PC Madeley. "Are you sure I can't help, if you have something to report? I'd be pleased to take the details."

"No," said Henry. Raising his voice and speaking clearly in the direction of Sergeant Rudge, he added: "I'll wait until someone in authority is available." He crossed the reception area to a row of three seats, sat in the centre one, spread out in either direction to mark his territory, then crossed his legs and arms.

PC Madeley sidled across to Sergeant Rudge. "Sarge…"

"I know, I know." Andy Rudge locked his computer screen, sighing heavily. "I'll see to it." He stood up and made his way round the reception desk. "If I'm still over there in a quarter of an hour, invoke the PITA protocol."

"Yes, Sarge." PITA stood for Pain-In-The-Arse and the protocol involved being informed of a highly important phone call that required urgent attention.

"Make that ten minutes."

"Sarge."

Andy Rudge wandered over to Henry and squeezed onto the seat next to him. "Henry," he said as pleasantly as he could manage. "How nice to see you. Must have been all of a week."

"Good morning, Sergeant. Last Thursday actually."

Andy Rudge reeled at the blast of foul breath that came his way and shuffled back a little in his seat. "That's right. You were in here confessing to the theft of some books."

"I couldn't help myself."

"We phoned the store manager, you know. He checked his stock and confirmed that none of the titles you mentioned had gone missing."

Henry appeared unfazed. "I might have got the names wrong. But I stole them. I'm guilty and prepared for the consequences. I'll go to prison if necessary."

Andy Rudge smiled. "We don't send people to prison for stealing a few books, especially when there's no evidence."

"Well you should do. It's a crime."

"Be that as it may, we won't be taking it any further."

Henry looked disappointed.

"So how can we help, Henry? I've got a lot on at the moment and time is at a premium. What is it today?"

Henry peered around to make sure he couldn't be overheard. "I want to make a confession."

"I rather thought you might. What have you done this time... thieving again?"

"You could say that. Yes, thieving I suppose. Only far worse than last week."

"Or the week before? A bottle of *Jack Daniel's* from *Morrisons*."

"*Tesco Express*."

"Ah yes, I remember now. They couldn't find anything missing either."

"This is much worse. Serious stuff. You really will be locking me up this time."

"Come on then, out with it. What have you done?"

"I've stolen some money."

"How much?"

"A hundred thousand pounds."

Andy Rudge whistled. "I'm impressed."

"Well you shouldn't be. It's a serious criminal act."

"It certainly is. What have you done, robbed a bank?"

"No, but I stole it off a man who did... sort of."

"Would you like to tell me about it?"

Henry hesitated. "Can we go somewhere a bit more discreet?"

"This will do fine," said Andy Rudge. "Fire away. But please, make it concise. Just tell me the facts."

"Don't you want to make notes?"

"Let's hear it first."

Henry thought for a moment and then began. "As you know, Sergeant Rudge, I live alone."

"You do indeed."

"I am also gay."

"I know that too."

"Well, last night I was in a bar... *The Blue Diamond*. I expect you know it."

"By reputation. I've never been inside."

"I'm not surprised, unless you're of the same persuasion. It's one of the places around here where I can go and be with my own, if you follow my drift."

"I do."

"Good."

"Please get on with it," said Andy Rudge impatiently.

"I am," said Henry, somewhat peeved by this. "It's all pertinent."

"Okay, but do come to the point."

"I met a man... in *The Blue Diamond*."

"Name?"

"Joe."

"Surname?"

"No idea."

"Go on."

"I'd never seen him before. We got chatting. He bought me a drink. Several in fact. One thing led to another and..."

"You took him home?"

"I did."

"That's no longer a crime these days, Henry, unless he was under age."

"He was not. Younger than me but not *that* young. In his early thirties I'd say."

"So tell me about the crime."

"I'm coming to it. This man, Joe, he'd come down from London that same day. Must have left in a hurry because he only had a briefcase with him. No other luggage. I lent him a toothbrush and the next morning I offered him a change of clothes, but for some reason he declined."

"I can't imagine why," said Andy Rudge, looking Henry up and down and trying not to smirk.

Henry shrugged. "Anyway, while he was in the shower, I noticed his briefcase on the coffee table in the lounge. It wasn't shut properly, and, being the inquisitive type, I thought I'd take a peep inside."

"Is that the one?" asked Andy Rudge, pointing at Henry's left hand.

"It is indeed."

"What did you find inside?"

"Money. A lot of it."

"A hundred thousand smackers?"

"That's correct."

"How do you know… did Joe tell you or did you count it?"

"Both."

"And is the money in there now?"

"No, I left it at home. I just brought the briefcase along to show you, as evidence."

"May I see?"

Henry handed over the briefcase. Sergeant Rudge tried to open the catches but it was locked. "The combination please?"

Henry looked around again to be sure no one was listening, then whispered: "One, two, three."

"Not very imaginative and not very secure."

"Blame Joe, not me," said Henry.

"How do you know the combination?"

"Joe told me."

"When? When did he tell you?"

"Actually, come to think of it, no he didn't. He left the briefcase unlocked and so the combination was showing."

Andy Rudge seemed unimpressed. He scrolled the tumblers round until they showed the numbers and opened the lid. The briefcase was empty. "And Joe. Where is he now?"

"Strangest thing. We had breakfast together, then he said he was popping out to buy some cigarettes… and he never came back."

"What, and left all that money behind?"

Henry nodded.

"Did he say exactly where he got it?"

"When he saw that I'd looked in the briefcase, he was angry at first. Told me to mind my own business. But then he calmed down and told me about it. Apparently, he works, or worked I should say, for a businessman up in London. A sort of private banker who lends money to people and charges them interest."

"A loan shark."

"Something like that. Anyway, he deals in cash mainly and one of Joe's jobs was to courier payments around, moving them from the office safe to a more secure one in the man's basement."

"Why didn't he do it himself?"

"They shared the work between then. I think he and Joe did a bit more than work together."

"Were they lovers?"

"Yes."

"So what happened?"

"Well, yesterday, Joe was on his way from the office to his boss's house with a briefcase full of cash – a lot more than normal because they'd managed to claw back a huge payment from someone. And, as Joe put it, he suddenly found himself on the wrong train and ended up in Hastings instead of Balham."

"With what in mind?"

"To steal it of course. Run away and set up a business of his own."

"And this morning he walked away and left it all with you."

"Yes."

"Why would he do that?"

"I have no idea."

PC Madeley appeared. "Sorry to interrupt, Sarge, but *Peter* is on the phone. He says it's urgent. I think you should take the call."

"Thank you," said Andy Rudge. "Tell him I'll be with him in a moment."

"Sarge."

"Now, Henry, exactly how can we help you? Why are you here? I'm not quite clear."

"To confess to a crime. Theft. I told you."

"But you haven't stolen anything. Joe did. You're actually reporting a crime."

"Yes, but I have the money. I'm an accomplice."

"I don't think so."

"Well I'd like to take responsibility. I want you to punish me… on Joe's behalf."

"Sorry, Henry, it doesn't work like that." Andy Rudge made to stand up.

Henry grabbed his arm. "Please."

Another blast of stale breath. "No can do. Take your hand away, please."

Instead, Henry gripped harder. "I insist!"

It didn't take much for Andy Rudge to extract himself. He was losing patience now, and not afraid to show it. He stood up and towered over Halitosis Henry.

"Now listen to me. I am not going to pursue this any further. Henry, I don't need to tell you that you're in here all the time reporting crimes you've supposedly committed. It's like a hobby of yours. There's never any substance to any of them. Last time it was stealing books, the time before a bottle of *Jack Daniel's*, and the time before that it was some clothing if I'm not mistaken… from *Marks and Spencer*."

"*TK Maxx*."

"Whatever. The point is you're in here all the time… every couple of weeks. You confess to crimes, all of them petty, and want us to arrest you and punish you. We humour you, and we play the game. But the fact remains that there is never a shred of evidence and, frankly, you are wasting valuable police time. This has to stop."

Henry held up the briefcase. "This is evidence,"

he said. "And there's nothing petty about a hundred thousand pounds."

Sergeant Rudge took the briefcase and examined it. "A perfectly ordinary, bog standard case. You could have bought it at any of half a dozen shops in and around Hastings. *Debenhams* for one, *Marks and Sparks* for another. *Argos* even." He opened the lid and made to tip out the contents. "Empty. Not a pound coin in sight."

"It's all at home, in a pile on the coffee table in my living room. No pound coins, all fifty pound notes. You are welcome to come round and see for yourself."

"Sorry, Henry, I don't believe you. Nor do I believe that your friend Joe – if he exists at all – would walk away and leave it with you, just like that. It doesn't make any sense."

Henry tried to look coy. "Perhaps I haven't been entirely honest with you. Joe and I argued about the money. The truth is…"

"Let's stop this now, Henry. I don't believe a word. You're a fantasist."

"I'd like to make a formal statement."

Andy Rudge pointed towards the door. "Enough's enough. Off you go."

Henry stood up, closed the briefcase and headed towards the entrance. As he did his sullen expression turned to one of anger. He looked Sergeant Rudge square in the face and shouted, "Bastard!"

"Ironically," said Andy Rudge, "abusing a police officer *is* a crime."

"Really?" said Henry, anger turning instantly to eager expectation.

"Yes. Regard this as a verbal caution. Now hop it."

Expectations dashed, Henry stood on the pavement outside, looking bewildered, not knowing where to go and what to do. Without any real thought process, he wandered down the street, into a pub and ordered a double *Jack Daniel's*. What next?

There was a young man leaning against the bar, on his own. Good looking, nice legs inside the tatty jeans. Probably in his mid-twenties. No, forget it. This was not the place to pick up. Just look.

Half an hour later, Henry was stepping off a bus at the end of his street. He walked to the front door, fumbled for his key and let himself in. His flat was on the first floor and he trudged up the stairs feeling inordinately weary. Inside, he took off his scarf and jacket and dumped the empty briefcase on the floor. In the kitchen he boiled the kettle and made a mug of filter coffee with a dash of cold milk. From a cupboard he pulled out a half-empty bottle of *J.D.* and added a generous slug. Then he made his way into the lounge, slumped down on the sofa and took off his sandals, stretching his legs out and waggling his toes. A big one peeped out from a hole in his sock. He took a sip of coffee. It tasted good.

He looked at the coffee table in front of him. What to do with all that money? He leaned forward, picked up a wad of notes and flicked through them. Must be at least two grand in this one alone, he thought. And the table was covered in them. Some loose notes had fallen onto the floor. He couldn't be bothered to pick them up.

In terms of the money, his conscience was clear. He had tried his best to report the crime – nay confess to it

– and the police didn't want to know. Okay, so he had a track record of not being honest and reporting things he hadn't actually done, or at best expanded on the truth. They didn't really understand, and he didn't himself, not fully. The idea of being locked up, incarcerated, that's what excited him and was at the core of it… and the notion of being punished by men in uniform. He liked that idea too. But he fell shy of actually committing real crime which, after all, was against the law.

This time had been different. The crime had come to him, so to speak, and he had been entirely honest – well, perhaps not entirely. But the money was real, and had been stolen. He was sitting looking at it for Christ's sake. Joe had been real too. Henry really had picked him up in the *Blue Diamond* and brought him back home. They had slept together and that morning he had looked inside Joe's briefcase and seen all that cash. Joe had been very angry and gone out to buy some cigarettes. And to calm down.

★ ★ ★

Up until that point everything Henry had told Sergeant Rudge had been true. The lie was about Joe not coming back. He had. He returned an hour later, even angrier than when he went out. He shouted at Henry, called him a nosey, interfering, disgusting old poof with stinking breath. Ranted for a quarter of an hour in fact. It culminated in a death threat. Now Henry knew about the money, Joe hissed, he would have to die.

They were standing facing each other in the lounge. Henry listened in awe, not saying a word; he was fascinated rather than upset or angry. He nearly giggled at the death threat. He didn't hear the insults; he was focused entirely on Joe the man. He thought how much more attractive, how sexier he was when all worked up like that. He was getting turned on.

Henry's mistake was to say so.

Joe hit the roof. His face turned scarlet with rage and he started to babble. From his jacket pocket he pulled out a gun. Henry's eyes widened. No fear, no anxiety, just curiosity. Joe was waving it all over the place. His hand was shaking – he was out of control, ranting about Henry and how it was his own fault he was going to die. Spittle flew everywhere and he started to foam at the mouth.

There came a point when Henry decided he'd heard enough. Joe wasn't turning him on any more; he was becoming boring. Unbeknown to Joe, Henry knew a thing or two about firearms. Guns fascinated him. He'd been in the army in his youth and a member of a gun club for many years. For a start he knew that possessing a handgun was illegal and had been since the Dunblane massacre. He could tell from where he stood that the gun was a nice piece – a *Smith & Wesson* Model 10 revolver with 4-inch barrel firing .38 calibre cartridges. Or in simple parlance, a six-shooter.

He could also tell that Joe had no idea whatsoever how to handle a firearm. He was scared of it, and his index finger seemed reluctant to make contact with the trigger. Henry watched, and waited for his moment.

With sudden agility that stunned Joe, Henry leaped towards him, grabbed his gun arm with both hands and twisted it so that it bent backwards in a way nature never intended. Joe yelped with pain. Henry diverted one hand towards the gun and snatched it from his grip. He pointed it directly at Joe's forehead… and pulled the trigger.

★ ★ ★

Henry drank the last of his coffee and *J.D.* and set his mug down on the floor. He looked across at Joe, sitting next to him on the sofa, bolt upright and staring wide-eyed into space. In the centre of his forehead was a ragged circle of coagulated blood. He sat exactly where and how he had conveniently fallen when Henry had shot him earlier that day.

It was wrong not to have told Sergeant Rudge about the murder. Henry knew that. He intended to, but when he hadn't been believed about the money it seemed hardly likely he'd be taken seriously about shooting someone dead. So he hadn't bothered. There didn't seem any point. Now all this money was his to enjoy, and he fully intended making the most of it. He'd already given it some thought. A Mediterranean cruise perhaps, or a trip to Vegas, or New York. Or all three! Then buy a nice property along the St. Leonards seafront instead of this pokey rented place in the seedier part of Hollington.

But first, Henry thought with a sigh of despondency, he had better do something about the body.

VICAR'S WIFE

The Reverend Adrian Prendergast, vicar of St. Peter's, and his wife Susan had enjoyed nigh on ten years of blissfully happy married life together. He had a delightful parish in Loades-next-the-Sea, a quaint village on the Norfolk coast. He wasn't an ambitious man but his Christian faith was profound and he took great satisfaction in tending to the spiritual and pastoral needs of his congregation which was small but for the most part mirrored his own deep religious convictions. He was held in high esteem by his flock.

The couple had met when Adrian first arrived at St. Peter's as a young curate. He was in his mid-twenties and Sue a couple of years his junior. She was one of the congregation and an avid churchgoer. Getting together had been a slow process; neither was experienced in such matters and by the time they had progressed to the point of becoming engaged, the incumbent vicar was due to retire with Adrian lined up to take his place. Their marriage and his promotion (if that's the appropriate word) followed swiftly one after the other. They loved each other and were a good match, compatible in every way a vicar and a vicar's wife ought to be.

There was only one aspect of connubial life that had been problematic over the years, and that was what Adrian and Sue euphemistically referred to, if they ever referred to it at all, as *the bedroom department…* or sometimes *you know what.* The problem was in two parts.

Firstly, Adrian was stringent in applying the rule that *you know what* was intended for the procreation of children and not for the mere enjoyment of the pleasures of the flesh. If you weren't trying for a child then it was strictly out of bounds. Sue felt otherwise and was keen to use bedtime as an opportunity to show affection towards her spouse, whom she loved dearly. Besides, after ten years they were still childless and as far as she was concerned every opportunity was fair game by Adrian's way of thinking. Nevertheless, she respected her husband's beliefs and her feelings were supressed; it was not something they could easily discuss, or even discuss at all.

Secondly, Adrian was extremely self-consciousness about his body. He never allowed Sue to see him naked. At bedtime he would habitually disappear into the bathroom to undress and return wearing pyjamas that revealed nothing at all. When it did happen, *you know what* took place in the dark; never in the morning when it was light. Sue on the other hand was relaxed about such things and quite comfortable wandering around in bra and knickers, or even completely naked, though she was aware that Adrian never looked at her when she did. Nor, if the opportunity ever arose, would she be averse to showing her affection fully as the sun rose and the day dawned. Although not tried and tested, she was a morning person in that respect, she felt certain.

Despite their differing, and mostly unspoken, attitudes towards this area of potential disharmony, it was very much kept in its place between them. In the grand scheme of things, *the bedroom department* was not a major issue; it was a side show. There were many other aspects of life, both spiritual and secular, of far greater significance.

To put the record straight, Adrian and Sue were neither prudes nor introverts. At times they bordered on the gregarious. Adrian was the life and soul of the party at all manner of social occasions within the parish; he could make a whist drive simply buzz with excitement, and a post-christening bash bounce along nicely. Equally, Sue shone at W.I. meetings – the chairwoman no less – and was the leading light in organizing charitable events such as jumble sales and car boot sales. Nor were they averse to a tipple now and then, above and beyond communion wine; there was nothing in the scriptures counselling against, in moderation.

In fact, it was alcohol that was almost invariably the key that unlocked the door to *the bedroom department*. Without it there was a strong chance that *you know what* would never take place at all. Once in a while they retired to bed a little on the tipsy side. Sue would take the initiative and kiss her husband, then take his hand as they lay in bed and place it somewhere on her body, by way of encouragement. If that led to anything, it was usually over quickly. Practice makes perfect, there is no doubt, and the lack of it has the opposite effect. Premature ejaculation was almost inevitable; frustrating for Sue. She would turn her back to him in bed afterwards, pray, and try hard to avoid the temptation to finish the job herself, not always succeeding.

With their tenth wedding anniversary looming, it was Sue's suggestion that they go away to celebrate. In all that time, apart from their honeymoon, which had been spent on a walking tour of Northumbria, they had not had a holiday. Adrian often said that he could not understand the need to take a break from a job that he loved so much. Sue had no argument to the contrary; however, she made a clear point over breakfast one morning that this would not be a holiday as such, rather time out to celebrate and reflect upon ten years together. It would have greater meaning if spent away from parishioners, pastoral duties, and their home turf. To her delight, Adrian nodded in acquiescence and that afternoon she began searching the internet. She knew to avoid anything too expensive or exotic as Adrian would turn it down flat. She was determined that it should be abroad, and somewhere hot, so she concentrated on package holidays in Southern Europe and around the Mediterranean.

By teatime she had found what she imagined to be the perfect location; a village on the Greek mainland called Stoupa, on the coast of the southern Peloponnese peninsula. Flights, transfers and accommodation in an apartment just a short stroll from the beach were all included; and the price was reasonable. The photos looked delightful. Adrian was interested in history, and an additional attraction for him, she thought, might be the fact that Stoupa was in the Mani region, where many events from the history of ancient Greece had taken place; the home of Olympia and the city of Sparta. At dinner, she told him all about it and afterwards showed him photographs on the Thompson website. He pulled a face at the price and mumbled a few things about getting cover for the parish while they were away. Then, to Sue's huge relief, he said: "Alright, let's go."

The next morning she had it booked.

Their anniversary was a month away, in early September, so the timing was perfect; the schools would be going back and the resort not too heaving with tourists. The wind tends to build up around the Med towards the end of the season, but it should still be hot. Adrian was very well organised and as the date for the holiday approached he gradually put in place all the necessary arrangements to ensure his parish survived during his week away. He had an assiduous curate in Nigel Pugh who could be relied upon to hold the fort, not to mention some trustworthy church wardens. Sue, meanwhile, freed up a morning to nip into King's Lynn and do some holiday shopping, consisting mainly of buying an adaptor plug, a money belt, a couple of second hand novels from a charity shop, and a new swimming costume. She toyed with the idea of a bikini but decided against; Adrian would almost certainly disapprove.

Their actual anniversary was a few days before their departure and they celebrated modestly at home with a few close friends.

When departure day arrived, Mr Rogers, the kindly if somewhat vulgar parish treasurer, insisted on driving them to the airport. He was outside the vicarage in his Vauxhall Mokka at 5am prompt.

"Bloody hell of a time to be up," he moaned.

"You did offer," Adrian reminded him.

"Too kind for my own good."

At Stansted they thanked him profusely and Mr Rogers promised he'd be waiting for them on their return. He had the details of their flight and would check it was on schedule before setting off to collect them – "to avoid a bleeding waste of a trip".

They were in good time and once they'd checked in their luggage they sat in the departure lounge and drank prosecco. Sue could tell that Adrian was preoccupied; no doubt mulling over in his mind the arrangements to make sure nothing had been overlooked. She hoped he would be able to chill out while they were away and not spend the entire week fretting over how they were coping without him.

She needn't have worried. As they flew out across the English Channel and traversed mainland Europe, he visibly began to relax. His shoulders lowered and he sat back in his seat, gazing out at the extraordinary spectacle of the world laid out below like a giant, textured three-dimensional map. A gin and tonic helped.

The plane landed at Kalamata airport from where they would be transferred by coach to Stoupa. When they stepped off the plane to walk to the terminus building, the heat hit them as if an oven door had been opened.

"Goodness!" remarked Adrian, loosening his tie.

"Take it off altogether," suggested Sue. Adrian thought about this for a moment then, tempting though it was, decided against what was a step too far for the time being. He did, however, remove his jacket and carried it over his arm.

The coach was comfortable; air conditioned and only two-thirds full. It was a beautiful journey, through Kalamata itself, following the long beach road before beginning a gradual climb up zigzag roads onto high ground with stunning views of the ocean, deep blue and hugely inviting. They were given an almost continuous narrative by a lady from the tour operator which, frankly, they could have done without. She seemed to be of the opinion that any silence was a weakness in their quality of customer service. It varied from tedious and banal (pointing out a rocky outcrop that looked to her like a crocodile and to everyone else like a rocky outcrop) to occasionally informative and useful (Greek plumbing is rubbish – always put your toilet paper in the bin, and never down the loo for fear of causing a blockage). It took an hour and a half to reach Stoupa, and once there the coach stopped off at various points to disembark people close to their allotted hotel or apartment. Adrian and Sue's was a two-bedroomed flat in a block called The Alexandra. It was set back down an alleyway off a road that ran parallel with the beach, on the first floor with a balcony that overlooked an olive grove; comfortable, secluded, and only five minutes' walk from the sea.

In short, it was ideal.

Once they had settled in, unpacked a little and changed, they wandered down to the seafront. The beach was sandy and stretched in a natural curve for half a mile or so from one promontory to another. Along the front were cafés, bars, shops and restaurants, each one as appealing as the next. It was more touristy than they had expected but not to the point of being disappointing. By then it was early evening and having perused the restaurant menus they chose one on the southern promontory, slightly raised up and affording a delightful view across the bay. It seemed more traditionally Greek than most of the others. They ordered lamb kleftiko and a carafe of local wine, then wandered back to their apartment and went to bed feeling tired but very content.

The next day they wandered down to the beach, paid for a couple of sunbeds and spent the day sunbathing, reading and occasionally dipping in the sea. Sue wore her new bathing costume which Adrian complimented her on. He wore shorts that hung down almost to his knees and, to Sue's dismay, socks and sandals. Fortunately he removed both after a while. He also wore a shirt at first but that too was discarded as the heat of the sun intensified towards midday. Lunch was a Greek salad, bread and a glass of retsina at the apartment, then back onto the beach. In the evening they wandered to the other promontory and had dinner in a restaurant that was virtually a mirror image of the one they'd chosen the night before. Another delicious meal with wine.

When they arrived back at the apartment and got ready for bed, Sue was hoping that *you know what* might happen. She was feeling very happy and relaxed and adored having Adrian all to herself. She wanted to show her affection towards him. But as they got in to bed, Adrian pecked her on the cheek, said goodnight and turned his back.

Their second full day was pretty much a repeat of the first, only that evening they tried a restaurant in the centre of the bay. It proved disappointing.

The next morning, they had breakfast in a café on the front and sat next to a couple roughly their own age who hailed from Warrington. They got chatting. The topic of Stoupa being a bit too touristy cropped up.

"Not the place to come to get away from the madding crowd," said the man, whose name was Bobby. "If you want to do that, best wander down't coast to Agios Nikolaos. It's a lovely fishing village, relatively unspoilt, about an hour's walk. We did it the other day, didn't we Pet?"

"We did," said his wife. "It were right nice." She pointed towards the road that led out of the bay to the south. "Just keep walking out of town along that road and there's a path signed where houses stop. Take a bottle of water, to keep you going 'til taverna half way."

An hour later, after a quick pit stop back at the apartment, Adrian and Sue were heading out of Stoupa en route for Agios Nikolaos. It was a charming walk, through olive groves on the edge of town then onto a path that followed the contours of the coast to their right with a backdrop of high ground verging on mountainous to their left. They passed the halfway taverna but decided against stopping and carried on until they reached their destination.

115

Agios Nikolaos was just how it had been described; relatively unspoilt with a tiny harbour and cafés and bars that still catered for the locals more than tourists. It was how Stoupa might have been fifty years before. They wandered around the village then sat down outside a harbourside bar and ordered iced coffees. They watched fishing boats come and go, manned by what Adrian referred to as ancient Greeks; old fishermen with deeply tanned, leathery skin and dark eyes that still sparkled with life. They talked incessantly and when their tasks were finished sat with even older men, presumably the previous generation of fishermen, to play cards and put the world to rights.

Adrian and Sue spent the day pottering around, lunching at a taverna overlooking the harbour, swimming from the rocky outcrops around the harbour, lying on a nearby beach reading, and eventually strolling back along the path to Stoupa in the late afternoon. Again they passed the halfway taverna without stopping, reached home and sat on their veranda sipping retsina and nibbling black Kalamata olives. It had been the perfect day; so perfect that they repeated it every day for the rest of their holiday. They had fallen in love with Agios Nikolaos.

Sue could not have been happier; with the exception of one area of disappointment. She had hoped that being away together, relaxed and in such a romantic setting, Adrian might have shown more affection towards her than usual. But by the penultimate day of their holiday, they still had not done *you know what* and Adrian had shown no inclination even to try. *The bedroom department* was not happening at all. One night she had tried to snuggle up to him in bed but he had turned away from her and with a "goodnight dearest" adopted a foetal position. Shallow snoring soon followed.

On their last full day they did the coastal walk again, then had lunch with a carafe of retsina before lazing on the beach until it was time to head back along the path. It was Sue's idea to stop at the taverna, out of curiosity more than thirst, although it did feel inordinately hot and the idea of an ice-cold beer was a temptation worth giving in to.

It was a simple, fairly crude building, set back from the path with a pleasant veranda shaded by palm trees and a sort of rockery in front that seemed only recently to have been laid out. There were a few other couples sitting drinking, some they recognised from passing on the path. The waiter spoke fluent English. His name was Georgios. He was in his forties, charming and wore surprisingly neat, well cut trousers and shirt. Sue thought he was good looking, although she would have preferred him clean-shaven rather than stubble-chinned. From the moment they arrived he flirted with her non-stop. Adrian seemed oblivious but Sue revelled in the attention. She particularly liked his habit of brushing against her as he served their drinks.

One beer led to another and late afternoon slipped into early evening. Having no particular plans for their last night, they decided to stay where they were for dinner.

It was idyllic sitting on the veranda, gazing out across the sea with the sun making its way gradually down towards the horizon, sipping their drinks and picking at a selection of meze dishes, accompanied by the omnipotent drone of cicadas. The beers were followed by retsina, rather a lot of it, and to round off a truly sumptuous meal, coffee with *Metaxa*, a brandy-based liqueur that Georgios recommended they try.

By the time they decided to leave, they were both quite drunk. Sue got up to visit the loo, the entrance to which was at the side of the tavern and not visible from the veranda. As she came out, she all but barrelled into Georgios who was standing immediately outside for no apparent reason. Suddenly she was virtually nose to nose with him and their bodies were touching. Instinctively she pulled away, but Georgios took hold of her arms and kept her close. She could feel his breath on her face and smell him; a clean, sweet, warm aroma. He stared into her eyes.

"You are very beautiful," he said.

"Why thank you."

"I wanted you the moment I saw you."

She stifled a nervous giggle. He sounded like a bag of clichés. Clearly this was not the first time he had stood there and said such things. Yet it was rather nice to hear – to know that a man thought that of her. "Very kind of you," she said graciously.

She felt his hands move round to her buttocks and squeeze them. He leaned forward and kissed her forcefully, his tongue filling her mouth. Under normal circumstances she would have been appalled and disgusted and pushed him away, screamed even. But she was drunk, and it felt really good, and she let it happen. She could feel his erection pressing against her.

"Georgios!" The voice bellowed from the veranda. It followed through with something in Greek which could well have been "Where the bloody hell are you?" Georgios pulled away, running a hand over her breasts as he did, then as a parting gesture down under her skirt and between her legs. Instinctively, defensively, she closed them together, only to trap his hand there for a few pleasurable moments. Then he was gone.

Sue tottered on her feet until she had regained her composure, patted herself down and returned to the veranda. Adrian had paid the bill during her absence, so they set off. She looked back as they left and saw Georgios walking to a table with a tray in one hand, waving at her with the other. He blew her a kiss.

They walked in silence for a while, taking it gently as the path twisted and turned; it was not well lit. There was no one else around. Sue was aroused. Being touched by Georgios had awoken something in her and the combination of his kiss, his hands on her body and the alcohol had stirred her.

"Nice place," said Adrian, slurring his words. "Good food, good wine, good service. We should have gone there before."

"We should," replied Sue. "And it's not the only thing we should have done before now."

"What do you mean?"

"This." They had walked around a narrow inlet and were on the opposite side from the taverna. She took his hand, marched him off the path and down a track through sand dunes onto a secluded stretch of beach, and started undoing his trouser belt.

"Susan, what *are* you doing?" exclaimed Adrian, trying to stop her. He invariably called her Sue. *Susan* was a reprimand.

"It's not what I'm doing," she replied, "it's what you're going to do to me. Something you should have done the first night we arrived... and the second and third for that matter." She tugged his trousers down and then his underpants, taking his limp penis in her hand and massaging it until it began to harden. Then she bent down and put it in her mouth.

"Susan! Stop that at once!"

She did not reply; could not reply. Her mouth was full. When she judged he was erect enough, she stood up, slipped her knickers down from beneath her light summer skirt, and undid the buttons on her blouse, exposing her breasts. "Come on," she said. "We're going to do it... here and now."

"Do what?" said Adrian, swaying and trying to keep his balance with his trousers around his ankles.

"You know very well." She tugged his penis. "You're going to put this inside me." She sat down on the sand and lay back, lifting up her skirt and spreading her legs. "Come on, Adrian."

"But... but we can't. Not here."

"Yes we can, and I won't take no for an answer." She put a hand between her legs and began to rub herself. She was already wet. Georgios had started it and now her sudden burst of sexual aggression was helping nicely.

Adrian stood above her, gazing down, seemingly unable to take in what his wife was proposing. Defensively he put both his hands down to cover

120

himself, but his erection poked out from between them. He felt instinctively that this was wrong, although what Sue had just done to him felt good. She'd only ever done it once before, early on in their marriage, and he had discouraged her from a repeat performance. But in his drunken state he had enjoyed the warm feeling it gave him.

"Come on, Adrian, get on with it, will you? I'm not leaving here until we've made love." He continued to stand there. Sue was losing patience. She stood up. "Alright, let's make it easy for you." She took his hand and pulled him towards the back of the beach where a row of boulders was set in a line, a crude attempt to keep the sand dunes from eroding. With trousers and pants still round his ankles, Adrian waddled like a penguin. "Take them off," she ordered. Adrian did as he was told. When they reached the nearest boulder, Sue slipped off her skirt, leaned forward across it so that her backside was sticking provocatively towards her husband and said: "There, you can keep standing. Just edge towards me and it will slip inside. Come on, darling, do it... please?"

Adrian was shocked. This was something else they had never done before, from behind, fornicating like beasts in the field... or on the beach to be precise. His mind was beginning to numb. Again, he just stood there. He couldn't think straight beyond a general feeling that this was very wrong.

"ADRIAN!" screamed Sue. "DO IT!"

He'd never heard her raise her voice before. This was even more shocking to him. Obediently he moved towards her until the tip of his erection was touching her bottom. Sue put a hand down, took hold of his shaft and directed it between her legs. It felt good as it began sliding inside her. She wriggled and pushed herself back towards him to help it on its way. Soon it was filling her completely. *Please don't finish too soon*, she said to herself. *Please let it last.*

She was in luck. Adrian was drunk enough that his sensitivity was numbed, but not so much that his prowess was impaired. He began to push himself in and out of her, getting into a rhythm. She started to pant, which seemed to encourage him more, and once his inhibitions were behind him he got well and truly into the swing of it, thrusting away energetically. For Sue it felt wonderful. Normally Adrian was timid, too timid, but this was anything but. He was really going for it.

Soon afterwards his rhythm came to an abrupt halt. Between thrusts he had pulled back further than was necessary, his penis popped out and he fell backwards onto the sand.

"Get back here this instant!" ordered Sue.

"I don't think I can. It's nice just lying here."

"Do as you're told!"

"I really don't think…"

"I don't want you to think, I want you to do it to me!"

Adrian staggered to his feet. He felt even more drunk than before, but managed to find his wife's backside again and pushed his penis in the general direction.

"Get on with it," said Sue, her tone edged with frustration. She too was drunk to the extent that just about all her inhibitions had vanished. Georgios's blunt, crude sexual advances had seen to that.

Adrian too was becoming frustrated. He was not in control, his wife was calling the shots, and drunk as he was he was not comfortable with this unprecedented role reversal. He felt the need to re-establish himself, not in any logical way, but how present circumstances allowed. He growled, grabbed her buttocks and pressed his erection at her. It felt some resistance. He pushed and felt it gradually entering her.

"Ahh!" cried Sue. "No!"

No? Surely not, thought Adrian. *It's what she wants – what she'd been goading me to do!* He pushed harder, feeling dominant. It felt good. Normally when they did *you know what* he never really experienced any great sensation, apart from the obvious one at the end. But this felt different.

"Adrian, stop!"

Her words fell on deaf ears. No way was he going to stop. He thrust even harder and felt himself penetrate right into her.

"Oh… oh!"

Sue went quiet. She stopped complaining, and seemed to accept what Adrian was doing to her. He was pummelling away, making guttural noises, like an animal. He was forcing himself on her for the first time in their marriage. He was being a man. With one hand she steadied herself against the boulder, with the other she rubbed herself. As Adrian reached his climax, so she reached hers. His final thrusts into her were intense, almost barbaric.

Adrian fell back again, drained and exhausted. Sue leaned forward against the boulder, gasping, her breasts pressing against the cool stone.

When it was over, a round of applause rose from the direction of the taverna. The English vicar and his wife had been in full view of customers on the veranda, courtesy of spotlights that reached out across the inlet. Fortunately for them, Adrian and Sue were completely oblivious to the fact. They heard the distant applause but had no idea it was for them.

Having put their clothes back on and sorted themselves out, they found their way back onto the coastal path and tottered back towards Stoupa in a daze. When they eventually reached their apartment, they took it in turns to use the bathroom then went straight to bed without their customary goodnights to each other.

Adrian tossed and turned all night, disturbed as he was about the evening's events. Sue slept like a log.

They stayed in bed later than usual. The coach back to Kalamata wasn't until midday so they had plenty of time to pack and get ready. They didn't talk much, only about luggage and leaving, nothing at all about the events of the night before. Conversation was similarly sparse on the coach and at the airport as they checked in and killed time in the departure lounge.

Only on the plane, in mid-air and after a couple of gin and tonics, did they have a discussion. Adrian began, fumbling for words in a way that was out of character for him; or would be on any other topic.

"Sue, about last night."

"Yes, Adrian."

"I find it very difficult… to talk about… *the bedroom department*. As you know."

"I do. But I'm glad you're broaching the subject."

"I… I'd had rather too much to drink."

"You and me alike. We were both quite sozzled."

"Yes, we were. I don't remember everything, but I do remember that you, that you, very much took the initiative."

"I did rather."

"I think that was only right."

"Well, Adrian, it was important to me that we should not bypass the opportunity to… to be close to each other, physically, at least once on this special occasion."

"I understand. I know that is more important to you than it is to me. The… the…"

"The sexual?"

Adrian blushed. "Yes, that's what we're talking about."

"That may be so, but you know that we've always said it's not a key aspect of married life. It's a side show, no more."

"We have indeed, thank you." He paused, struggling again to find words. Then with an enormous effort he suddenly found them. "Sue, it has always been something of an ordeal for me. The idea of… *you know what*… not to mention my strong feelings about the act being solely for procreation, and not for pleasure."

"It's never anything else with us," said Sue. "Every time there is that hope."

"I know, I know. But there in Greece, on holiday, it seemed to me that every evening when we returned to

125

the apartment, if we had, you know, done *it* – *it* would have been purely for pleasure. I have a problem with that, as you know."

"I do. My feeling is…"

"However…" Adrian interrupted her and closed his eyes as he came to what was clearly the peroration of his speech. "However, on the beach last night, doing what we did, how we did it, with you leaning against that rock like that." His face took on a pained look. "That was the first time it didn't seem to matter. It felt different. It was wrong to do it like, you know, from behind like that… sinful on various levels. But there was something about it, as if it was meant to be. I know I should feel guilty, but I don't."

"And because you don't feel guilty, you feel… guilty?"

Adrian half smiled. "Something like that."

Sue looked across at him, on the verge of saying something but holding back as if not sure whether to or not. "Adrian, there is something you need to know. It felt different because it *was* different. We not only did it from behind, you… oh dear, how do I put this. If we're talking about *the bedroom department*, let's say that you… came in through the back door, not the front."

Adrian looked at her for a moment or two, puzzled by this allegory. Then as its significance struck home, his newly tanned face paled in an instant. His jaw dropped and he clutched the sides of his seat with claw like fists.

"I… I…" He looked her straight in the eyes. "Are you certain?"

"Yes, dear. It isn't something you can easily be mistaken about."

"Oh my Lord! That too is a sin."

"Is it?"

"Genesis 13:13, 19:5-7, Leviticus 18:22, 20:13, Romans 1:27... I could go on."

"A man with another man perhaps, but consensually between husband and wife within marriage, I don't think so. Doesn't Corinthians 7:5 cover it?"

"Hmmm." Adrian appeared unconvinced. "Are you... are you okay?"

"A tad sore."

"Oh, my Lord!" Adrian leaned forward and cupped his head in his hands. "What would the archdeacon say?"

"He will never know," said Sue emphatically. "It's none of his business. I have no intention of telling him, and I sincerely hope you don't either."

"I may have to confess."

"No, Adrian, this is entirely between us. No one needs to know."

Adrian shook his head. "Not for a man in my position." He was becoming tearful. "And now I feel extremely guilty indeed... for having..."

She took his hand and held it tight within her own. "Adrian, it was a mistake... a drunken error. There was no intent there. You have nothing to feel guilty about. If anyone does it should be me for goading you on."

"You should have stopped me, once..."

"I tried, but you weren't listening."

They slumped into another silence, both full of thoughts and mulling over what had been done and the things that had been said. The plane landed and they disembarked. As they waited at the luggage

127

carousel, Adrian took Sue out of earshot of the other passengers.

"Sue, I've been trying very hard not to feel guilty… after what we talked about on the plane. You're right, it wasn't intentional, and if anything is to blame it was the alcohol. Neither of us was in control and we did something that could be construed as sinful if that were not so. I can reconcile myself to that. But… but… I still have a very strong sense of guilt.

"Why?" asked Sue. "What then is it that makes you feel that way?"

Adrian turned away to avoid looking her directly in the eyes. "When we… when I was doing what I did…"

"Yes?'

"When I… did that to you. I… I… I…"

"What, Adrian? You what…?"

"I really enjoyed it."

Sue took his head in her hands and turned him so that he had no choice but to stare her directly in the face. She smiled at him and kissed him gently on the lips. "So did I."

As they pushed their luggage trolley into the arrivals lounge, Mr Rogers was there to meet them.

"Welcome home," he said, shaking Adrian's hand and pecking Sue on the cheek. They loaded their bags into the boot of his car and got in, Adrian and Sue in the back. As he drove off, Mr Rogers said: "Sue, you look terrific, positively blooming. You must have had a bloody great time."

"Thank you," said Sue, smiling, genuinely delighted to hear this. "Yes I did. A lovely time."

"And how about you, vicar. Have you enjoyed yourself?"

"I have indeed. Thank you… yes."

"Lucky bugger."

Adrian froze. He stared ahead, eyes focused on the back of Mr Rogers' head. How on earth did he… how could he possibly…

He felt his hand being squeezed reassuringly. He looked across at his wife who was still smiling. She winked at him. He unfroze. Of course… just Rogers being his politically incorrect self. A wave of relief flooded through him.

He squeezed Sue's hand harder, smiled at her and winked back.

RUDE WORDS

Liam hated visiting the care home. The thought of it filled him with dread every other Sunday morning as he drove down the M23 towards Burgess Hill... or Bugger's Hole as Peggy, one of the other Sunday visitors he'd got to know, called it; and that was about right as far as he was concerned.

He parked in the visitors' section of the car park and wandered towards the main entrance. The façade of the Victorian building – surely a workhouse in bygone days – appeared grimmer than usual on this damp, overcast November day, surrounded as it was by a medley of trees in the last throws of shedding their leaves to reveal naked winter branches.

Sometimes Shirley came with him, but he knew she hated it even more than he did and he never minded if she offered an excuse, to clean the house or do the washing; anything. At Christmas and on Dad's birthday the kids came along, usually under protest and for a short visit only. So more often than not Liam made the trip alone, stayed as long as he could bear, then drove home feeling guilty for finding it such an ordeal.

Dad had gone downhill rapidly after Mum died. At eighty-four he found himself living alone for the first time in his life. That was two years ago and his life had become chaotic for a while until they moved him into the home. His memory shot, he couldn't remember anything from one minute to the next; where he lived, where the shops were and, if he drove anywhere, where he had parked the car. On one occasion, he'd driven in to town for a haircut (only to be told he'd had one a few days earlier) and afterwards spent an hour wandering around the multi-storey searching for his car. A security guard joined in and he couldn't find it either. The car was reported as stolen and Dad had been given a lift home by the police. The next day it was found parked in a side street next to the multi-story, where Dad had left it.

The car was sold now, so too the house and just about everything else apart from Dad's clothes and a few other belongings, plus some mementos of childhood Liam and his sister, Ellen, had retrieved prior to the clearance; photos, some books, football programmes, games, that sort of thing.

The memory loss was a mixed blessing. On the one hand, Dad was happy; a lack of recall meant he couldn't dwell on the quality of his life, or rather lack of it, and he had settled into an existence free from worry, anxiety and any responsibility whatsoever. A fool's paradise if you like. On the other, it was incredibly frustrating for Liam, and others, trying to make conversation with someone who barely recognised his own son and who asked him the same question over and over again. In years gone by Dad had had a fantastic memory and his general knowledge was stunning. He'd travelled the world as an export sales manager and could quote facts and figures about any country you cared to name, plus a few you'd never even heard of. Which made this all the worse. Curiously, there were good days and bad days. There were moments of clarity, as if a fog had lifted from the landscape inside his head, which were a delight. But for the most part his retention period could be measured in minutes.

Being a Sunday, the most popular day for visiting, reception was manned. Most of the staff knew him by now and the overweight frump sitting at the desk nodded him in with the meagerest hint of a smile on her sour face. "He's in his room," she mumbled with profound indifference.

Dad was always in his room. As far as Liam could ascertain he only ever left it at mealtimes and for Sunday visits; the rest of the time he seemed to spend alone, flicking through newspapers that were weeks old, or magazines that were months old, or staring at the walls and ceiling with just his transistor radio on low for company. There was a television in the lounge but Liam knew Dad rarely went there, if ever; possibly he could not remember how to find it. A strange irony. For decades at home he had sat staring at the telly every evening, mindlessly watching anything that came on.

His was the last room at the end of a long, drab corridor that smelled of a combination of urine and damp, with just a hint of Febreze Spiced Apple. Whenever Liam walked down this corridor, the words of Carmen the Costa Coffee lady at work floated into his head. One Monday morning not so long ago, after a weekend spent celebrating a birthday with a nought in it, he had remarked as she prepared his Americano: "Sixty now, Carmen – officially old." In her droll, acerbic Caribbean accent she had stung back with: "You ain't old 'til you're drippin' piss, my darlin'."

Now he knew what she meant. The care home reeked of it.

Liam walked in without knocking and called cheerily: "Hi Dad, it's me, Liam." Then as an addendum: "… your son."

Predictably, Dad was sitting in the only chair in the room, staring at the wall, listening to BBC Five Live. He looked at Liam vaguely with no hint of recognition, then stood up and held out his hand. Father and son had never done this, shaken hands, and indicated to Liam that Dad had no idea who had just walked into his room.

Today was not a good day.

"Your son," Liam repeated.

Dad nodded. "If you say so."

This would have been hurtful had something similar not happened a dozen times before. "Of course I am," said Liam brightly. "How are you, Dad?"

"Fine."

"Everything alright?"

"Fine." He glanced around the room. "Have you been here before?"

"Many times, Dad." Liam pointed to the digital clock on the shelf above the bed. "Nearly twelve… do you fancy some lunch?"

"I don't mind."

"Come on, let's head off to the dining room, shall we?"

"Alright. Do you know the way?"

"I do."

"You've been here before then."

"I have indeed. Come on, I'll lead the way."

"I'll get my coat."

"No need, it's only down the corridor. We're not going outside. Unless you'd like to go somewhere… the pub maybe, or the fish and chip restaurant in town?"

"I don't mind."

"Well let's keep it simple and eat here, shall we?" It was Liam's preference. He found it stressful taking his dad out for lunch. It took an age, and ordering was complicated when Dad couldn't remember what he'd chosen from one minute to the next. In the care home Dad ate anything that was put in front of him, but anywhere else he became overtly fussy and particular; the meat was tough, the vegetables undercooked, the gravy runny, the custard lumpy… "not like your mother used to make".

The dining room was busy. Liam recognised some of the other visitors and smiled and nodded at a few. He saw Peggy, fussing over her mother, and gave her a wave and mouthed *Hello*. She rolled her eyes, mouthed back

134

Bugger's Hole and grinned. Some visitors were absorbed in their elderly folk and engaged in conversation or helping them with their meals; others seemed indifferent, eager to be distracted by anything that wasn't to do with an ageing relative. Liam wondered how he came across to others; probably somewhere in the middle ground between the two.

It was a canteen arrangement; you took a tray and moved along the serving area and watched dollops of this and lumps of that gradually filling your plate. There was a choice of roast beef or pork, as always on a Sunday. Liam chose pork and Dad beef. You could help yourself to gravy, mustard, apple sauce or horseradish, if you could find room. Just before the end was another sour faced woman who could have been the slimmer, older sister of the woman at reception.

"Do you want stuffing?' she declared, a serving spoon containing a congealed mess hovering uninvitingly in the space between them.

No, but you do, thought Liam. Then out loud he said: "Ordinarily I would say yes, but not today, thank you all the same."

"Please yourself."

They made their way across the dining room and set their trays down on a table by the window. The view was of an orchard of apple trees with fruit rotting on the boughs or as windfalls on the overgrown grass beneath. In one corner, on a narrow terrace, stood a swing seat with the cushions removed, undulating slightly with the gentle breeze, and beyond the trees, next to a disintegrating wooden fence, a rusty Zimmer frame lay on its side, as if abandoned on the very spot where its owner had expired. It had been there as long as Liam had been coming here.

Dad was hungry. He tucked into his meal with gusto, which made Liam wonder when he had last eaten; he'd been looking thinner recently. This was not the most expensive of care homes; it was all he and Ellen could afford. The amount resulting from the house sale had proven disappointing and it was plain from the conditions that you got what you paid for. So if they skimped on meals he wouldn't have been at all surprised. He'd queried things on a couple of occasions and been given assurances by the manager, Mr Castellani, that the establishment prided itself on high standards of governance and that his father was in the very best of hands. There was nothing more he could do, but it added to his sense of guilt, and encouraged him to remember to buy a lottery ticket every Friday on his way home from work.

"Enjoying that, Dad?"

"Hmmm."

"Did you have any breakfast this morning?" Dad shook his head. "Why not – weren't you hungry, or wasn't there any?" Dad shrugged. "Which was it?"

Dad shook his head, which meant: "I can't remember."

"Okay." Liam picked at his meal but it really was highly unappealing and he wished now that he'd insisted on going to the pub. He watched Dad tucking in, so tried again and managed a roast potato… or it might have been a parsnip.

Dad put down his knife and fork and took a sip of water, his hand shaking slightly. "How's Marie?"

"Marie?"

"Your wife."

"You mean Shirley. Marie was my first girlfriend when I was at college forty years ago."

"If you say so."

"Shirley is fine thanks. So are the kids."

"Kids?"

"Robin and Sam."

"Boys, that's nice."

"Sam is a girl. Samantha." This was a continuing disappointment to Liam, that Rob and Sam's grandfather didn't even recall their existence, let alone their names. "Rob is twenty-nine, Sam twenty-seven," he added as a reminder.

"Thank you." He shovelled a greasy forkful of beef into his mouth then sat back and gazed out of the window vacantly as he chewed. "And Clara?"

Liam sighed. Dad hadn't asked about her for a while and he'd hoped she had dropped out of his memory for good. Clara was Dad's sister, Liam's aunt; dead fifteen years from cancer. Not wanting to upset or confuse his father any more than necessary, he said: "As well as can be expected." Dad looked perplexed. Perhaps he remembered more than Liam imagined. Had it been a mistake to lie? More guilt piling up.

When Dad put his knife and fork together, Liam said: "Shall we go and sit in the lounge and have a coffee?"

"I don't mind."

"Or would you prefer some tea?" Dad looked

confused. "I'll get you tea," said Liam, rather than waiting and hoping for a decision.

"Alright."

The lounge was next to the dining room and overlooked the same orchard. They sat in a couple of armchairs separated by a low, heavily-stained coffee table and sipped their drinks. The conversation had become sparse now there were no practicalities to deal with. It had always been this way. When it came to making talk beyond doing stuff, there was a void. They had nothing whatsoever in common.

Dad had become far less communicative since moving into the care home. He'd never been a great conversationalist, preferring to listen to others rather than take the initiative, speaking mostly when spoken to. The memory loss hadn't helped, and Mum dying and the move to the care home had compounded the problem. Liam was worried it may be a symptom of depression and had discussed it with Mr Castellani who had brushed the idea away with a wave of his hand. "Part of settling in," he said. "That's all. It's very common."

Liam tried a few openers but received nothing back in return. Had he watched television recently; had he heard from any of the rest of the family (not that there were many – Dad had a brother down in the West Country and a cousin in New Zealand, and that was about it); was he friends with any of the other residents? If Dad spoke at all it was to say "No"; mostly he said nothing at all.

Liam thought he'd try football. Dad had been a lifelong supporter of Brighton and Hove Albion F.C. and had followed their ups and downs long after he'd stopped going to matches. They had lived in Hove for much of Liam's childhood, just a twenty-minute walk from the ground

"How are the Seagulls doing, Dad?"

There was a glimmer of a hint of a spark in his eyes at the mention of the Gulls. "Not bad." He looked uncomfortable and struggled up out of his chair. He shuffled across the room to the gents and after what seemed an age eventually returned, sat down again and finished his reply. "Not good, not bad. They win some they lose some."

Encouraged by this response, Liam continued the same thread. "Nothing's changed then. I've lost touch. Sometimes I drive past the Amex stadium – you know, where they play these days – and wonder how they're doing. Looks impressive but I can't imagine it has the same atmosphere as the old ground… The Goldstone."

"Hmmm."

Liam thought back to his youth and the excitement of those first trips to see the Albion. It was like nothing he'd ever experienced before, standing on the terrace surrounded by hundreds, thousands, of cheering, shouting people. And when Brighton scored, that adrenalin-fuelled mass celebration. For a lad in his early teens those were heady memories.

"You know, Dad, I loved going to The Goldstone with you as a kid – being in the crowd and cheering the Gulls on. They were great times."

"Hmmm."

"Do you remember?"

No response.

"I do, vividly. I can remember the very first game you took me to, against Aston Villa in March 1972. We beat them two goals to nil. Great result. Willie Irvine scored the winner. A fantastic goal, like a bullet right into the top right hand corner of the net. Unstoppable! Surely you remember that?"

"Hmmm."

"What was the manager's name then? The one before Brian Clough came and made a pig's ear of things, briefly. Pat something." Liam knew the name very well but hoped this might prompt an answer. No response. "Saward, that was him... Pat Saward. I must have been about fourteen. We always stood about halfway between the goals, just in front of a refreshment hut. I remember the noise. I can hear it now. Deafening at times. And the smell of cigarettes – really strong. I'd never been so close to so many smokers before. It permeated my clothes. Mum was none too happy when we got home! But I loved it. Such an amazing atmosphere."

Dad was staring out across the orchard, either conjuring up memories of those Goldstone days or devoid of any thought whatsoever, Liam could not tell. He was beginning to feel despondent. He'd done this before, played on the football memories, and with good results, ending up in a nostalgic chat. But today he was getting nowhere. Dad seemed to have sunk into a world of his own.

"Something else I remember about that first match, Dad." He leaned forward and lowered his voice to make sure no one could overhear. "I've never told you this before, but on the terraces that day... that was the first time I ever heard rude words. You know, the really rude swear words. The four-lettered variety. When the fans were chanting, every other word was an F and whenever the referee gave a decision against the Seagulls he was a C."

Dad continued staring into infinity, giving nothing away. Then gradually his brow furrowed as he mulled over what Liam had just said, giving it some serious thought. Slowly, he turned to look at his son. The vacant expression in his eyes cleared and a brightness took its place, as if that foggy landscape had cleared inside his head.

Liam hadn't seen this for quite a while. "You okay, Dad?"

"Hmmm."

Dad focused on Liam, making direct eye contact for the first time.

"What's up?"

"How did you know?"

Liam looked at him, puzzled. "How did I know what?"

"They were rude."

"Sorry, I don't know what you mean."

"If you'd never heard those words before, how did you know they were rude?"

"Well, I…" Liam looked across at his dad, not at all sure how to respond. He was taken aback; stumped. "Well now, I suppose… I'm not sure. Good point."

It was a very good point. Dad had made him think. How *had* he known? With hindsight he knew very well what they meant in all their various meanings, vulgar and otherwise. He'd used them enough times, though never in front of Dad, which was why he had been so cagey about making reference to them at all, and by initials only. He sat in silence and pondered. Such a simple question, yet no simple answer sprung to mind. Had he known they were rude at the time? Or had he tagged them as rude later on with knowledge gained at a later stage in his life? Though not much later, not at fourteen in the early seventies. Perhaps he had sensed they were rude, by the tone in which they were used, often aggressively. If not rude then disapproved of for young ones, ring-fenced for adults only, at a time when he had yet to leave childhood behind, let alone adolescence. Telling Dad that he'd never heard them before might, on reflection, not be entirely true. Surely someone at school had used them. Gary Hudson was a bit of a rebel, so too the Lake twins; he remembered vividly them using expletives, usually directed at teachers they hated. But had that been later, in the sixth form when they had all turned into moody, longhaired pre-university oddballs? He truly could not remember.

Dad was still looking at him, waiting for and expecting an answer. Liam was none the wiser and at a loss for words. So all he could do was look back at his father. This had not happened for many years, decades, and possibly never at all – a meaningful exchange of looks instead of brief eye contact then one or other glancing away to avoid any further awkwardness.

"Dad, I have to confess, you've got me there."

"Got you?"

"Yes, got me. You have well and truly got me. I have absolutely no idea."

"About what?"

"How I knew they were rude words." A grin began to form at the edges of his mouth, which developed into a full-blown smile. Then he was giggling, then chuckling. And to his enormous delight, Dad copied him at each stage, culminating in a mutual laughter that had the other residents and their visitors turning around to gaze at them. It fell short of a hug, of bodily contact, but only just. Even so it was the closest father and son had been for many years, possibly in their entire lives. Did Dad fully appreciate the depth of his question and the mental effort required to provide an intelligent, insightful reply? Or was it asked in all innocence with no insight whatever? Liam couldn't tell, nor did he care. It had, for a sublime moment, broken the ice – nay the glacial mountain – between them and brought him close to his Dad.

When he escorted Dad back to his room and said goodbye, Liam felt tearful. For once he didn't want to leave. On the drive back home, before he had even reached the A23, he began to feel emotions welling up inside him, a concoction of good and bad. There was always guilt, but this time also regret, loss, even shame; on the other hand, there was happiness, elation and delight at having enjoyed at least a moment of rapport with Dad. Hopefully there would be more. It was just a case of finding keys to unlock his head. More triggers like rude words. *Rude words* – of all things!

Liam pulled into a layby, turned off the engine, sat back and wept. He cried and cried until he was drained and his eyes stung from the saltiness of his own tears.

Willie Irvine scoring the winner for Brighton and Hove Albion against Aston Villa on 25th March 1972. Liam and his dad are in the crowd just behind the leaping goalkeeper.

Photo courtesy of The Argus / Brighton and Hove Stuff

MATLOCK MEG AND
THE RIBER HOARD

She was standing outside *Superdrug* when the pirate ship first came into view. Stepping out of the air-conditioned store into hot direct sunlight had made her feel woozy for a moment. A mist seemed to float across her eyes, colours drained from everything in sight and there was a loud buzzing in her ears, like a thousand bees with pollination in mind. She reached out an arm and clutched on to something next to her. Out of the corner of her eye she thought it was a man, but the touch felt like plastic so it couldn't have been. A statue perhaps, or a mannequin of some kind? She couldn't tell. For a split second there was nothing but blackness. Then in an instant, as if by some sorcery, a drug kicked in – she revived and was alert again. Everything was vivid and clear.

The ship had made its way along Bakewell Road and was turning onto Causeway Lane, in full sail, looking both majestic and terrifying at once. The sails billowed, the Jolly Roger rippled in the breeze, and the crew lined the decks waving their cutlasses as one; some had eye patches, others peg legs or a hook for a hand, and a couple had all three. They were shouting. She couldn't hear what they were saying but it was almost certainly "Ahaaar!"

Oddly, none of the other shoppers seemed to notice, which was strange because pirate ships are unusual in Matlock, especially sailing through the town centre on a Tuesday morning. An elderly gentleman crossed the road in front of it at a snail's pace, seemingly oblivious to the great bows bearing down upon him, or the huge bare-breasted figurehead towering above his head. But miraculously he reached the other side unharmed.

Positioned as far forward as it was possible, with one foot on the figurehead's back and a hand gripping a sail rope, like the mighty prince of all pirates, stood a man. Even from a distance she could see his finely chiselled features and the shock of dark hair beneath the scarlet bandana wrapped around his head. He wore black pirate boots, tangerine pantaloons, a white silk shirt open to the waist, and a black belt from which hung an ornate knife and a cutlass. His chest was deeply tanned and covered in thick hair. Six feet tall, he was lean, virile and breathtakingly handsome! She had never seen the face before, yet instinctively he was known to her. A familiar stranger.

He gazed ahead, scanning the shoppers along the pavements, eagerly looking for something, or someone.

It took no time for him to spy her. His deep blue eyes widened and his mouth stretched into a huge grin. He raised his arm and waved.

Suddenly there was a commotion on board. The pirate glanced behind him and saw a sinister figure standing on the raised deck at the stern. Jackson Richard Coplan, better known as Black Jack! The evil beast he'd taken prisoner in battle and was transporting to captivity. He must have escaped from the hold, no doubt helped by one or more of the scurvier members of the crew whose heads were easily turned by empty promises of gold doubloons and caskets of fine rum. Yes! He could see the main culprit. Next to Black Jack stood the foul smelling, hunchbacked mulatto that was Rancid Rajinder, the scurviest of them all.

The mood was changing by the second. Black Jack was rallying the crew to his side, shouting and gesticulating wildly, inciting them to mutiny. And the crew were listening. Some nodded their heads, others turned to stare menacingly at the handsome pirate, their faces dark with the sudden realisation of how badly they had been treated by their captain all this time, if only they had had someone to point it out. There was a surge of movement towards the figure at the bows.

The pirate knew instinctively his time was up and that he must act. Pulling his cutlass from his waist, he sliced the bottom of the rope he was holding. Gripping the rope high up with both hands, he launched himself over the bows into mid-air, swinging in a great arc and landing perfectly on both feet – directly in front of her.

"Meg!" He gripped her by the shoulders, pulled her

towards him and kissed her full on her lips, long and hard. When he eventually pulled away, she gasped. It was the most passionate kiss she had ever experience, sending a shiver down the entire length of her spine and a tingle into her toes. "Meg! I recognised you immediately. How could I miss that cute little turned up nose!"

She gazed up into his eyes, her mouth wide open. "My name's Beryl," she said. "Beryl Smedley."

"Ahaaar!" he cried, his head tipping back as he guffawed loudly. "No time for games, I'd know my Meg anywhere." The ship was passing broadside on to them now and they were drowned out by shouts of derision from the mutinous rabble. Some were trailing ropes over the side of the hull, intent on giving chase. "Avast!" he said urgently, grabbing her arm. "We must make ourselves scarce. Do you have horses?"

"No, but my Fiat Punto's parked in the multi-storey."

"I have no idea what that means," said the pirate. "Like a horse I suppose. Lead the way… quick!"

"I haven't finished my shopping yet."

"No time! We must leave now."

"What does *Avast!* mean? I've often wondered."

"It means halt, but only sailors know that so I use it whenever the fancy takes me with landlubbers."

"Where are we going?"

He pointed towards the top of a hill on the outskirts of town. "To yonder castle."

"What, Riber?"

"That be the place… that mighty fortress in the hamlet of Riber! Once a stronghold, sadly gone to rack and ruin."

148

"It's luxury apartments now."

He seemed disappointed at this intelligence. "I didn't know that. Our destiny and our destination nevertheless. Hurry!"

Behind them the sound of marauding pirates was getting louder. They were flooding down ropes onto the pavement and weaving their way between shoppers on the trail of their prey.

Beryl and her pirate cut down a side road, through a mall and onto another street. The noise of pirates receded and was a faint hum by the time they reached the car park. Beryl stopped at the pay machine, fed her ticket in, paid and slipped it into her jacket pocket.

"Four English pounds to stable your horse?" exclaimed the pirate. "Outrageous!"

"It's even worse in Chesterfield," said Beryl knowledgeably.

Her Fiat Punto was on the third level. Bright red, it stood out like a ripe tomato amongst the silver and black Fords and Vauxhalls surrounding it. She slotted into the driving seat comfortably, but the passenger seat was a squeeze for a six-foot pirate with a cutlass. He eventually managed to shut the door.

She started the engine, but did not move off.

"Go!" he commanded. "Go now! What is wrong?"

"Put your seat belt on please."

"This feeble strap? You are not serious, woman! I have travelled the seven seas of the world, fought battles galore, come within inches of death a hundred times, and now you want me to strap myself into your coffin on wheels?"

"It's the law," stated Beryl.

"I will not do it."

"Then we're not moving."

The door to the stair well burst open and a dozen fearsome looking pirates all but tumbled out onto the ground not fifty yards away. He put his seat belt on.

Beryl moved off. It was a piece of great fortune that the exit was in the opposite direction from the stairs. As she drove away she could see nothing but pirates in her rear-view mirror, waving cutlasses and chasing after them at full pelt. Usually she was a very wary driver, but today she decided against caution in favour of self-preservation and sped down the ramps of the car park until they were on the ground floor and at the exit barrier.

"Ram it!" ordered her pirate passenger.

Beryl fumbled in her pocket. "Hang on, I've got the ticket."

"Smash it to smithereens!"

"It's here somewhere."

He grabbed the steering wheel. "Do as I say. How does this thing work?"

"Stop that!" yelled Beryl angrily, slapping his hand. "It won't do you any good. You need the pedals." Beryl felt inside her jacket pocket. "Here it is." She wound down the window and slotted the ticket into the machine. The barrier went up. "Let go of the wheel now please, err… goodness, I don't know your name."

"Of course you do. I told you before, no game playing."

"Remind me?"

As if to answer her question, a dirty hand at the

end of an even dirtier sleeve thrust its way into the car through the open window, reaching across Beryl towards her passenger. An unshaven face filled the rest of the space. A blast of foul, stale rum breath hit her. "Ahaaar, Pete, you scummy piece of dog filth. Time for your comeuppance!"

Beryl pressed her foot onto the accelerator and the car jerked forwards. The figure at the window screamed as he was dragged along, then the face and the hand disappeared. In the mirror, she saw him rolling over on the floor, sending other pirates tumbling like skittles.

"So, your name's Pete," she said.

"You know very well it is."

"Pirate Pete. Not very original."

"I like it."

"Well I don't. I think I shall just call you Mr P."

As they turned onto Causeway Lane, the ship was ahead of them, almost at the Matlock Town football ground. Pirates were hurrying to catch up and climb back on board, and to suffer the wrath of Black Jack for letting Pirate Pete slip through their fingers.

"Look!" said Mr P. "They're ahead of us, and the castle is in sight. They know what's up there and will do anything to reach it first. Can't this wreck go any faster?"

"I'm doing thirty-five as it is. I'm breaking the speed limit."

"We should be on horseback. You can't beat it."

"Actually this is a Fiat Punto 1.2 MPI and has seventy-two horsepower," boasted Beryl, who had read the owner's manual.

"Pah! Seventy-two worn out old nags overdue for the knacker's yard! One stallion at its peak is all we need."

"I'll see if I can push it up to forty as we get out of the town centre."

"That's my Meg. Come on, girl, let's outrun that ship!"

"Shouldn't be difficult to outrun a ship, on dry land and going uphill."

"That's the spirit!" He ruffled her hair which sent another shiver down her spine. "Onwards and upwards to stake our claim to the hoard!"

★ ★ ★

She stood on the top one of the crenellated towers of Riber Castle, peering down into the valley below, Mr P by her side. The view was clear across to Matlock. To the left was the road to Matlock Bath and the Heights of Abraham; to the right, miles of open countryside pitted with villages until eventually you reached Chesterfield and its curious twisted church spire.

There was no sign of the pirate ship.

She looked away, and down to her body. Somewhere en route, she wasn't sure precisely where, the jacket, polo shirt and jeans she had put on that morning had vanished. She had first been aware of the change when she pulled up and parked her Fiat at the rear of the castle. Mr P had climbed out immediately and she followed him. It was then she sensed a change and looked at herself. She wore a dark woollen hooded cape, contrasted by a soft black silk bodice, laced down the front with ribbon ending in a bow, with a full black silk taffeta skirt, rouched at one side to reveal a crimson lace petticoat and rich claret velvet jacket, gathered at the shoulders with narrow sleeves that covered the tops of her hands. Around her waist, she had a thick brown leather belt adorned with a large silver buckle to which a pistol was strapped. On her feet, she wore pirate boots. On her head, a large brimmed hat with a black feather.

In the reflection of a window she saw her face; that too had changed. Her wavy blonde hair was longer and she wore blood red lipstick and jet black eye liner.

The effect on Mr P had been dramatic. When he saw her, he kissed her again, roughly this time, pulling her up against his body. He was aroused. His blood was up. He pulled the bow on her bodice and it fell open.

"Avast!' she said playfully, and only halfheartedly because in truth she did not want him to stop. "Not here," she pleaded. "We might be seen."

"Who cares!"

"Mr Smedley, for one. Me for another." They were standing on a lawn in front of the entrance to the castle, totally exposed, though the place appeared to be deserted.

"I know where," said Mr P. He took her hand and all but frogmarched her into the castle, up several flights of stairs and onto the roof of the tower, with its stunning vista of the Derbyshire countryside. "Here!" He lifted her off the ground and encircled his arms firmly round her thighs.

When he eventually set her down gently on the roof again, Mr P ran his fingers through her hair. "What a woman you are, Meg," he whispered with unexpected tenderness.

"My name's Beryl," she insisted, breathlessly.

He smiled and shook his head. "You're my Meg."

She patted down her skirt. "What next? I'm feeling drained."

He took her hand. "Come, we have much to do and little time to do it in. Black Jack and his motley crew may be here at any moment."

"What are they after?"

"Numerous things." From inside his shirt he pulled a tattered piece of parchment. "First of all this – a map of Riber that tells where the treasure is hid. A hoard beyond your wildest imaginings. Second, the treasure itself. Third, me. They would love to capture me and make me walk the plank... or keelhaul me."

"What does keelhaul mean? That's another pirate word I've never understood."

"It's a terrible thing, Meg. They tie you to a line that's looped under the ship, then they throw you overboard and drag you under the keel from one side to the other... or it might be from bow to stern. The hull's usually covered with barnacles, so you're cut to ribbons. If they pull you slowly you might sink below the hull and avoid them, but then you'd be under water so long you'd likely drown."

"That's awful!"

"Fourthly..."

"Yes?"

"Fourthly, you."

"Me?"

"You, Meg. Black Jack would relish getting his hands on my woman to ravish and have his way with her. But

154

have no fear, I'm here to protect you and be sure that never happens."

"Thank goodness," said Beryl. "Twice in one day would be a bit much."

Hand in hand they made their way back down into the castle until they reached the entrance hall. Mr P lay the parchment on a mahogany table. "What do you make of this, Meg? I'm no good with maps and puzzles and working stuff out. I'm a man who does things. Look at this and tell me where the treasure is hid."

Beryl studied the parchment. "Where did you get this?"

"I stole it off Black Jack."

"That wasn't very nice. No wonder he's after you."

"It was pirate justice! He too stole it… off Evil Paul Crew. Cut his throat to get it."

"That's awful!"

"Not awful. Evil Paul Crew stole it an' all… off Larry Parry. Murdered him in his sleep."

"What dreadful people!"

"That's what pirates do. Possession is ownership with this parchment, and I have it, so it's mine. I did no killing for it, mind, but there's others that did. We're up here at Riber in the wake of dead man's shoes."

"Horrible."

"Time presses on, what does it say, this map?"

It wasn't a difficult task. The small rectangle was taken up mostly by a crude plan of the castle and the surrounding grounds. Underneath, written in faded ink, was a verse:

This missive gives you all the power
If on July the sixth can afford
To rhyme with beast and then with flower
Tis all you need to know, my lord;
And when sun doth shine at midday hour
You'll find the key to Ribers hoard.

"Well now," she said. "It's a rubbish poem, and there ought to be an apostrophe in Riber's. But it's quite simple really. Words that rhyme with beast and flower that have something to do with a castle. Beast, east, flower, tower. It means the East Tower."

"Which one is that?"

She pointed at the map, blushing. "The one where we just…"

Mr P grunted. "And what about the rest, about the midday hour and the key?"

"I assume it means that if you stand on top of the tower at midday the sun will shine on something that will give a clue to the location of the hoard."

"What time is it now?"

She looked across at a large clock on the wall. "Quarter to twelve."

"And today's date?"

"July the sixth. What an incredible coincidence!"

"This is a fantasy," said Mr P, winking at her. "Anything is possible. Fifteen minutes to go, no time to waste. Let's go back there now, and hope the sun is shining."

"It was a moment ago."

They climbed again up the stairs to the tower roof

which was indeed bathed in sunlight. In fact, there wasn't a cloud in sight. Mr P took Meg's hand and kissed it, then ran his hand along the side of her face and neck. He looked deep into her eyes with an intensity that melted her to the core. She knew that this man, rough round the edges though he may be, adored her. He had not *had* her earlier – he had made love to her, in his own rugged way. Emotionally she felt totally content for the first time in her entire life.

They stood in silence, glancing occasionally towards the sun. "How will we know when it's midday?" she asked.

"We shan't need to," said Mr P. "Something will show itself. I know."

Silence again. They looked around expectantly. Nothing seemed to offer a clue as to what might happen. There wasn't a breath of wind now, even on the top of a tower on a high hill. A swift landed on the crenellation next to them and twittered to itself happily. The faint rumble of a train in the distance was the only other sound of any kind.

Suddenly Mr P felt his hand being squeezed tight. "Look!" cried Meg. She was pointing up at the weathervane that rose above them on top of a wooden pole in the centre of the roof. The pointer had a majestic cock perched on it that crowed in the direction of the wind. Today it was motionless. Beneath was a static crosspiece indicating the four compass points in ornate ironwork letters – **N,S,E,W**. The extended arm of the **N** was casting a shadow against the side of the tower, pointing like a gnarled finger at a particular stone low down in the wall. "Is that it? Is that what we are looking for?"

"You could be right!" said Mr P. He strode across and bent down on one knee, examining the stone. He ran his fingers round the edge, touching the grouting. "It's loose," he said. He took the knife from his belt and began to scrape around the sides. "This cement is parchment thin." Shortly he put the knife away, slid his fingers into each side and tugged at the stone. Nothing happened, so he scraped some more with the knife and tried again. Still nothing. On the third attempt the stone came away a fraction.

"It's moving!" said Meg excitedly.

One final application of the knife and the stone plopped out of its place in the wall and fell to the ground. Mr P peered inside. He put his hand into the space, felt around for a moment, then pulled it out. In the palm of his hand lay a large, ornate and very tarnished key. He examined it carefully, then peered inside the space again, feeling all around to see if there was anything else to be found. There was nothing.

"A key," said Meg. "But to what?"

They took turns to examine the key from all angles. They could see no inscription, no markings, just a key.

Mr P sat back on his haunches. "Now what!" he exclaimed, a look of exasperation on his rugged face.

Meg looked equally baffled. "I don't know," she said. "I don't know." She turned the key round in her hand, as if for inspiration. Then she looked at the gap where the stone had been. "Are you certain there's nothing else in there?"

"Certain," said Mr P. The sun was still shining directly onto the space. From his squatting position, he could see directly into it and the sun was like a natural torch lighting it up. "No wait." He lay flat on his stomach and pushed his face right up to the entrance of the gap. Attached to the stone at the back he saw a brass plaque. He squeezed a hand in and tried to pull it away but it was stuck solid. He peered at it. "There's an inscription, Meg."

"What does it say?"

"Just letters. **N**, then **S**, then **E**, then a question mark."

"Compass points. Like on the weathervane. The missing letter is **W**."

"So, do we head west?"

Meg looked upwards, squinting at the crosspiece on the weathervane. The sun was in her eyes, so she moved round to the other side of the tower with the sun behind her. On the lines of the **W** she could just make out some writing.

"On the weathervane!" she called out. "Another inscription. How do we get up there to read it for heaven's sake?"

Mr P studied the pole and kicked the wood at its base with his boot. A splinter flew off and the weathervane above rocked slightly. "We don't," he said. "The weathervane comes down to us." He leaned against the pole, pressing his shoulder into it. With feet firmly rooted on the surface of the roof, he began pushing at it, harder each time. Meg heard a cracking noise from the base, where the wood was set in a kind of metal shoe and held firm by nails. The more Mr P pushed, the louder the cracking sound. She looked up. The weathervane was swaying perilously now and she moved aside, well away from where inevitably it would land. Then a loud crack as the pole split and began to topple.

"TIM – BER!" yelled Mr P.

The weathervane crashed to the roof. Compass points **S** and **E** had taken the brunt of the fall and buckled on impact. The cock was now crowing innocuously at the crenellated wall of the tower. **W** was conveniently positioned at roughly knee level as Meg and Mr P gathered round to read the inscription.

"What does it say, Meg?" said Mr P.

"Look," she replied. "Just a few words. You read them."

"No, you."

She looked at him suspiciously. "You handed me the parchment to read – now you won't read these few words. Do you have a problem with literacy, Pirate Pete?"

Mr P looked sheepishly at her. "If you mean can I read, the answer's no. That's woman's work, not a man's… especially not a pirate!"

Meg chuckled. "You sound really silly," she said.

"I never had the chance for any schooling. Tain't my fault."

"I'll teach you one day."

"I'd like that." He turned his attention to the compass point. "What does it say?"

"Simple. It just says *Beneath the Ice House*."

"What does that mean?"

"It means we should look underneath the house where they store ice."

"I know that, woman! Don't mistake me for a fool."

"I'm only teasing you, Mr P. Don't be cross with me."

"Where is the ice house?"

"Somewhere in the grounds I imagine, so we need to go down the tower again."

All of a sudden there was an almighty boom. It came from the front of the tower, in the direction of Matlock. They rushed to the side and gazed down into the valley below. In the distance a plume of smoke floated in the air above the port side of the pirate ship, which appeared to have made its way along Starkholmes Road and was moored beneath the castle. Another boom rang out and they saw a cannonball fly through the air and vanish into trees to their left.

"Look!" exclaimed Meg, pointing downwards. Making their way up the hillside was a swarm of pirates, clambering over fences, crossing fields and slashing randomly with their cutlasses at anything in their path. "Black Jack wants his map back."

"Come!" said Mr P. "Not a moment to lose!"

They hurried down the stairs and out into the grounds at the rear of the castle. Both stood and gazed out across the grounds; they saw a lawn, a cark park, trees, and a number of outbuildings of various shapes and sizes.

"It must be one of those," said Mr P, nodding towards the outhouses. He took Meg's hand and started in that direction.

"No wait," said Meg, holding him back. "I used to play up here when I was a kid. Ice houses are often round, a bit like an igloo, and with moss or greenery over them. I think I remember seeing something like that." She tugged him in a different direction. "Over here. Yes, I'm sure it's over here."

Mr P let himself be led. They crossed over the lawn towards some trees, the beginnings of a wood that bordered onto the land surrounding the castle. As they reached the edge they heard another great boom and seconds later a cannonball landed just to their right, splitting a tree in half. It faltered then crashed to the ground.

"Well blow me sideways!" exclaimed Mr P.

Meg grinned. "Let's find the ice house first."

She led the way through the trees, following a path that didn't appear to be well trodden. Soon they reached a clearing. In the centre was a conical hut, green from a covering of lichen, with a front door in the centre of a rectangular brick surround. It looked in reasonable condition, if somewhat neglected.

"As you described," said Mr P.

"An early fridge."

"A what?'

"Never mind. Now, the clue was *Beneath the Ice House*. Shall we take a look inside and see what the floor has to offer?"

Mr P strode forward. "Let me." He approached the door, which was wooden and looked very solid, and pressed his shoulder against it. He pushed. It didn't give an inch, so he pressed harder. Nothing. He pulled back a foot or so and hurled himself at the door, but to no avail. He switched shoulders and tried again, and a third time. Next, he stood back further and kicked it firmly with the soul of his boot. He marked the wood but it didn't give.

"Can I try?" asked Meg meekly.

"No, wench, this is the job for a man." Mr P kicked the door again, and again. He turned around and backed into it with his feet rooted to the ground like two anchors. Nothing he did made any impact. The door remained unmoved and intact. Eventually he stood back, wiped the sweat from his brow and swore.

Meg stepped forward, gripped the door handle and turned it. The door opened. "It's not locked," she said.

Mr P looked positively emasculated and swore again.

Inside it was dark at first but their eyes soon grew accustomed to the gloom. On either side of the confined space were wooden latticed shelves. There was nothing in the centre and the circular floor dipped down to a point well below ground level, looking rather like a large bowl.

"To keep the ice cold as long as possible," explained Meg. She walked into the middle and inspected the floor. "This is solid stone," she said. "I can't see that anything could be hidden underneath here."

Mr P nodded his head. "I think you're right. No way is anything down there."

"So now what?"

"I don't know."

"Let's take a look outside. Maybe there's another way to reach underneath." They made their way back through the door and wandered around the side of the ice house.

It was overgrown with thick brambles and Mr P had to hack it away with his cutlass. Clearly no one had been round there for years, decades even. Meg followed in his wake, stoically ignoring rips to her dress and scratches to her skin. When they reached the back of the building, the brambles were at their thickest. Mr P stripped to the waste and attacked them with cutlass in one hand and knife in the other. Eventually he had cleared them enough to be able to see the brickwork. His efforts this time were worthwhile. Low down in the wall was a small door, a half-sized version of the one at the front.

"Give me the key," demanded Mr P. Meg handed it to him. He slid it into the keyhole, pausing for effect before turning it. The key clicked inside the lock and the door instantly moved a fraction. "Here we go – the key fits. This has got to be the place." He pushed at the door and it opened gradually, creaking as it went, until it was flat against the wall.

They both bent down and peered inside. "It's terribly dark in there," said Meg. "Darker than the front. We need a torch."

"Aye, you're not wrong," replied Mr P. "But we don't have one. Too small for me to get inside… more a cupboard than a room. Do you think you can squeeze in, Meg?"

"I'll give it a try." She bent low into a squatting position and edged forwards. "It's pitch black in here. I can't see a thing."

"Close your eyes for a while then reopen them," suggested Mr P. "It'll accustom you to the dark." Meg did as he said. "Any better?"

"Much better, thanks." She half disappeared into the room, then stopped. "Right, the first thing I can see is a barrel, several in fact. They're blocking the way. Are they what we're looking for?"

"I don't know – I don't think so. Are they heavy? Can you move them towards me?"

Meg puffed and grunted. "Hang on. Yes, they're not huge actually. I can tilt and roll them."

Minutes later four barrels were lined up outside next to Mr P. "Quarter casks, I reckon," he said. On the side of each were stenciled the word *GUNPOWDER*.

"Not what we're after," said Mr P. "Could come in handy though." Meg was still inside the room. "Is there anything else in there?"

"Hard to tell. It's still murky in here, it would help if I knew what I was looking for." She shuffled into the space as best she could.

"A trunk or a casket is my guess," said Mr P. "Or a box or a case. Anything that might hold the Riber Hoard!"

"What *is* this Riber Hoard?"

"It's the treasure that we seek. Left here many years ago by Zakariah Parry, an evil son of the Devil who would have carved up his own grandmother for some pieces of eight. He spent his life gathering together treasures beyond your wildest imagination. When he died, a clue to its location was left on that parchment for his son Larry who as I've told already was murdered in his bed for it."

"Ow!" cried out Meg.

"What's up?"

"Stubbed my toe on something." She felt in front of

her with her hands. "A box of some kind. It's big. I can feel studs all round it. I think it could be made of leather."

"Can you lift it… bring it out into the open?"

"There's a handle. Very heavy." Mr P heard puffs and grunts and scraping noises. "I've shifted it a few inches but I don't think I can manage it any further. It feels like it's as heavy as lead."

"Here let me try." Mr P reached inside the space. "Guide my hands." He felt them being taken by Meg and pulled into the darkness. His body filled the doorway and it was a stretch, but eventually the fingers of one hand made contact with the handle – and he pulled. What had been heavy for Meg was a gentle lift for him and the leather box came sliding towards him. Then it was in his arms and he and Meg were back outside, round the ice house, and sitting in the clearing inspecting their find. It was indeed a leather box, studded on all sides with reinforced edges and a stout handle at both ends. The lid was held in place by rope wound round the box and tied securely; underneath was a lock. Mr P took his knife to the rope and had it removed in seconds. From beneath his tunic he pulled out the key again and tried it in the lock. It was not a fit, far too large.

"What now?" said Meg.

"Desperate measures," said Mr P. With his knife, he stabbed at the leather to one side of the lock. Once it had penetrated, he sawed into the leather and gradually sliced round the lock. Moments later it came loose and fell onto the grass. He lifted the lid. They peered inside and saw what appeared to be a sack, tied at one end with more rope.

Meg's curiosity was boiling over by now. She grabbed the sack impatiently, tugged the rope to loosen the end and held it over the leather box, allowing the contents to spill out. From within poured a multi-coloured shower of jewelry, gems, precious stones, and gold and silver nuggets. She gasped. When the bag was empty she ran her hands through them all. She recognized diamonds, rubies, sapphires and emeralds; some were loose stones, others were embedded in rings or necklaces. There were bracelets and head combs, all studded with gems of one sort or another.

"Well I never!" said Meg. "This little lot is worth a fortune… an absolute fortune!"

Mr P's eyes were out on stalks. "By heavens, woman, you're right. This is even greater a hoard than I imagined!" He too ran his hands through the contents of the box. He picked up a large, loose diamond, put it between his teeth and bit down on it. He winced. "The real thing," he acknowledged. "Stronger than my teeth." He picked out an ornate comb, made of ebony and lined along the top with half a dozen blood red rubies, and slipped it into Meg's hair. "There, you'd look a picture wearing that."

Meg giggled. "I would, only shouldn't we be concerned about Black Jack and his men? They must surely have reached the castle by now."

"Blast the man! I'd like to hang him from a yardarm, and whip him with a cat o' nine tails as he swings there."

"Meanwhile," said Meg. "Back in the real world…"

Mr P roared with laughter. "The real world! I don't think so, my wench! Even so we must make a plan. We need to get away from here as fast as we can with this hoard. We need a plan of escape. What say you, Meg?"

"I agree. So, we are hidden at present in these woods at the back of the castle, the pirates are making their way up towards the front – probably close to it by now – and my car is in the car park. The plan surely has to be to get to the car and drive away with the hoard avoiding Black Jack's thugs in the process."

"Easy!" said Mr P, slamming the lid of the treasure case down and slotting it under his arm. "Let's head that way right now." He strode off through the woods at such a pace that Meg had trouble keeping up with him. As they reached the edge where the trees thinned out, he slowed down to a gentle stroll, then stopped altogether allowing Meg to catch up. She knew why he had stopped before she could see out of the woods. The noise of marauding pirates was raucous and unmistakable. She edged forwards until the veil of trees barely still hid them. In front of her were the castle grounds with the castle itself beyond. The grounds were a heaving mass of activity.

There were pirates everywhere.

★ ★ ★

Half an hour later, they were still standing in exactly the same place.

"Easy!" said Meg sarcastically. Mr P gave her a blanching look, his manhood bruised once again. Meg squeezed his side. "Now now, don't go mardy on me. We need to work together on this. We're stuck here, we need to find a way out."

"What do you suggest then?" said Mr P grumpily.

Meg thought for a moment, looking one way and then the other. "Well, we're here, and the car is over there" – she pointed to their right – "and between the two are a lot of nasty men who want to tear us to pieces."

"Or do worse to you."

She shivered. "Ugh, perish the thought."

"So what's your magic solution?"

Meg thought some more, then said: "A distraction."

"What do you mean?"

"Well, in order for us to get from here to the car we need to get those pirates shifted. One way of doing that would be to give them something to focus their attention on." She pointed dramatically to her left. "Over there!"

"What do you have in mind?"

"An explosion – as loud as possible."

"An explosion! And how in the name of Hades do you intend to…" He stopped in mid-sentence and glanced back towards the woods.

Meg grinned. "The penny has dropped," she said.

"Gunpowder! And we can use the rope off this here case as a fuse." His gaze turned towards their left. "Do you know what's over there?"

"Not exactly, no," said Meg. "It's been so long since I was here. More outbuildings I seem to remember. But it doesn't really matter what we blow up, it's the distraction that counts."

"Wait here." Mr P disappeared into the trees and presently returned with a barrel on each shoulder and some strands of rope tucked into his tunic. He stood erect with legs apart and a gleam in his eye.

"My, you make a picture, Mr P," stated Meg, admiring the perfect example of manhood standing before her. She shook her head to clear it. "So, make your way round there just inside the tree line until you've outstripped the pirates. Set up your gunpowder with a long enough fuse to get back here in good time."

"As you say, Meg." He bent forward and kissed her on her lips. "My God, you'd make a cracking pirate princess. Come and be mine when this is all done. With the Riber Hoard we can live in luxury together on a boat I'll have specially built. A love boat!"

"Go now, Mr P, or it will never happen!"

He headed off through the trees again, only in a different direction this time. All Meg could do was stand and wait. Peering through the trees she could see the pirates clearly. She counted at least fifty. They were milling about, searching outbuildings, talking to each other and standing guard. Black Jack was in the thick of it. Pirates kept coming up to him and speaking; reporting, it seemed to Meg, probably of their failed attempts to find her and Mr P. He looked angry. After one such briefing, a scurvy looking character got a fist in the face for his trouble.

Black Jack moved away from them, towards the woods as if in disgust. He was close to the edge of the tree line now, barely feet away from Meg with just a few trees shielding her from his view. She heard him curse. He took a wad of tobacco from his pocket, bit off a chunk and chewed. Between the branches and leaves she saw brown liquid dribble from the corner of his mouth into his beard; the colour of both was identical.

170

She could hear him breathing, and she could smell him, he was that close.

She felt a tickle inside her nose. She wriggled it from one side to the other, trying to make it go away. But the more she wriggled it, the worse the tickle became. It really was the worst possible moment to sneeze.

★ ★ ★

Mr P had set the two quarter casks next to each other and twisted together the two pieces of rope fuse that now fed out of the top of each, so he only had to light the end of one. They were tucked behind what appeared to be an old stable; wooden and in need of repair. The wood was dry and brittle. It would burn well.

He took out his tinderbox, struck the flint vigorously until the tinder glowed, then blew on it gently until it had caught enough to ignite a sulphur-tipped splint. This he applied to the rope. It took a while to catch but once it did the rope burned solidly. A perfect fuse. When there was no doubt that it would stay alight, Mr P departed, making his way back into the woods, round to the place where he had left Meg. When he reached the spot, he looked about in all directions. She was nowhere to be seen.

From beyond the trees he heard the excited babble of pirates, louder and more animated than before, punctuated by cheers and whistles. He peered through the foliage and saw figures circled around something, but he could not see what. Their backs were towards him, forming a wall of pirates. His gaze was fixed upon them. After a while a gap appeared which allowed him to see into the middle of the circle. To his horror he saw Meg, pinned against a wall, her hands tied behind her back, her silk bodice all but torn down to the waste. Black Jack was leering at her. Next to her, on the floor, lay the case containing the Riber Hoard.

Mr P's blood boiled instantly. "Scurvy scum!" he yelled and, throwing caution to the wind, pushed his way through the foliage into the clearing. When he reached the two pirates closest to him, he grabbed them by the ears and cracked their heads together. They fell like ninepins. He strode into the circle.

"Black Jack! Step aside and leave my woman be, you son of a dog!"

Meg craned her neck towards him. She looked angry and defiant rather than victimized. "Mr P!" she beseeched. "Please deal with this evil monster before…"

Black Jack stopped her mouth with his hand. "Ahaaar!" he bellowed. "We have some goods of yours here, and was just about to enjoy them for ourselves."

"Leave her be!" commanded Mr P through gritted teeth. A pirate stepped out of the circle, intent on blocking his way. A single punch to the jaw saw him tumble unconscious to the ground. Another tried the same and found himself tipped upside down and body slammed. A third received such a hard kick between the legs that he twisted sideways in agony, gasping for breath. And a fourth, who had swung at Mr P with a cutlass, screamed as his weapon was wrenched from him and used to sever his own arm.

Black Jack pulled his cutlass from its scabbard and

confronted Mr P head on. Meg was forgotten. The two men faced each other with cutlasses poised… and the fight began. Black Jack struck a blow towards Mr P's neck but was parried. He tried again, aiming lower this time, but this too was countered. The sound of clashing swords was crisp in the air and they flashed as sunlight shone off their blades. Black Jack was fast and accurate, but Mr P was his match and not a single blow hit home, though he felt the blade whizz past him numerous times. Then he managed to break through and drew blood from Black Jack's forearm. Almost immediately, Black Jack reciprocated and bloodied Mr P's cheek. The pirates were egging their leader on, cursing and cheering. Black Jack seemed inspired by them and cut faster and harder with his cutlass. The blows eventually overwhelmed Mr P who was forced to back away from the onslaught. A pirate stuck his foot out and Mr P went tumbling backwards onto the ground. Black Jack lunged forwards, tugged his knife from his belt and knelt down on one knee, ready for the kill.

A huge explosion ripped through the air. Everyone stopped dead, including Black Jack, then turned and looked in the direction of the noise. A plume of black smoke rose from behind the outhouses in the corner of the castle grounds, and flames were rising up. Everyone had turned to look, apart from Mr P. When the pirates turned back again, Black Jack was lying on the ground, a bloody gash across his face, stretching from his left ear to the bottom of his right cheek. He lay motionless.

Mr P got to his feet, clutched his cutlass tight in one hand, and Black Jack's knife in the other. He backed towards Meg and stood protectively in front of her. Some of the pirates had started running off towards the explosion; others stood as still as statues, looks of puzzlement, fear and astonishment on their faces.

"Who wants some?" shouted Mr P. "Come on, you cowardly bunch... who's next?" A pirate rushed at him, screaming loudly, a wooden club in his hand. Holding his knife by the blade, Mr P threw it directly at him. It embedded itself in his chest, and the pirate slumped in a heap. "Anyone else?"

The rabble gradually began moving backwards, slowly at first, then faster until they were in full flight. Mr P turned his attention to Meg. "My angel, I let you down. I am sorry." He untied her hands and legs and covered her up with the rags that were left from her bodice.

"Not your fault, my love," said Meg. "I have myself to blame – I gave myself away. No harm done, apart from being touched by that beast. Is he dead?"

Mr P looked down at Black Jack. "I think not. But he won't be hassling anyone for a while until that face of his is mended. Shall we get out of here?"

"Oh yes please. Look, the explosion did the trick, they've all run off in that direction as we hoped. We can reach the car now."

Mr P picked up the case, and with his other hand took Meg's arm and led her towards the car park. The little red Fiat he had scoffed at earlier now seemed a very welcome sight indeed. "Our chariot awaits," he said, grinning. "Let's hope those seventy-two old nags don't fail us."

"They won't," said Meg. "They never have before." They climbed in and Mr P threw the case onto the back seat. "Where to?"

"Anywhere there are no pirates… present company excepted!"

Meg started the engine and off they went, away from the castle, through Riber village and out onto country lanes. With no plan or direction in mind, she instinctively found herself heading back towards Matlock. They approached the town centre from the same direction they had left it, driving along Causeway Lane. It seemed natural to head back to the place where their adventure had begun and before long they were back in the multi-story car park, in exactly the same bay. They strolled out into the street, hand in hand, Mr P clutching the case containing the Riber Hoard. No one seemed to notice the fact that a pirate was wandering around, nor did they seem to pay any attention to how Meg was dressed, not even her badly torn bodice. Eventually they were in Causeway Lane, outside *Superdrug*, the very spot where Meg had spied the pirate ship for the first time.

"We've come full circle," said Meg. "What now?"

Mr P did not reply. He put the case down on the pavement and took Meg in his arms. He covered her lips with his, running his hands through her hair as he did. The kiss was very long and Meg felt she was being enveloped by her pirate lover, absorbed into him somehow to the point where it seemed their bodies were melded together as one. It was overpowering. Her head began to swim. Her eyes were closed and there was a buzzing in her ears. She blacked out.

★ ★ ★

"You alright, me duck?"

A woman's voice. It sounded distant and ethereal. She couldn't see where it came from; in truth, she couldn't see much at all. That buzzing in her ears again, and a sound like water rushing across a beach as it was sucked back into the sea. All very strange. She had no idea where she was.

"What's your name?" A man's voice this time.

"Meg… no, Beryl."

"Not sure of her own name," someone commented.

"What day is it, love?"

"Tuesday… I think."

"Not sure of the day." The man again. "Concussed probably."

"What's the name of the prime minister?"

"Theresa May." Then as an afterthought she added: "More's the pity."

"That's more positive," the man said, chuckling. "It can't be all bad then. You're going to be fine. Just a bump on the head."

Her vision was returning and she could make out the outlines of several people peering down at her. Beyond them was the sky, mostly blue with a few puffy clouds. She must be lying down out of doors somewhere. Across the road was a park. If she wasn't mistaken it looked just like Hall Leys Park. Surely not – there was nowhere to lie down opposite there. Just shops. "What's happening, what's going on?" she asked.

The man replied. "You fainted. You're in Matlock,

outside *Superdrug*. You've got a lovely bruise on the side of your head where you hit it on the pavement. Other than that, you're okay. I'm the store manager. Would you like us to call an ambulance?"

"No, please don't. I'll be fine in a moment."

"Here," said the woman. "Drink this."

A glass of water was put to her lips. She drank. It was cold and refreshing and immediately perked her up. She could see clearly all around her now. She was sitting on the pavement, propped up against the wall of *Superdrug*. Next to her was her shopping bag. "What time is it?"

"Just after twelve."

"What, twelve noon?"

"Not midnight, that's for sure."

She sat upright. "It can't be. I was up at Riber all afternoon, having…" She decided not to say what she had been having.

"It's only just gone twelve, I can assure you."

She stood up and looked down at herself. She was back in her jeans and polo shirt. The cape, torn bodice, skirt, petticoat and jacket were all gone. She picked up her shopping bag.

"Are you feeling well enough to go?" asked the store manager.

"I'm fine," she replied. "Thank you for taking care of me. I'll be on my way now." She turned to walk away and cannoned straight into someone – or something – next to her on the pavement. It looked familiar. It was a pirate.

"Mr P!" she gasped.

"Ahaaar!" said the store manager, in a poor imitation

177

of a pirate's voice. "Let me introduce you to Cut Throat Keith, our plastic pal. Named after our regional manager whose idea it was. Personally, I don't see the connection between a chemist shop and a statue of a pirate, but he seems to think otherwise... and the kids love him. They think he's Cap'n Jack Sparrow."

Beryl gazed at the figure. It had a hook for a hand and a peg leg, and looked nothing at all like her Mr P. She wandered off along the street, her feelings wavering between bewilderment, embarrassment and amusement. She'd been blessed with a lively imagination all her life, but nothing like this had ever happened to her before. A dream, a fantasy, yet so vivid that she felt she had lived every second. She could feel his lips on hers, his hands on her body.

She paused momentarily and looked over her shoulder in the direction of Riber Castle. It was just visible from where she stood, bleak and austere. She could make out the East Tower. She blushed.

When she reached her car, she sat in the driver's seat and looked across to where Mr P had so recently been her passenger. She could smell him, she was certain. Whatever had happened, she was now well and truly back in the real world, and now she had to drive home and get some chores done before her husband came home from work and wanted his tea. As she pulled her seat belt across to strap herself in, her hand brushed against something in her hair. It fell away and landed in her lap.

It was an ebony comb, studded along the top with blood red rubies.

WOOF JUSTISS

Helo, my naem is Zulu, Im a polees dog.
I wos born at the Metrpolitun Polees Dog Trainin Establishmunt, or MPDTE four short, wich is in Keston in Kent. My mum an dad wur both polees dogs so its in my blud. At 8 weaks old I went tu liv with Polees Cunstble George Brunel hu is a polees dog handlur, an his famly. They are luvly peepl an kind an treet me very wel an I am very hapy with them. They liv in Croydn wich George cawls a shitehoal but I quite leik it. Theres sum smashin parcs an we go warking wen not on dyuty in the Shurly hills and sumwear cawld the Hapy Valy at Chaldun, both graet. George oftn sez wurk hard play hard. I agrea with him.

George chose Zulu as a pet naem cuz my burthdy is on 22 Janury, the anivursry of the batle of rorks drift aparuntly, wich is wot the film Zulu is all abowt. Its won of Georges favrites. I also have a propr kenel naem wich Im very prowd of. But its no gud wen weir on dyuty an George is givin me opurashunal commands. Can yu imajin. "Stop him Metpol Rawnsley Lamberhurst!" The pursun Im chasing wud just larf.

Anuthr fave film of George is Leif of Brian. He leiks tu say the leins wich is funy if yu no the film but not if yu dont. Sumteims he warks intu the polees stashun, poynts tuwords the sels and in a sily vois showts "Weleas Wodewik!" Uther teims he cawls our bos Bigus Dikus, but not wen hes arownd. Sumteims wen he meets new coleegs he sez "I hav a weif yu no". Sum new coleegs larf at this. Then he sez "do yu no wot she is cawld, she is cawld Incontinentya Butux." Moor larfs at this. But its not tru, Georges weif is cawld Wendy. She is a very neis laidy an luvs me an feads me an maeks a big fus of me. Shes a bit moody at tims an can get queit stresy, but not with me, only with hur two kids, theyre both boys whos naems are Shutup Ivan and Stopit Craig.

By the wey, sory abowt the crap spelin an tiepin, I no its not graet, but they didnt teech riting at MPDTE. Im doin my best.

The famly who liv nex door tu us also hav a dog, but hes just a pet not a wurking dog leik me. Their faerly posh or leik tu think they ar an so dus there dog, yet hes got the most comn naem yu culd imajin. Rover! So funy! It dusnt soot him, he uses long wurds an culd tawk for Inglund. He moans abowt his naem, I sed it culd be wurs, they culd of cawld him Spot or Lassy. I think hes jelus cuz Zulu is such a cool naem, also cuz I work an he dusnt, he stayz at hoam awl day. Probubly on benefits. We get on moastly but sumteims I find him a bit borin. He wonts tu go on abowt polutics an filosofy an stuf wen awl I wont tu do is naw on a neis bone an lik my bawls. He went on four munths abowt Brexit aftur the refurendum, sed hed hav votd remayn givn the chans an its al downhil from now on an Grate Britan is no longer grate an is goin to the dogs. Thats not a neis thing tu say cumin from a dog I sed, an he gaev me a luk leik I was styopid an sed it was mearly a figur of speach. I sed I dint reely cair eethr way, he told me Im shalow, so I told him tu woof off.

I startd my traening at MPDTE wen I wos a yeer old. Im a Jurman Shepurd. Most of my dog coleegs are ether Jurmun or Beljun Shepurds, moastly Jurman, we are wots nown as GPs, genrul purpus dogs an part of the Dog Support Unit, DSU four short. Were tawt tu surch for misin peepl, objekts dropd by scalywags as George cawls them such as raps an splifs, traking sents on the ground, controlin hosteil crouds, that sawt of thing. Last but not leest chasin an detaynin peeple wen chalenjd tu stop an they don't, wich I leik best about the job, sumthing yu can reely get yur teath in tu.

Iv been a polees dog now four six yeers and Im very prowd tu sai I hav given gud survis all that teim. Me and George hav a supurb wurking relashunship an we hav court lodes of scalys. (In privut George cals them sumthing els, not scalys, but its very rood.) In thos 6 yeers only ons have I behavd badly, or I think the wurd Georges bos usd was inapropratly. That is wot I wont tu tel yu abowt.

Wed been cawld tu a Fayl Tu Stop, wich means sumwon the polees wont tu speek tu has, wel... fayld tu stop! Run awai or drivn off, probly cuz there a scaly up tu no gud. On this ocyshun we wur owt an abowt in Croydn in our speshuly adaptd respons veicle, George driyvin an me in my kenel compartmunt, air cundishund, soundproofd, al modcons. Also their is storij spase four speshlist ekwipmnt. George says this is wear he keaps his nukledustrs an catle prods an joynt roling parafinaylyur. Moar of his joaks... . I think.

He got a cawl on his radyo sayin theirs bin a Fayl Tu Stop on the Lundn Rode neer West Croydn trayn stashun, yung lad dryving a Voxaul Corser, heding in the direkshun of the Mayday hosptl and Forten Eaf pond. I say Mayday but musnt cawl it that eny longr, thay changd the naem tu Croydn Univursty Hosptl a few yeers bak cuz tu many peepl kept cawling it the Maydie. Wendy says thats unfare, she shud no, shes a nurs but not at Maydie, she wurks for Epsum an Sunt Helyer. But she had both Shutup Ivan an Stopit Craig at the Maydie and says she caem out on boath ocayshuns with awl major orguns in tact and no C Diff, wotever

182

that is. She rekuns Epsum is much wurs. She sed wons at Epsum aparuntly they tuk the rong kidny out of a payshunt. They left the bad won in an remoovd the helthy won by mistaik. The man dyed... wel yu wud wudnt yu.

Wear wos I. O yes, wen the cawl caim thru abowt the Fayl Tu Stop we wur in Selhurst neer the Cristal Paliss futbawl stadyum wear George gos on satrday aftrnoons tu get depresd. George put his foot down an we reechd the Forten Eaf pond rounderbowt just in teim tu sea the targit veicl cureer up the Lundn Rode an go LEFT LEFT LEFT ontu the A23 tuwords the Purly Way. Ther wur tu polees cars alredy on its tayl with bloos an toos goin so we tagd along four a weil, in caes thears a decamp or the perp gets agresiv an is resistin arest. The chaes shot ahed an owt of site, so George tuk it easy an drowv in the generul direkshun wich sootd me nisly, I wos quite hapy chillin in the bak.

We went past the twin towrs, thats IKEA, or Hurdygurdyland as George cawls it. He puld in at a burgur van outseid sum big shops for a cofee. I got a nise boal of watr. He gaev me a bit of fus an we playd with a bawl for a weil. Then his radyo blared an we hurd the chaes had gon awl up the Purly Way, past the airudroam almowst as far as the big Tesko at Purly. Now their heding bak in our direkshun, the targit jumpin leits an evrythin. George put me bak in my kenel an got behynd the weel. Then in no teim at al he saw the targit with bloos an toos on its tayl comin tuwards us. They tuk the slip rowd off tu IKEA. Goerge puld ontu the mayn rowd then LEFT LEFT LEFT ontu the sliprowd aftr them.

"Maybe hes goin shopin, Zulu," cawls George. "Buyin a Billy bookcaes or sumthin." Im thinkin not at this teim of neit he isnt. Even if they wur opn its mor leik hes after sum sweadish meetbawls in the restront. Ive never taestd them but Iv bin in their wons chasin sum scalys an they smelt reem. I lurnt the wurd reem from wochin The Only Way Is Esix on tely. Good program.

I cud heer the radyo. The targit wos trapd in IKEA car parc, gowin rownd in surcels aparntly. The uther respons veicles had closd in.

"I sea him," sed George. "Hes cornerd. Hes not givin up litely."

George puld tu a holt an rushd rownd tu let me owt, putin me on a short leed. I cud smel trubl alredy. "Cum on Zulu," he sed. "Lets sea wot we can do." We ran tuwords the cornr of the car parc. By then the targit wos stuk in a smal spase and goin bak an forward, a polees car on won side, a brik wal on the uthr and a shop in frunt. Ther wer polees on both seids, won with a tasur gun, anuther with a baton redy tu smash the winscrean. They wer showtin reely lowd.

George led me tuwords the car from the reer, intendin tu get rownd the frunt so the drivr culd sea thers dogs abowt tu scair him. But befour we cud, the drivr sudnly slams intu rivurs tryin tu run

184

us ovr. George manijd tu get out of the wai but dropd my leed. I ran rownd the frunt and barkd awai leik mad, showin my teath an lookin meen. An ges wot, the scaly only treid tu run me ovur agen! Droav strait at me, nearly squoshin me betwean the shop frunt an the wal. I jumpd ontu the bonet, then he revursd so I jumpd off agen quik. Then he treid tu run over anuthr polees man. He didnt giv a shit.

Next thing the polees man with the batun smashd the seid window, glas evryware, then stuk a hand in the window an puld out the kees. Nise won. Next he had the doar opun an he an George dragd the scaly out by his sholdurs an had him fase down on the flor. They manijd tu get both hands behynd his bak an hancufs on. George red him his rites. Wile this wos goin I wos standin cloas by redy tu inturveen if rekwird, but I wosnt needed. I didnt have anything tu do. Thing is, I wos right next tu them an the scalywags bum wos stikin up in the air in frunt of me. It wos leik it wos starin me in the fase, an it wos just tu temptin an I culdnt resist.

So I bit it.

Wel, I wos angry, he tride tu harm George. He soar wot I did an showtd tu bak off. So I did an went tu grownd as traned.

Soon moar bloos an toos aryvd as reyinforsmunts (triky wurd for a dog that) an the scaly wos dragd ontu his feat and shuvd in the bak of a van. I cud sea the scaly limpin a bit, an their wos sum blud on his bum. Surv him rite.

185

George put me on the leed an tuk me bak tu the respons veicle. I wos feelin gilty now cuz I new I shudnt of bit the scalywag. He was in cufs and proan an not a thret by then. I expectd a telin off an deservd won. So no won wos mor surpisd than me wen George givs me sum fus, a pat on the hed and said: "Gud boy, Zulu. Wel dun!"

I smild. Dogs can smil yu no, wen their hapy. Its not awl tale wagin.

Next day George an me wur orderd tu go an see Bigus Dikus, remember hes our bos, reel nam Detectiv Cunstubl Timothy Gorse. George chukls about his nam cos he knows his films an its the nam of won of the polees men in Cary on Cunstubl, plaid by the skiny blok with speks who George sais wos a pansy an sed "O helo" awl the teim! We wotchd it tugethr recently, its very funy, my favurit caractr is cawld Polees Cunstubl Cunstubl, that maed me larf.

George wosnt larfin this mornin. Dc Gorseses expreshn told us imediatly this poleesmans lot wos not a hapy won (hapy won). He told us he had receevd a cumplaint abowt us, or rathr abowt me not George, from the dyuty solicitr last nite. The bos had red the report of the incidnt an apreciatd the seris of events, the scaly (he didnt use that wurd, thats me) an that he fayld tu stop, wos resistin arest and his behaviur drivin leik that wos totly unacseptubl. But the cumplaint wos about wot hapnd aftr that, wen he wos proan and in cufs wich wos a difrent matr. The solicitr wos claymin his

cliunt woz vishusly atakd by a polees dog, me, an it
wos an unesesarily and unprovokd asorlt. Hes rite in
a way, but the scaly disurvd it. Evn so I wos feelin
very gilty now, Id got George intu truble an thats
not gud. My eers wer down, an I put on a sulun
expreshun an gav Dc Gorse my doe eyd luk, yu
no leik Princes Diana was so gud at. Georges weif
Wendy can do it supurbly. I hurd her wons telin her
frend Joana Lumly (not the famus won, her frend
at bingo) that she lurnt it from wotchin Princes
Diana an it wurks a treet on George espeshly wen
her kredit card is maxd owt.

Sumteims wen George is in a bit of a pikle he
sais "Hang on lads Iv got a grate idear... um, um",
just leik Mykul Cain in The Italyan Job, evryone
nows that won. Rite now I wont tu sai that tu him
coz I think hes genuinly wurid an it wud maek him
smeil. But I cant speek so thats that, Im a dog for
crist saek.

Dc Gorse got up from his desc and caem rownd
an stud in frunt of us both. He lukd George in the
eiy, then he bent doun an lukd at me an Im thinkin
hear it cums, wot George cawls a boloking. My
eers wer evn futhr down an I wos doin the Princes
Diana luk big teim. I wos temptd tu lik his fase but
decidud betr not, meit be deemd inapropriat. Then
he sed "George" (gud sine, furst nam not Pc Brunel)
"yu hav a fein dog hear, with a fawltles record,
an I am not prepard tu acept this incidunt was
anythin moar than poleese dog Metpol Rawnsley
Lamberhurst, also known as Zulu, doin wot he thort

was rite in protectin his handlr an othur polees personel undr very dificlt curcumstancs an doin his dyuty. I shal be takin it no futhr."

Then he patd me on the hed an sed: "Woof justiss Id cawl it."

Ha ha woof justiss, thats the bos maekin a joak. Neis won Bigus Dikus. George larfd an so did I, dogs can larf yu no, wen they thinc sumthins funy.

An that wos that, the story of the won an only misdemenur in my carear. I hurd latr that the scaly wos only 17, no lisens, no insurans, with previus, an pisd. He got a 20 huors community servis an six poynts on his lisense wen he eventuly gets won. George sed its disgustin, meit as wel giv him a fortneits holidy in the Maldeevs tu reflect on his shortcumins.

As four me, I no I shuldnt hav don it but tu be honist I hav tu sai if the saem situashun arows an I was cunfruntd with that scalys bum wen hed just treid tu run ovr George Id bite it agen. I wud.

I'm dew tu retir soon. Dont rely wont tu but Im getin on a bit an long in the teeth four chasin scalys awl dai and neit. Im lukin fourwurd tu sum pees an quite, so long as I cun stai with George an his famly as there pet. A gurlfrend wud be neis, start a famly, mak sum litel polees dogs.

Im enjoyin writin an wont tu do a propr autobiogrufy telin my leif storey, Iv alredy thort of a graet titel...

ZULU – WORIER AGENST CREIM!

Maybe maek a gud film won day, Stevn

Speelburg directin, no won els wil do. Rover next dor dusnt think much of the idear. He sais that anthrupumorfism is a vulgr omniputense thes days, an the rot set in with Wolt Disny. I havnt a clu wot hes talkin abowt.

Wen Iv got mor teim I wont tu improov my spelin and lurn tu teip betr, I know its paw. That wos a joak by the way, paw. Maebe not the best joak evr but then luk at it this wai... not bad for a dog eh?

DOTTY

Mrs. Dorothy Roberts – Dotty to those who knew
her well, Mrs Roberts to anyone else – had few
pleasures left in life. At eighty-six, widowed, with her
two children and four grandchildren living in different
parts of the other side of the world, few remaining
friends she hadn't outlived, and struggling to get by on
a meagre state pension, there was, frankly, little to take
pleasure in.

Admittedly she lived in a lovely part of the country,
Dunton Green, on the Kentish stretch of the North
Downs Way, a couple of miles from Sevenoaks. Born
and bred in Tunbridge Wells, she hadn't moved far;
Kent had been home to her all her life. The housing
association flat she lived in was basic and functional
but pleasant enough. There were convenience shops
nearby and the public transport into Sevenoaks wasn't

bad; not great but not bad. Her lifestyle lacked the finer things, yet it was comfortable. For her age she was in good health, and remarkably agile. By and large she had much to be grateful for, even if pleasures were few and far between. Like many who had exceeded their three score and ten and outlived their spouse and most of their contemporaries, she was finding loneliness the hardest challenge of old age.

One small, some might say mundane, solace did, however, bring her a sense of satisfaction, if not out and out pleasure; her daily morning walk down to the local shop to buy a newspaper, which she took home via a gentle stroll around the nearby recreation park and then read from cover to cover, even the sports pages, sitting in her armchair with a nice cup of tea. *Twinings English Breakfast*. No other brand would do. *Golden and well rounded*, it said on the packet, and the packet was right.

Mrs Roberts had had a good upbringing and education, was well-read, and although a housewife for most of her adult life, she had taught for a while in a private school; English Language and Literature. She prided herself on being a bit of a pedant. For example, it bothered her that there was no apostrophe in *Twinings*. She knew from research in the library that Thomas Twining had started the business in the eighteenth century. So, if the family name was Twining, an apostrophe was necessary to designate possession of the tea, or the business that produced the tea. She had written to them about it and received a polite but brief reply thanking her for her interest and saying how sorry they were that she was disappointed in their trade name. It had, however, been their trade name for over two hundred years and there were no plans to make a change.

Each morning she bought a different newspaper. She had no preference; the easy reading style of the tabloids appealed to her just as much as the more scholarly treatment in the broadsheets, or what had once been broadsheets. Chopping and changing between them kept her up to date not just with the news but with their diverse perspectives upon it. Today it happened to be *The Guardian*.

Punctuated by sips of tea, she read every word and then went back to the beginning to reread the articles that had stuck in her mind first time round, as was her habit. On this occasion, she didn't get past the first on her list; a short but intriguing piece about goings-on in a court hearing the day before:

Thursday 11th August 2016

Judge and defendant exchange insults in court

A judge who was verbally abused by a defendant reciprocated at a court hearing where he was being sentenced for breaching an antisocial behaviour order.

John Hennigan, 50, who had breached the order by using racist language towards a black woman and her two children told Chelmsford crown court judge Patricia Lynch QC that she was "a bit of a cunt". And Judge Lynch replied: "You are a bit of a cunt yourself. Being offensive to me doesn't help."

When Hennigan screamed back "Go fuck

yourself", the judge replied: "You too." He reportedly also shouted "Sieg Heil" – a pro-Hitler chant used in Nazi Germany – and banged the glass panel of the dock as he was jailed for 18 months.

Hennigan, from Harlow, Essex, has dozens of previous convictions for offences including drug and firearm possession and common assault.

Mrs Roberts found this extraordinary. Fancy a judge using the C-word, a female judge at that... and in court! She wasn't sure whether to disapprove of her for stooping to Hennigan's sordid level, or admire her for parrying the moron's verbal abuse in language that he would understand. Mrs Roberts had never used the word in her life, not even in private. She was no prude and had no problem with swearing; indeed, she had done her share over the years when circumstances demanded, usually when Richie, her now long departed husband, had been guilty of some misdemeanour or other. But the C-word was the worst imaginable swear word and it had never passed her lips. She remembered once reading somewhere that someone – Germaine Greer it might have been – had said that in a world where the use of the F-word was commonplace and had lost its edge, the C-word was the only word left in the English language with the genuine power to shock.

"If high court judges are using it now," mused Mrs Roberts, "perhaps that too is losing its power."

The story about the judge fascinated her. Why was the C-word so offensive? She determined to find out more about it the next time she was online. She didn't have a computer in her flat, she used one in Sevenoaks Library. It wasn't that she was averse to new technology; it was down to cost. She couldn't afford one. Good heavens, she'd been embracing new technology all her life; telephones, fridges, televisions, cars, washing machines, freezers, microwaves, mobile phones. Everything was new technology when it first came out then gradually became part of your life depending on how long it took you to appreciate the benefits. Richie had taught her that. He'd been a civil engineer, until his health failed, and always the first to lock onto and own a new gadget. She remembered doing the shopping with him when the first mobile phones appeared back in the early eighties, staring at him with embarrassment as he talked loudly to his mates through what appeared to be a house brick glued to his ear.

She was due to visit the library the next morning. Books were another of the few pleasures old age had failed to diminish. She loved libraries, always had done, and was an avid reader; fast too, invariably with at least several books on the go. There had been times when she would take three or four books out a week. But not these days; they were heavy and a struggle to carry on and off buses. Her habit nowadays was to take out one at a time and visit the library more often, every other day or so rather than once a week. It was an excuse to get out of the flat, otherwise she would never leave it for days or weeks on end. God's waiting room.

One of the librarians, Mrs Anderson, had worked there for twenty years and knew her well, and always had a smile and a welcome for her. She would ask about the book being returned – what was it like, did she enjoy it, was it the author's best – and was usually impressed by the response. Mrs Roberts was clearly an erudite lady with insight who absorbed what she read and had a critical flair. Once in a while the feedback could be terse and to the point if the book hadn't met her expectations – "piffle" or even "crap" on occasions – which, coming from someone who bore a strong resemblance in both appearance and manners to Joan Hickson playing Miss Marple, left Mrs Anderson in fits of giggles.

The library in Sevenoaks was about a twenty-minute bus ride away; according to the timetable buses ran every half an hour, though the reality was usually rather different. Mrs Roberts was the only one at the bus stop this morning. She had timed her arrival to be ten minutes before the bus was due. She waited patiently for twenty-five before the familiar shape of a blue single-decker turned the corner into view. Over the years she had got to know all the regular drivers. Mostly they were pleasant and accommodating; with the occasional exception. Today was one of the exceptions. She could tell as the bus drew nearer it was the miserable fifty-something with the Bobby Charlton comb over who never smiled, was abrupt at best and more often than not plain obnoxious.

"Good morning," said Mrs Roberts as she stepped onto the bus. "At last."

"I came, didn't I?" grunted the driver. "No pleasing some people."

Mrs Roberts decided not to labour the point and started to make her way towards an empty seat. The bus was only half-full so there were plenty to choose from.

"Oi, where d'yer think you're going?"

Mrs Roberts turned around and looked at the driver.

"I beg your pardon?"

"Haven't you forgotten something?"

"No, I don't think so."

"Bus pass."

"Do I need to? I would have thought you'd know me by now, and I'm hardly borderline senior citizen. Most drivers don't usually…"

"Bus pass."

"Well, really!" She fumbled in her handbag, walked up to the window of the driver's cab and pressed her pass up against the Perspex. He didn't even bother to look at it, so she put it away and took a seat. Hopefully on the way home she'd get that nice young woman with the nose piercing and the tattoo of a python on her neck.

Mrs Roberts arrived at the library just before eleven o' clock. Today, rather than perusing the shelves for an interesting new read, she headed straight for the upstairs room, containing a row of five computers which could be used for a maximum of an hour at a time, although the librarians only enforced this rule if they were busy. This morning they were not. Only two were occupied: at the far end was a grubby-looking youth wearing headphones who was grunting and appeared to be playing a highly unsavoury video game. Then there was a gap. At the third along she recognised a fellow silver surfer, Mr Pardey, a retired solicitor whom Mrs Roberts knew slightly and avoided whenever possible as he was very boring. He nodded by way of a greeting, and Mrs Roberts nodded back. She had a choice; either sit next to Mr Pardey or leave a space and use the computer at this end of the row. It was a no brainer. She sat down at the end.

"Good morning, Mrs Roberts," said Mr Pardey, in his soft I'm-in-a-library voice, smiling and nodding.

"Good morning," she replied in a tone intended to be friendly but with a hint of matter-of-factness, hoping to avoid a prolonged conversation, or preferably any at all.

"What are you looking at today… recipes, clothes, holidays?"

"Oh nothing in particular."

"Online dating perhaps?"

"I should think not!"

Mr Pardey sensed this wasn't going anywhere, so he returned his focus to the article he was reading. An avid collector of milk bottles, he had found a fascinating piece about Dr Hervey D. Thatcher, the New York druggist generally regarded as the father of the milk bottle. Mr Pardey dreamed of one day owning an *Original Thatcher*.

Mrs Roberts' computer screen was dark but ready and waiting for her. A slight movement of the mouse had it bursting into life and prompting her to enter her library card number and pin. Glancing around to make sure no one was watching, she typed them both in and pressed *Enter*. Up came the default browser page. *Google*. Next, with the index fingers of each hand alternately, she carefully tapped *C-U-N-T* into the search box, then clicked on the little magnifying glass icon that denoted *Search*.

First to come up was a concise dictionary definition. Two definitions in fact; both nouns, one anatomical, the other vulgar. Below this were broader definitions, a thesaurus listing alternative words – some she recognised (vagina, pussy, twat), others were new to her (snatch, minge) – followed by a series of articles about its origins, analysis of why it was regarded as so offensive, and references in literature from Chaucer by way of Shakespeare and James Joyce to D.H. Lawrence.

Already the search brought up mention of Judge Lynch's use of the C-word in court earlier in the week. Opinions seemed to be divided about it. On the one hand, social media comments were predominantly supportive:

> *What a legend Judge Patricia Lynch QC is.*
> *Judge Patricia Lynch QC has a cracking reply to a racist thug in her courtroom. I think it was a reasonable response given the circumstances.*
> *What a wonderful lady – we need more judges like her.*
> *It is hard to give children role models nowadays but Judge Patricia Lynch QC is definitely one.*

On the other hand, *The Telegraph* was reporting that the Judicial Conduct Investigations Office (JCIO) which handles complaints made about judges both inside and outside court had received complaints regarding HHJ (Her Honour Judge) Patricia Lynch's comment in court. They would be considered in accordance with the Judicial Conduct (Judicial and other office holders) Rules 2014. To what extent the public were appalled enough to object was unclear. A spokesman added that they "never comment on how many complaints have been received".

Mrs Roberts couldn't really understand what the fuss was all about. Having spent a good half an hour absorbing all the information she could glean, it seemed to her that the judge had merely thrown the awful man's insults back at him, using his own words. He deserved no less. She particularly enjoyed reading in another account that after the vile racist had raised his arm in a Nazi salute and shouted *Sieg Heil* he had started singing an offensive song about the Jews, to which Judge Patricia Lynch QC responded: "I'm sure we're all very impressed. Now take him down." This raised her admiration even higher. She supported what the judge had done and said and felt inclined to write to her and tell her so.

Whilst reading up on the etymology of the C-word, a fascinating snippet had come to light; she found it repeated in various *Wikipedia* entries. Apparently its first recorded usage anywhere was on thirteenth century street signs in a number of English towns including Oxford and London – Gropecunt Lane!

She chuckled out loud.

Mr Pardey heard her. "What's funny over there?" he asked.

"Oh nothing."

"Careful now, Mrs Roberts, they say that's the first sign."

Of what she chose not to enquire and ignored him.

Unsurprisingly, she read, when she had regained her concentration, these were streets where prostitutes plied their trade; red light districts in modern parlance. It was common in medieval times for a street name to reflect the business that went on there – Fish Street, Silver Street – although Gropecunt Lanes had over the years been modified to less graphic equivalents; Grape Lane, Grove Lane and in the case of Oxford to the entirely innocuous Magpie Lane. It occurred to Mrs Roberts that if it appeared on public notices in those days, surely the word was neither vulgar nor offensive. Looking ahead, Mrs Roberts couldn't help but think that if it was good enough for Chaucer, Shakespeare and D.H. Lawrence, it was good enough for her. (James Joyce didn't count – his books were crap.)

There was an unfortunate incident at this point in Mrs Roberts' research. The urge to spend a penny had been building for a while and reached a point where it could no longer be ignored. She gathered up her handbag, preparing to leave her computer in order to pay a visit. Mr Pardey stood up and shuffled towards her.

"Not leaving already are we, Mrs Roberts?"

"Just off to powder my nose."

"Shall I keep your place for you?"

"That won't be necessary, I'll only be a few moments."

"What was it that made you laugh just now – a recipe, a holiday review?" He leaned forward and peered at her screen.

"Oh nothing. I suppose I ought to lock the computer before I go." She fumbled on the keyboard, struggling to remember the odd combination of keys you needed to press, but not quickly enough to prevent Mr Pardey from seeing the screen.

"Social history, eh? I do enjoy looking back into the

200

past. Street names in the late medieval period – how interesting. What's this, Grope… Gropecu…"

She remembered! Control… Alt… Delete… Enter. *This Computer is Locked.*

Mr Pardey stepped back, looking bemused and pale and more than a little taken aback. "I say, I really don't think it's appropriate…"

Mrs Roberts did not hear him. She was halfway across the room, heading for a door in the corner with a stick man and a stick woman on it, above a stick person who appeared to have wheels instead of legs.

When she came back, Mr Pardey was back at his computer; he glanced across at her, frowned disapprovingly, and focused his attention again on the father of the milk bottle in 1880s New York. Mrs Roberts didn't really care whether he approved or not. Nevertheless, he had bothered her and so she decided to pack up and leave.

Around the corner from the library was a *Starbucks* where she settled down with a small cappuccino. She would have preferred a nice cup of tea but they didn't serve *Twinings English Breakfast* in *Starbucks*, nor did they serve whatever brand they did have in a proper teacup, or provide something to put your teabag in when you'd fished it out of the glass; a disgusting American habit, she presumed, which meant either plopping it onto your saucer and wetting the bottom of the glass so it dripped over you when you drank from it, or using a stack of serviettes, hoping you had enough to stop it from seeping through onto the table. In terms of good practice in tea making, it was a shambles. But their cappuccinos were very nice.

It had taken her some time to pluck up the courage to venture inside when it first opened; everything looked so contemporary and daunting. And the prices! She remembered the first time she eventually took the plunge and went in and asked for a cup of coffee. The array of different types had been bewildering. The man (with 'Barista' printed on the back of his shirt; she had looked up the meaning later – *from the Italian for 'bartender'*) had been very helpful and explained them all to her; latte, mocha, macchiato, cappuccino, Americano, espresso. Mrs Roberts liked her coffee frothy, so she settled on a cappuccino. The young man then asked, "What size would you like, Short, Tall or Grande?" to which Mrs Roberts replied, "Don't be so pretentious… a small one, thank you."

Mrs Roberts enjoyed drinking coffee in *Starbucks*, although for her the prices meant that it was an occasional treat rather than a regular event. Like *Twinings*, the pedant in her was perturbed by the lack of an apostrophe in their name. She had written to them, explaining that according to *Wikipedia* their company was named after a character in *Moby Dick*, one of the three mates on board the whaling boat *Pequod*, in which case there ought to be an apostrophe, *Starbuck's*, to denote ownership. She also complimented them on their decision not to call themselves *Pequod*, as had nearly been the case according to *Wikipedia. That would have been just too silly*, she wrote. So far there had been no reply from Seattle.

Mrs Roberts sat on a comfy sofa, sipping cappuccino and thinking about the C-word.

When had it become so offensive... and why? She hadn't fathomed that out yet and it continued to puzzle her. In the twelve-hundreds it had been used on public street signs, and in subsequent centuries in works of greatly respected literature. Yet nowadays, in complete contrast, and in the most enlightened times in history where the second most offensive word in the English language – the F-word – was commonplace, the C-word was well and truly taboo.

Or was it?

Perhaps her own middleclass morality was showing; hers and millions of others like her with ultra conservative attitudes firmly rooted in the standards of times long gone. Mostly old people who knew what was best for the semi-literate youth of today and were dragging their feet against the rip tide of popular feeling as in so many things. The selfish geriatrics who apparently had forced the Brexit vote and blighted the lives of future generations. If so, the lady judge had surely just breached a huge hole in their anachronistic dam.

When she had finished her coffee, Mrs Roberts decided she would potter around the shops for a while, then return to the library and continue her research. Hopefully Mr Pardey would have gone by then.

She might even begin drafting a letter of support and admiration to Judge Patricia Lynch QC.

★ ★ ★

In *Boots*, who also needed an apostrophe, Mrs Roberts bumped in to an old friend, Susan Grosvenor, a fellow widow; thus a potter around the shops turned into lunch and a good old chat.

"Good to see you, Dotty. How have you been?"

"Oh, the usual. You know, trying to make ends meet, struggling to get my old bones out of bed every morning and make the most of each day."

"You were always good at that," said Susan Grosvenor with a hint of envy. "Unlike me, I'm a layabout by comparison, more so since Leonard passed away. So what's taking up your time at the moment?"

Inevitably, as it was so fresh in her mind, this prompt brought up the topic of Judge Patricia Lynch QC. Susan Grosvenor had read all about it.

"What do you think, Susan?"

"Disgusting!"

"Don't you think it was acceptable under the circumstances?"

"Absolutely not! Fancy a high court judge using such foul language… and a woman… and in her own courtroom! She should be defrocked, or debarred, or whatever they do to judges when they behaved appallingly."

"I think they usually give them a peerage," remarked Dotty musingly. "But she only repeated back the insult which the man in the dock called *her*."

"Not just any old insult. It was *that* word. She used *that* word!"

"The C-word."

"Dotty! You shouldn't say it, not even the first letter like that."

"Is that such a terrible thing nowadays?"

"Yes it certainly is. *That* word is disgusting. Just

204

because he used it at her was no excuse to repeat it! She ought to be a role model. Two wrongs don't make a right."

Mrs Roberts nodded understandingly. "Yet most of the views I've read on social media are very supportive of her," she said.

"That's also disgusting," stated Susan Grosvenor. "The great unwashed revelling in it as usual with their extreme right wing views. They're the real Brexit bunch. Trolls, isn't that the correct word for them? That woman should not have stooped so low as to bandy insults with a moron like that. She's brought the entire legal profession into disrepute."

"Isn't having her removed from office a little extreme… a little right wing?" suggested Mrs Roberts.

Susan Grosvenor, who was well on her way to being in high dudgeon, glared at her and turned up her nose as if suddenly confronted with a foul smell. "No!"

There was an awkward silence. Mrs Roberts took a bite from her egg and cress sandwich.

Susan Grosvenor sat rigidly in her seat as if in a trance. Then, out of nowhere, a grin appeared on her face and she laughed out loud. "Yes! How pompous of me. Of course it is. You're absolutely right, Dotty. Perhaps we should change the subject."

Change the subject they did and talked about friends from the past, some still around but mostly dead and gone. They parted company on the best of terms, promising to meet again soon.

Mrs Roberts wandered back in the direction of the library. It had been an interesting encounter, and a reminder to her of Germaine Greer's point. *That* word still had the power to shock, and to engender strong emotions. Perhaps she, Mrs Roberts, was too broadminded, or rather more so than her compatriots who, let's face it, were of a dinosaur generation dating from long before the birth of sexual intercourse, identified by Philip Larkin in that poem of his (she could never remember the title) as 1963, *between the Chatterley Trial and the Beatles' first LP*. He was wrong of course, Mrs Roberts knew. Sex had been a very enjoyable part of her life long before either. The difference, it seemed to her, was that until then it had all been done in secret; under the surface; in private. It wasn't talked about, and certainly not using those infamous Anglo Saxon four-letter words. The Chatterley Trial had been something of a watershed. She ought to refresh her memory about the details.

But amidst all the bluster, Susan Grosvenor had made a very good point indeed, a simple one but a very good point nevertheless. Two wrongs do not make a right. Perhaps, after all, Judge Patricia Lynch QC had been out of order to use the language she did in court.

Mrs Roberts weighed this in the balance as she walked through the entrance of the library.

★ ★ ★

Mr Pardey was nowhere to be seen, thank heavens. The grubby-looking youth had gone too and a dowdy woman of indeterminate age Mrs Roberts had never seen before had taken his place. She resumed her old seat at the nearest computer.

Further reading revealed that although not taboo in the Middle Ages, the C-word had started to become so even in Shakespeare's day and the Bard had used it cautiously, implying rather than stating it. Probably the most famous example appears in *Hamlet* (Act III, Scene 2 to be precise) when the eponymous Prince of Denmark asks Ophelia, "Lady, shall I lie in your lap?" Ophelia replies, "No, my lord." Hamlet, pretending to be shocked, responds, "Do you think I meant *country matters*?" The double meaning of the first syllable of 'country' was no coincidence.

By all accounts, the next two hundred years brought about a considerable change in attitude, and for no obvious reasons that Mrs Roberts could identify other than the rise of Puritanism and the sobering influence of the likes of Oliver Cromwell. By the end of the eighteenth century the C-word was generally frowned upon and had all but vanished from print, apart from in very private publications.

And so it remained until the second half of the twentieth century. For the United Kingdom, it was the Lady Chatterley Trial in 1960 referenced by Philip Larkin that opened the floodgates. Penguin Books Ltd. were prosecuted under the Obscene Publications Act 1959 for intending to publish D.H. Lawrence's *Lady Chatterley's Lover,* which included liberal use of both the F-word and the C-word. Lawrence had published the novel privately in 1928, but no real attempt was made to do so publicly until Penguin. In March 1960, ahead of the intended publication date, they presented fifteen copies to the police, effectively challenging them to prosecute

– which they did. A summons was issued in August at Bow Street Magistrate's Court in London and the trial began towards the end of October. *Wikipedia* summed up the result rather neatly, Mrs Roberts felt:

The jury found for the defendant in a result that ushered in the liberalisation of publishing, and which some saw as the beginning of the permissive society in Britain.

Although fifty-six years ago, she remembered it well and had followed the six-day trial in the newspapers as it evolved. She was thirty then and enjoying a healthy sex life with Richie. When it was published a month after the trial, they were both keen to read this notorious book; a bargain at only three and six in paperback! Getting hold of a copy was the problem. Bookshops all over England sold out on the first day – a total of two hundred thousand copies. *Foyles* in London sold their three hundred copies in fifteen minutes and took orders for three thousand more!

When they eventually managed to get their hands on the book, Richie read it first and feigned disapproval when his wife insisted on doing the same. They didn't discuss it, but for weeks, if not months, their sex life took on an edge to it, a rawness, which was new and very exciting.

Mrs Roberts was feeling tired. She looked at her watch. Good heavens, five-thirty! The library would be closing soon. To round off her day, she did another quick Google search on Judge Lynch's name and came up with an interesting comment she had missed before from a journalist relating to her use of *that* word:

It wasn't shocking that it was said in a court of law, just the fact that it was a judge who said it.

Mrs Roberts didn't know whether to agree or not because she had never been in a courtroom and had no idea what language *was* used. It seemed common sense to assume that proceedings were undertaken politely and respectfully without resorting to sexually explicit insults; this was certainly reflected in what she had seen on television. Judge John Deed would never allow it.

It was an interesting point though; the shock element was the fact that a judge had said it. So, was the offensiveness of the C-word on a sliding scale depending upon who was using it, and to whom, as much as where it was uttered? For two football hooligans – on the terraces, in a pub, in the street, or in *Sainsbury's* – it would be par for the course because they were what they were; mindless thugs in any location. But coming from a judge, whether in the high court or in *Sainsbury's* – or perhaps *Waitrose* in their case – its use was always going to be shocking. (Incidentally, the pedant in Mrs Roberts approved of *Sainsbury's* branding, for obvious reasons.)

Now feeling very weary, she logged off her computer and popped to the loo again before saying goodnight to Mrs Anderson and making her way to the bus stop. There was a bit of a queue and the electronic sign in the bus shelter indicated the next one on her route would arrive in seven minutes. She'd believe that when she saw it.

A young lad stood up from his seat in the shelter and indicated she was welcome to it. Mrs Roberts thanked him and sat down gratefully. She felt a bit woozy. The lunchtime sandwich had been a good few hours ago and she felt her stomach rumbling. What would she have for supper, she wondered – lamb casserole out of the freezer perhaps, or the rest of the spinach quiche with new potatoes and beans? She wondered what high court judges had for supper.

The bus arrived after twelve minutes. Mrs Roberts took her place at the end of the queue. When she stepped on board and approached the driver, to her dismay she saw it was the awful man with the comb over from this morning. Her heart sank.

"I suppose you want to see my bus pass, do you?" she said with more than a little irritation in her voice.

He glanced at her disdainfully. "Do vacuum cleaners suck?"

The meaning, including the implied vulgarity, was lost on Mrs Roberts. She pulled out her pass and again pressed it against the Perspex. Again the driver looked the other way and paid it no attention.

She put the pass away and turned to walk down the bus. Then she paused, looked up at the driver and, in a firm but perfectly measured tone, said, "Actually, young man…" and proceeded to speak the phrase that had preoccupied her thoughts all day; the phrase that felt perfectly appropriate for the moment and the use of which, she was quite certain, Judge Patricia Lynch QC would have wholly approved.

The driver's eyes widened and his jaw dropped. The passengers in the bus, which was full, had heard it as clear as a bell. They stared towards her in absolute silence, not moving an inch, like a still photograph. The proverbial pin could have dropped; and so it stayed for a few brief seconds that seemed to last an hour. Then someone clapped, then someone else clapped, then the whole bus was clapping and cheering.

Mrs Roberts was taken aback. She was confused, and didn't quite know what to do, suddenly finding herself the centre of attention and lauded in such a fashion. So she did what she often did when out of her comfort zone; she simply smiled. The smile was followed by a nod of appreciation and she mouthed "Thank you" several times in different directions, as if on stage acknowledging an appreciative audience. The applause showed no sign of abating, so finally she put down her shopping basket and handbag and, slowly and graciously, curtsied as low as her eighty-six-year-old limbs would permit. Once back up again, she gathered her bags and sat down in the nearest empty seat, just as the bus pulled off.

It was a snapshot moment. One of those key events in life that instantly embed themselves into your head, never to be excised, where they remain forever. We all have them and they are a blend of public and personal incidents. For Mrs Roberts they were… her first day at school… V.E. Day… her first kiss… her eighteenth birthday… losing her virginity… her wedding day… giving birth… Coronation Day… the death of her mother… Churchill's funeral… the 1966 World Cup Final… the Aberfan disaster… the first moon landing… the 1981 royal wedding… becoming a grandmother… Richie passing away… Princess Diana's funeral… and, last but by no means least, the day she told the driver of the number 452 bus from Sevenoaks to Dunton Green that he was a bit of a cunt.

What a day! Goodness, she would sleep well tonight. But not before – yes, now that all the hoopla was over she had made a decision as she sat staring out of the window, watching the world go by. Spinach quiche for supper after all, with new potatoes and green beans, washed down with a nice cup of tea.

Twining's, naturally.

RUNNER

Jez, Chris and Toff had spent the day at Sandown Park races, and fared well. They came away with pockets crammed full of banknotes and their heads spinning from a combination of booze and high spirits. Their mood could be described as ebullient, not that they would have been familiar with a four-syllable adjective – Jez possibly, Chris unlikely, Toff no chance. As Jez drove them out of the car park at a snail's pace, queuing to get onto the Portsmouth Road, they had one thing on their minds. Food.

"Fancy a Chinese?" said Jez.

"Prefer Indian," said Chris.

"Chinky for me," said Toff.

The majority verdict won. Chinese. They were heading towards Surbiton.

"What about that one on the Brighton Road, near

the railway bridge?" suggested Jez as he weaved his way round the Scilly Isles roundabout. "What's it called?"

Chris googled it on his phone. "*The Mandarin Palace*. Do we have to? I fancy a curry."

"Chinky!" yelled Toff. "You're outnumbered."

"He's right," said Jez. "Chinky it is."

They parked in Victoria Avenue and walked around the corner onto the Brighton Road. *The Mandarin Palace* was a hundred yards up on the right. Just beyond it a train rumbled over the bridge.

"Have we done this one before?" said Chris.

"Don't think so," replied Jez. "Bit close to home."

"We've done most of them round here at one time or another."

Toff peered through the window. The restaurant was half full. "Looks posh," he said, seemingly unimpressed. "What about that one down by the station?"

"This'll do fine," said Chris.

"Not too posh for us," agreed Jez who took the lead, as he invariably did, and marched through the door. "Alright?" he said to the rotund, neatly dressed man who greeted him.

"Good evering," said the man. "My name Ping. Welcome."

"Alright Ping." Said Toff. "What's your surname, Pong?"

Mr Ping grinned and bowed slightly. "You have reservation?"

"Yeh," said Toff. "I've got one. I'm worried your chicken is cat. My Aunty Joyce lives just round the corner and her Tiddles went missing last week."

214

Mr Ping grinned some more. "Ah, the old ones always the best."

"What's that supposed to mean?"

"Nothing, nothing. You booked?"

"No," replied Jez. "Table for three."

Mr Ping consulted a booking sheet on a clipboard. "No probrem." He indicated a table towards the middle of the restaurant, along one side. "This one flee."

Jez ignored it and eyed up the table in the window, which had a grey metal sign in the centre that read *Reserved*. "This one'll do."

"Reserved – so solly."

"Not any more," said Jez, picking up the *Reserved* sign and throwing it on to the table next door. He sat down. Chris and Toff joined him.

"Regular customer has this table," explained Mr Ping anxiously.

"You sayin' they're more important than us?" asked Toff.

"Not exackery, I…"

"First come first served," said Chris.

Mr Ping hesitated then decided not to pursue it any further. "Okay okay, you sit there." He walked to the back of the restaurant, spoke to a colleague – presumably about where to seat their regulars when they arrived and how to explain why their usual table was not available – then returned with some menus. "You like drink?"

"Is the Pope Catholic?" said Chris.

"I know I not," replied Mr Ping. "Don't know about Pope!"

"Uh?" said Toff. "What's he on about?"

215

"Me joke, me joke. What you want to drink?"

"Three lagers," said Jez. "And no heads."

"Okay, I get and come back for food order."

"You do that, slitty eyes," murmured Toff, loud enough to float after the receding Mr Ping who, if he heard, chose to ignore it.

Jez perused the menu. "What's it to be… crispy aromatic duck with some pancake rolls to start?"

"Bring it on," said Toff.

"Poppadoms and an onion bhaji for me," said Chris.

"Tough, you're having what we're having. Then what, go our own ways? I fancy Szechuan king prawns."

"I'll have sweet and sour chicken," said Toff. "With e-fri-ri."

Chris stared at the menu, seemingly unimpressed by anything he saw. He pulled out his mobile and started sending a text.

Mr Ping returned bearing a tray and a large bowl. "Your drinks, genermen – free lagers, no head, and some plawn clackers."

"They look like prawn crackers to me, mate," said Toff, stuffing one into his mouth whole. "You ought to learn to spleak Engrish plopper." A cloud of cracker bits filled the air around him.

"Ready to order?" asked Mr Ping stoically.

"No," said Chris, still tapping away on his phone.

"Well make your mind up," said Jez. "I'm starving."

Mr Ping noticed a customer gesticulating at him from another table. "I give you more time. I'll be back."

"Alright Arnie," sniggered Toff. He pulled out his phone too and stared blankly at the screen, scrolling up and down. Jez took his out and joined them. They sat in silence and remained that way until Mr Ping returned with a notepad and pencil.

"You decide yet?"

"We're ready," said Jez. "Crispy aromatic duck for three to start, with pancake rolls. Then I'll get Szechuan king prawns, with egg fried rice and some seaweed. Toff, you still having sweet and sour chicken?"

"Yeh, in the style of Hong Kong, Mister Pong."

"With egg fried rice?"

"Yeh, e-fri-ri."

"Any sides?"

"Nah."

"Chris," said Jez. "What about you?"

"Uh?"

"What do you want?"

"I can't decide."

"Jesus, here we go again. You do this every time."

"Do what?"

"Go into a moody if you don't get your own way. Look, if you want an Indian, go and have one. The *Red Rose* is just over the road. If you're staying with Toff and me, tell Mr Pong here what you want."

"Ping not Pong," corrected Mr Ping.

Chris rested his phone on the table and looked at the menu. "Do you do curry?"

"Yes we do cully."

"Alright, chicken tikka masala with pilau rice."

"We do chicken cully Chinese style, no Indian."

"Well that's no good. Alright I'll have just a chicken curry, with plain rice."

"Any side dishes?" asked Mr Ping.

"Yeh, loads. Sesame prawn on toast, Peking dumplings, tempura prawns, house special noodles and… two portions of seaweed."

"You'll never eat all that," said Jez.

"He right," added Mr Ping. "You eat all that, you exprode, like Mister Cleosote. Make big mess."

"Well that's what I'm ordering. Don't matter anyway, if we ain't…"

"Alright," Jez interrupted. "That's our order. We can share it all."

"Okay," said Mr Ping with a tone of resignation. "That what you want, that what you get. Customer always right." He wandered off to the back of the restaurant and disappeared through a swing door with a circular glass window. Moments later, a chef's head appeared at the window and stared at the threesome at the window table; a fierce looking face with thick eyebrows, a flat nose and bad teeth, all framed by cropped dark hair and two day stubble. A face with an expression that said: "Crazy bastards."

An hour later, the table was a mess, strewn as it was with the remnants of the meal. None of the crispy aromatic duck remained, nor of the pancake rolls, but there was a good deal of everything else, including two portions of seaweed and some special noodles that hadn't been touched. They were on their third round of lagers.

Halfway through the meal, the couple who reserved the window table had arrived. Mr Ping greeted them with practiced obsequiousness and shepherded them towards a table half way down the dining room.

The man was elderly – tallish, smartly dressed with silver hair and thin-rimmed glasses; his wife, similar in age, shorter, elegant in a bright summer dress. They were not happy. The man came over to the table where the three were tucking into their meal.

"I say you lot, Mr Ping tells me you stole our table." None of them replied. "Did you hear me?"

"We heard," muttered Jez.

"Well, what do you have to say?"

Chris looked up. "What makes it your table? Do you own it?"

"It was reserved for me and my wife."

"Well we got here first."

"We always sit at this table. Mr Ping had it reserved for us and he says you moved the sign."

"So what?"

The man was bristling with indignation. "You're rude, impolite and selfish."

"Nope, we're Jez, Chris and Toff. Pleased to meet you."

"You know very well what I mean."

Jez nodded. "Yep, I suppose you're right there."

"So what are you going to do about it?"

"No mate," said Chris. "What do you *want* us to do? We're sitting here eating our food. You expecting us to move tables in the middle of our dinner just so you can have your usual spot, like you own it? *Really*?"

The man was taken aback, suddenly appreciating the reality of the situation and not knowing precisely what he did expect of them.

"No, I…"

"You should learn to chill, old man. Take things easy… be more flexible. Especially at your age. Blood pressure and all that."

Realising there was nothing to be done, the man took several steps backwards.

"An apology would be nice."

"Hasn't Mr Pong done that already?"

"Your manners are appalling," said the man as he turned away.

"Hey grandad," called Toff. The man looked at him quizzically. "Bring us another lager will you?"

Later, over shots of Jägermeister, the three were again all staring at their phones. Chris was first to look up.

"So how much d'you reckon we made then?"

Toff shrugged. "I won about three hundred."

"Double that for me," said Jezz.

"Same here," said Chris. "Would have been more if that last mare hadn't decided to walk round the course. Probably still going. *Winged Messenger* – pah, should of known better."

Silence prevailed again. Chris yawned; Jez followed suit.

"We gonna do it then?" said Toff absentmindedly.

"We sure are."

"What's the plan?"

Jez leaned forward and lowered his voice. "The usual. I'll ask for the bill, then I'll go and get the car. When you see me out the front, you run. Chris in the front, Toff in the back. Right?"

"Right," said Toff.

"Right," agreed Chris.

Jez stuck his hand in the air, whistled and called out: "Oi, Pong... bill."

Two minutes later, Mr Ping laid a circular silver platter on the table. The bill lay on it underneath three *After Eight* mints. Jez picked up the long, thin strip of paper, skimmed over the contents and handed it round. He stood up and, for the sake of Mr Ping, who was watching from the far end of the restaurant, laid a twenty pound note on the table as his share before walking out of the door.

As they waited for the car to pull up outside, Chris and Toff counted out banknotes as if working out how to split the bill fairly. In the process, Jez's twenty was scooped up and added to the reckoning. Every now and again, they glanced out of the window, trying to appear blasé.

All the while, Mr Ping hovered in the distance, next to three other waiters. The fierce looking chef watched from the kitchen through the circular window. They had read the signs and were prepared. The chef turned and shouted at one of the other chefs who picked up a set of keys and hurried out of a back door.

Jez seemed to take an age.

"Where's he got to?" whispered Chris.

"Probably having a fag."

As Toff spoke the words, a car pulled up immediately outside the restaurant entrance, a black BMW that had seen better days. A familiar figure sat in the driver's seat. The window was half down and Jez's features were clearly visible, looking calmly towards them.

The wads of banknotes disappeared into pockets.

221

Chris and Toff looked at each other. Chris nodded and said: "Go."

They leapt from their seats and through the door into the street. Chris ran round the front of the car, opened the passenger door, climbed in and slammed it shut. Toff stumbled on the pavement and fell against the rear door. He grabbed the handle and pulled, but his weight was against the door and nothing happened.

"Hurry up, you knob!" yelled Jez. "Get in."

"I'm trying!"

"Well try harder!"

Toff eased back, the door opened and he tumbled onto the back seat. He just managed to pull the door shut as the car screeched forward, cutting across traffic and narrowly missing a car coming towards them. They were under the railway bridge and up the Brighton Road in seconds.

As they sped away, an almost identical BMW, only newer, cleaner and more powerful, turned out of Victoria Avenue and drew up outside *The Mandarin Palace*. Mr Ping appeared at the restaurant door, closely followed by the fierce looking chef, who was carrying a baseball bat. They climbed into the car and sped off in pursuit.

★ ★ ★

"Piece of piss," smirked Chris.

"Yep," agreed Jez. "Food tastes better when you don't pay for it." He shifted down a gear as they approached the Ace of Spades roundabout, then they were straight over and making their way through Hook, heading towards their home turf of Ewell.

"I hate Chinks," said Toff. "Serve 'em right. Love their food, hate them."

"Look what the bastards did to our soldiers in the war. Tortured them, starved them and worked them to death building railways. Payback time."

"That was the Japanese," said Jez.

Toff shrugged. "Whatever."

"Let's rip off a Paki place next time," said Chris. "Have a good curry."

"Okay, it's your call next." Jez yawned. "Jesus I'm knackered. Good day, what?"

"Yeh, good," agreed Toff.

At the next roundabout Jez turned left and from there it was a straight road into Ewell. Five minutes later they were pulling up in the parking area of their estate. He switched off the engine and sat back in his seat, eyes closed, allowing the calm to flow over him.

They heard the sound of another car pulling in behind them but paid no attention.

"British is best," said Chris smugly, also lounging back in his seat. "We're more smarter, more wiser, more intelligent. How can anyone think otherwise."

Toff was lying sideways across the back seat. "Too right. Skin colour tells you everything you need to know about someone. The darker it is the worse it is. Chinkies are like halfway. You just have to look at them slitty eyes to see they're worthless. Good for cooking and serving in restaurants but that's about all."

"Hmmm," mumbled Jez in agreement.

"I mean, can you name a decent Chinkie footballer?"

There was contemplative silence. No one could.

"What's happening tomorrow?" said Chris. "We doing something? Where are we eating for free? Any suggestions?"

The driver's side door next to Jez opened, fast and with force. Hands grabbed him firmly by the shoulders and tugged him out of his seat. A second later, the same happened on Chris's side and he too was pulled from the car. Toff was suddenly the only one left inside. He looked up in bemusement and said: "What the f…" Then the door behind his head opened and he too was dragged out; backwards.

They were bundled together in a corner of the car park, standing back to back, like a three-edged statue. To one side of them stood the fierce looking chef, the baseball bat in his hand; to the other, the driver of their BMW, sliding a metal nunchaku between his hands and making a clicking noise with them. In front stood Mr Ping, legs apart, arms folded. He stared at the threesome for what seemed like an eternity. Toff was shaking, so was Chris. Jez appeared in control, but inside he was scared because he knew what was coming. There would be pain involved. Eventually he plucked up the courage to speak.

"Hey, Mr Ping. Fancy seeing you here." He tried to sound light-hearted, nonchalant even, but failed.

No reply.

"Sorry about shooting off like that and not paying earlier – slipped our mind."

Mr Ping moved closer to Jez and looked him in the eyes, but said nothing.

224

"I've got the money… here in my pocket."

"Yeh," contributed Toff. "Loads of cash. Happy to pay you."

Mr Ping started to giggle, then suppressed it by putting a hand over his mouth. "We no want your money. We want pay *you*. Pay you a lesson and teach you some manners. That why we chase after you."

"That's good of you," said Chris. "But we'd just be happy to settle up and be on our way."

Mr Ping walked round and stared him in the face. "Too late for that – too late for words. We just let baseball bat and nunchaku do talking."

Chris whimpered.

"We've got manners," said Toff. "Just forgot them, that's all."

Mr Ping turned his attention to Toff and walked round until they were face to face. "You say we serve cat instead of chicken."

"I never did."

"I hear you."

"Well okay then… just a joke, that's all."

Mr Ping took the baseball bat from the fierce looking cook and waved it in Toff's face, then pressed it delicately against Toff's nose. "You call me slitty eyes."

"Another joke."

"Not funny."

"I guess you're right. Sorry."

"You left or right-handed?"

"What?"

"You hear."

Toff looked puzzled. "Right-handed. Why?"

"That the arm we blake."

"You're kidding me!"

Mr Ping moved along to Chris. "You left or right-handed?"

Chris paused for some time before answering hesitantly. "Right."

Mr Ping giggled again. "You lie. We blake left arm… also left leg for lying."

"Jesus, no, please!"

"You," said Mr Ping, addressing Jez. "You left or right-handed?"

Jez's face was pale, his lips quivering. He was too scared and confused to consider whether or not to lie, so he told the truth. "Right."

"Okay," said Mr Ping. "I no sure you lie or tell truth, so we blake both to be on safe side… also for being ringleader."

"You're not really going to are you, over a few quid?" Jez's voice sounded hoarse, as if he was struggling to speak at all. "We'll pay. Double, triple if you want…"

"If you got loads of money, why you not pay for meal in first place?"

Toff replied. "Like Jez said, it slipped our mind, that's all."

Mr Ping shook his head. "Now you lie. You take piss so we blake both arms and one leg. I feel in good mood today so let you choose which leg." He stepped back a few paces so he could see all three. "Why you look down on us? Why you treat us like shit? Why steal from us and try to ruin our livelihood?" There was no response from the threesome. "Why you think you superior?"

226

Again no response.

"Because your eyes not slitty?" He stepped forward and poked Toff in the side. "Or you more interigent? Maybe that it. If that what you think you clazy because it obvious to me you not."

"Just mucking about, that's all," said Chris, his voice quivering.

"Maybe you behave like this coz you speak from moral high ground? Better educated, better mannered, better behaved? I no think so. If you think that you clazy. Evidence show otherwise." Mr Ping sighed. "Okay so now our turn to muck about." He handed the baseball bat to the fierce looking chef. "Go ahead, start blaking bones." He pointed at Toff. "Him first."

Chris started to cry. Snot dribbled out of his nose. He wiped it on the sleeve of his jacket. But it was Toff, not Chris, who at this moment became the centre of attention. His eyes had glazed over with fear. When Mr Ping identified him first for a beating, he started to shake more violently. A dripping sound came from the ground beneath him as he lost control of his bladder and started to wet himself.

The chef looked disgusted as well as fierce. He raised the baseball in the air.

"Please!" begged Jez. "You can't do this – not to Toff."

Mr Ping gave him a quizzical look and held a hand up for the chef to stop. "Okay, who we do it to instead? You decide."

"That's not fair."

"Life not fair, get use to it."

"Why are you doing this?"

227

"Teach you lesson in respect. That why."

"Okay, okay," said Jez. "We get the message. We disrespected you – it was a mistake and we're very sorry. We've learnt our lesson, we really have. Now please let us go!"

"Sure we let you go, but first we blake bones. Make sure lesson not get forgotten. If not Toff, how about other one. What his name?"

"Chris."

"Okay we blake Chris arm first, if that what you want."

"No!" pleaded Jez. "I don't want."

Chris now followed Toff's example and wet himself, profusely, the splatting sound like water pouring out of a leaky drainpipe. He staggered as if about to fall over. He was still crying.

"Please!" repeated Jez. "Just let us go." His voice was loaded with emotions; panic, fear, terror even. "Please!"

Then a strange thing happened.

Mr Ping seemed to freeze for a few moments. He stood and stared at them, as if in a trance. When he spoke, his voice had changed; metamorphosed from stereotypical, parody Chinaman to pure Oxford English. The tone and quality were so different that it could have been emanating from another person.

"Now listen to me. I have no intention of wasting any more time on you. Frankly, you're not worth it. I have a restaurant to run and we have neglected our duties, and our customers." He put a hand into his trouser pocket and pulled out a long thin piece of paper. He held it in front of Jez's face. "Do you recognize this?"

Jez nodded.

"What is it?"

"Our bill."

"That is correct – your bill. Total amount, ninety-eight pounds and forty pence. Now we are not in fact going to harm you, nor was it ever our intention. To scare you, certainly, and by the looks of it, and the amount of urine being discharged, I believe we have succeeded very well. I am first and foremost a businessman and if there's one thing I hate more than anything else it's a bad debt. I hate bilkers, or runners, or whatever you choose to call yourselves."

Mr Ping patted Jez's jacket and felt a bulge that indicated an inside pocket. He slid his hand in and pulled out a wad of banknotes. He peeled off six twenty pound notes and returned the rest from whence it came. "I've taken a hundred for your meal, plus twenty as a tip and to cover the inconvenience you have caused. I'm sure you won't have any objection under the circumstances?"

Jez, Chris and Toff shook their heads in agreement.

"Splendid. I'm glad to hear it." He nodded towards the fierce-looking chef and the driver to back off. They did so, one smacking the baseball bat into his palm and the other rattling the nunchaku. They looked disappointed. "Now, you can be on your way… assuming that is that we fully understand each other. Am I right in believing so?"

All three nodded in unison.

"I play a part, you see. I am not at all like the Mr Ping who greeted and served you earlier. Believe it or not I was educated at public school – Charterhouse to be precise. Subsequently I have taken over the family business, so to speak. You Caucasians seem to want a caricature Chinaman to serve and entertain you in my restaurants. No doubt because you and your parents and their parents before them were brought up on a diet of Carry Ons and Benny Hill… even Chu Chin Chow depending on how far back they go. So that's what I give you."

"Restaurants?" said Jez.

"I beg your pardon?"

"You said restaurants, plural."

"I own twelve. I flit between them." He scrunched up the bill and shoved it into Jez's pocket. "And you are welcome to dine in any of them, anytime. However, if you do I would be obliged if your two friends here would change their pants first. They smell decidedly pissy."

The fierce looking chef and the driver got into their car. Mr Ping opened the passenger door. "I would also be obliged if you would pay your bill in future, like decent, reasonable human beings – the superior British that you imagine yourselves to be. Come into *The Mandarin Palace* and I'll give you the names of my other restaurants. They're all fairly local."

As the car pulled away, the passenger window lowered and Mr Ping called out in his restaurant voice: "You come soon so I no forget you. You all looky alike to me."

MY

TALE

Michael Powell and Emeric Pressberger are to be thanked for my love of Canterbury. They were responsible for some of the finest British movies ever made, under the title of The Archers, long before it was filched by the BBC for their long running radio series, and it was seeing their 1944 film *A Canterbury Tale* fifteen years or so ago that had me driving down into Kent to seek out locations. My eyes were opened to what is now one of my favourite places on Earth. It's no coincidence that I feel the same depth of affection towards their film. For me it's impossible to separate one from the other and they are permanently intertwined in my emotional psyche.

I cannot walk along the High Street and turn into Mercery Lane without seeing and hearing a military band marching along as it approaches the cathedral and enters

The Old Buttermarket. I cannot walk along Rose Lane without hearing the clipped tones of a local woman standing in a bomb site saying: "It is an awful mess, I don't blame you for not knowing where you are. You get a very good view of the cathedral now." I cannot walk past the Westgate without hearing three wartime pilgrims – an America G.I., a British soldier and a Land Girl – in conversation with Mr Colpeper, the local magistrate. Colpeper is also… ah but I'll say no more in case you haven't seen it.

Nor can I sit in the tea room by the cathedral entrance without hearing two ebullient G.I.s talking about tea and marijuana and blessings. The latter is why pilgrims make their way to Canterbury, to visit the cathedral where the St Thomas à Becket was savagely murdered. They come to receive blessings, or to do penance.

Like the three fictional pilgrims, I too am fortunate enough to have received a blessing in Canterbury.

I went there for a weekend with my girlfriend at the time – Nicola. She was from Swindon, had two kids, was divorced but still did her ex-husband's laundry, worked in an office and had once been a knitting pattern designer. Her brother-in-law was a well-known artist. Her kids had gone to stay with their domestically challenged father for a few days, so we stole down to Kent and checked into what was then the *County Hotel* in High Street, opposite *The Beaney Institute*.

I had a bad cough, or what I thought was a bad cough. It turned out to be viral bronchitis, though I didn't know that at the time. Needless to say, I was coughing a lot, and at times out of control. I must have been a nightmare to sleep with.

232

We pottered around the city, walked along the walls, had lunch in *The Weavers*, and went in the cathedral of course. On the Saturday evening, we had dinner in a charming Italian bistro in Best Lane and for some inexplicable reason – probably to impress – I blew an inordinate amount of money on a bottle of wine that proved to be very ordinary. (I've never repeated the exercise, having learned since that quality wine does not necessarily come at a price.) Slightly intoxicated, we made our way back to the hotel, all of two minutes' walk from the bistro, and proceeded to – as G.I. Bob Johnson in the film might have put it – *fool around*, which did my cough no good whatsoever.

On Sunday morning we had breakfast, checked out, and decided to stroll around the city some more until it was time to head home. This time we ventured into lanes and alleys a little further afield, pretty much at random. We made our way down Palace Street, past the King's School to the rear of the cathedral where Michael Powell himself had studied as a boy, and then got lost. Somewhere – Lord knows where – we came across a second-hand bookshop, something I can never resist. It was on four levels, packed from floor to ceiling with shelves of books on every imaginable subject. An absolute treasure trove for a bookworm like me. We went inside.

My cough had abated somewhat by then, at least for the time being. I was well in control in *Film and Cinema*, *Music and Musicians*, *Military History* and various types of *Fiction*. I could have spent a small fortune in each but managed to resist and enjoyed a pleasurable half an hour or more browsing. Nicola and I went our separate ways, occasionally bumping into each other.

It was when I wandered into *Poetry* that the proverbial brown stuff hit the wind machine.

I am keen on the work of Roger McGough and sought out a couple of his collections; *Blazing Fruit* was one. Not to purchase. I already had a copy as I had set one of the poems in that collection to music some years earlier: *Last Lullaby*. I have no idea what else I looked at, T. S. Eliot perhaps, or one of the poets I had been forced to study at school and subsequently come to enjoy without pressure; Thomas Hardy, Walter de la Mare, Edward Thomas, Tom Gunn, Ted Hughes, Robert Frost. And I would certainly have been on the lookout for any Spike Milligan.

On a far shelf, a large book with a bright green cover caught my eye. My daughter will tell you that animals come to you when searching for a pet; an inexplicable bond that exists as soon as you make contact. I can assure her that the same happens with me and books. I gradually honed in on the green cover as I meandered around the room, which was deserted apart from myself. The writing on the spine was indistinct, so I pulled out the tome and took a look at the front cover.

THE LIMERICK
The famous Paris edition, complete & unexpurgated.
1700 examples.

I adore limericks. It's a standing joke with my nearest and dearest that I can write prose but am clueless when it comes to verse, and whenever I make an attempt it always turns out as a limerick. They are, by and large, synonymous with vulgarity which I assume is part of the attraction. I opened the book.

There were indeed 1700 limericks within, each one numbered, as if to justify the cover title. They were listed in order of subject matter, ranging from *Little Romances* to *Chamber of Horrors* by way of (to name just a few) *Sexual Intercourse, Buggery, Abuses of the Clergy* and *Weak Sisters*. I started to flick through at random. Some were amusing, some funny, the occasional one hilarious. Some of the rhymes were neat, some clever, others inspired. I had decided after reading a dozen or so that I simply had to own this book. Scribbled in pencil inside the front cover was the price – £8. A bargain!

Amusing and delightful though the limericks were, even the best had eked out of me no more than a chuckle… until I came across number 788. It was tucked away innocuously under a section entitled *Gourmands*. Here it is:

> *There once was a baker of Nottingham*
> *Who in making éclairs would put snot in 'em.*
> *When he ran out of snot,*
> *As likely as not,*
> *He'd pull down his pants and jack off in 'em.*

I laughed out loud. And once I started laughing I couldn't stop. Then I began to cough, and once I started I couldn't stop coughing either. Soon I was having difficulty breathing.

I was making a lot of noise. Nicola came in to see

what was going on. I thrust the book at her and managed to blurt out "Buy this for me please" before rushing out of the room, down the stairs and into the street, where I sank onto the pavement with my back against the shop wall... and coughed and coughed.

By the time Nicola came out carrying the book in a brown paper bag, I had managed to regain some control over my respiratory system. I was told I looked purple in the face and that my eyes were bloodshot. When the coughing had abated, I stood up and we wandered around the streets, back towards the centre, until we found somewhere to regain our composure – *Tiny Tim's Tearoom* in Saint Margaret's Street. Even though it was still only late morning, we ordered scones with jam and cream and a pot of tea.

Nicola was curious to know what had set me off in the bookshop and started to take the book out of its bag. I begged her not to; not while we were eating.

By the time the scones had been devoured and we were sipping a second cup of tea, I had explained about number 788. Nicola opened the book, found the limerick in question and read it. She tried at first to feign disapproval, but failed miserably and let out a giggle. She started browsing through, chuckling sporadically. Then she stopped at a page and read a set, one after the other. As she progressed, she burst out laughing several times. Heads turned in the tearoom.

She stopped and slammed the book shut. "740!" she gasped. I took the book and began reading what turned out to be a whole series of limericks recording the scatological adventures of the extraordinarily talented

Farter from Sparta. Nicola, I should have mentioned sooner, was asthmatic. She had started to wheeze and took an inhaler out of her handbag and drew deeply from it. I struggled on with the saga until the final limerick when our eponymous hero tries to fart the storm section of the *William Tell Overture* and ends up shitting himself. Ironically it was an ill-timed cough that had been his downfall.

Nicola was still struggling; chuckling and choking and gasping for breath. I started coughing again. I plopped a ten pound note onto the table, hoping it would cover the bill and, much to the relief of the patrons of *Tiny Tim's Tearoom*, rushed out with Nicola close behind.

Hunched up on the pavement again, I was having real problems, coughing and spluttering. I could exhale but I couldn't breathe in. For a few moments, I was genuinely frightened and thought I was going to die.

Nicola leaned over me and pushed her inhaler into my mouth. "Try this," she said. "Breathe in."

This was not as simple as it sounds. Breathing in was the problem... I couldn't do it. But with a prodigious effort I managed it and as I did Nicola squeezed down the top of the inhaler. I felt some of the spray enter my lungs. Almost instantly I could breathe more easily.

"Again," said Nicola. I did as I was told. Soon I was breathing normally. It was a huge relief. I had no idea what was in the inhaler but I didn't care. The relief was all that mattered. "You should go and see your doctor," she said. "That's more than just an ordinary cough you've got."

And that was my blessing. To have discovered

courtesy of a book of limericks that I had viral bronchitis. On my return home I booked an appointment with my G.P. who made the diagnosis and I soon had my own inhaler.

My relationship with Nicola was not destined to last, but I still have the limerick book. It has given me enormous pleasure over the years. Tucked away within the 1700 limericks are some absolute gems. My all-time favourite is not in fact the one about a baker of Nottingham. It begins *There was a young man of Calcutta*, but it's far too vulgar to repeat in full, and by comparison makes the baker of Nottingham seem a martyr... which, curiously, rhymes with farter.

Far more recently I received a second blessing in Canterbury, of sorts. But that's another story.

13

UNLUCKY FOR SOME

Paula belched. "Lainey, it's a numbers game... dating." She made her statement as emphatically and precisely as she was able under the circumstances – the circumstances being that between them she and Elaine had drunk a bucketful of wine. Unusual to be doing this on a Sunday evening, but Monday was a bank holiday so what the hell. Besides, it was a beautifully warm evening, exceptionally so for early May, and they were sitting on the terrace of a pub on the edge of the Oracle overlooking the River Kennet, having eaten well, and setting the world to rights on a diverse range of topics from the ageing process to, inevitably, men and relationships, Elaine being unhappily single and Paula even more unhappily married. Both in their mid-thirties, they used to work in the same school – Paula teaching, Elaine doing admin – until Elaine moved on. It was their six-monthly catch up.

In terms of looks, they were like chalk and cheese. Elaine was the striking one; slim, petite with a shock of red hair, a pretty face and a natural elegance that brought her more than her fair share of male attention. Paula was short and dumpy with dark hair; attractive features but not outstanding. There was irony in Paula pontificating on the subject of dating when she had no recent personal experience, not since she met her husband in her late teens. Elaine was in fact the veteran.

"How many has it been this time?" asked Paula.

"What do you mean?"

"You know what I mean. How many dates have you had since you split up with Tim and went back on *Plenty of Fish*?"

"His name was Tom."

Paula giggled. "Whatever. There've been so many."

"You liked Tom."

"Until he dumped you for no reason, I liked him until then. Just as well you never moved in together."

Elaine considered Paula's question carefully, then started counting on her hands. She paused: "Including second dates?"

"Have there been any?"

"Cheeky mare, you know very well there have!" Elaine continued totting up and declared: "Excluding second dates… twenty-six."

"In how long?"

"Three months and a bit."

"That's an average of two a week!"

"Whatever back to you."

Paula belched again, as if making room for more wine, then filled the gap with a large slurp of sauvignon blanc. "And how many have you, you know…"

"Bonked?"

"That's what I was referring to."

Elaine started counting again with her fingers. She went through them all on both hands, including thumbs, and started a second run.

"Lainey! You are kidding I hope?"

Elaine grinned. "Of course, what do you think I am! Two actually."

"So that's an average of one in thirteen."

"Jeez, the down side of having a maths teacher for a friend!" She too drank some more wine. "From what you've said, thirteen is probably about the number of years it's been since your Duncan performed his matrimonial duty."

"Yep," confirmed Paula. "Ross is twelve now, add nine months and that's about right."

"Seriously, has it been that long?"

"Apart from a couple of boozy birthday fumbles. I'm thinking about reapplying for my virginity."

"Don't you miss it?"

Paula hesitated as if not wanting to admit the answer. "Yes."

"Doesn't he?"

"It would appear not."

"Do you miss it a little or a lot?"

"Big time."

"Have you still got your…?" asked Elaine, making a buzzing noise.

"Couldn't manage without it. Spend a fortune on batteries."

They guffawed together, loudly and raucously, the way only drunken people can.

"Get yourself a bit on the side," advised Elaine. "It'll work out cheaper."

"I could never do that."

"I beg your pardon! I seem to remember a Christmas do a few years back, and a certain gym teacher…"

Paula coloured up instantly. "That was a mistake, a one off, never to be repeated. I was pissed. Besides we never did it – not everything."

"So what were you doing together in the school hall store room for an hour and a half?"

"We just… I let him…"

Elaine held up her hands. "Woah! Actually, I don't want to know so soon after a chilli con carne! God knows how you manage without it. If I haven't had it for more than a couple of weeks I get twitchy."

"Me too, so I get my pocket rocket out."

"Not as good as the real thing."

"Oh I don't know, it doesn't snore or fart. And the batteries last a lot longer than Duncan ever did!"

More raucous laughter.

"So are you basically content on your own then, Lainey – happy with a fortnightly bonk if it comes your way, and a bit of male company?"

"NO! I am not. I want to be married like you and I want to have kids. I'm thirty-four and the old biological clock is ticking big time. I want a husband to come home to and who loves me like crazy."

"You can have mine."

"Thanks but no thanks. I'd have married Tom if he'd asked. I really loved him and thought he was the one. I was wrong."

"Remind me again why he dumped you?"

Elaine thought for a moment. "The short version is he needed space."

"What for?"

"He never said."

"After how long together?"

"Two years, four months, one week... approximately." Elaine paused for wine. "I've never told you this before but when I met Tom I started seeing a therapist. I wanted it to work so much I thought I'd try and sort out all my demons – see if I could get to the bottom of why all my relationships have failed. I still go occasionally."

"Can't have helped, otherwise you'd still be together."

"It's helped in some ways. I've certainly sorted out a few hang ups from my childhood. But to be honest I'm still of the opinion it simply boils down to finding the right person. The right man for you."

Paula gave her renowned look of smugness. "See, like I said, a numbers game." Then after a pause: "Was Tom a good lover?"

"Pretty good... very gentle, very loving. He kept me satisfied."

The conversation reached a natural pause and both women reached for their wine glasses.

"So now what?" asked Paula. "Keep hunting?"

"That's what I'm doing. He's out there somewhere, I've just got to find the bugger."

"Twenty-six so far, not to mention all the others over the years. How many does it take?"

"How long is a piece of string!"

"Maybe you're trying too hard. Maybe two a week means you're speeding your way through all the available men in the area to the point that you're gonna whizz past Mister Right without seeing him for what he is. Perhaps you ought to slow down."

"Hang on!" said Elaine in exasperation. "One minute you're saying it's a numbers game, the next you're saying I should go on fewer dates! Make up your mind, bird."

"I didn't mean it like that."

"What do you suggest then, Paula?"

"I don't know. I just wonder if maybe you ought to spend a bit more time with each bloke and get to know them better before flitting on to the next one."

"What's the point if you know within ten minutes you don't fancy him, or…?"

"It's not all about sex."

"… or there's no common ground, I was about to say."

"You can't tell that in ten minutes, surely?"

"Take my word for it, you can."

Paula sat back and thought. "Maybe it's the raw material that's wrong then. Maybe the men on *Plenty of Fish* aren't what you're looking for. Why not fork out and go onto a paying site?"

"Been there, done that, more than once. A lot are the same as on *Plenty of Fish* and the others are mostly solicitors and accountants… and teachers. Bore the tits off you."

"Thanks!"

"Come on, Paula. Is there anyone on the teaching staff at Bishop Walton you'd want to spend the rest of your life with?"

"Umm… no."

"I rest my case."

Paula thought some more. "How does it work then? How do you find all these men to go dating with?"

"They send messages to you, you take a look at their photo and profile and decide whether to reply or not."

"So don't you reply, if you're not interested?"

"I used to reply to everyone, but not anymore. No matter how politely you say 'thanks but no thanks' you're likely to get abuse in return, and not very imaginative abuse either. *Lesbian, fuck you*, that sort of thing. Simpler not to. If you don't hear back then you know it's a no."

"How many messages do you get?"

"It varies. Sometimes a couple, maybe up to twenty a day at weekends."

"Christ, all those men! How do you pick out the ones you meet?"

"Well for a start you immediately delete all the ones who don't have a photo…"

"Why?"

"Because they're either married or pig ugly."

"That's a bit harsh."

"Harsh but true."

"Then what?"

"Then you delete the ones who live too far away."

"How far is that?'

"More than ten miles from Reading as far as I'm concerned."

"Are there many?"

"Quite a few. I get them from all over the country. Abroad too… mainly from Ghana of all places. They have usually fallen in love with my photo and think I'm the woman of their dreams. After my money and a British passport of course."

"Fair enough."

"Then the ones who just say 'Hi'. If they can't string a sentence together I'm not interested."

"Anyone else?"

"Anyone with their top off, or holding a fish."

"Are there any left?"

"Enough to get a couple of dates every week."

"And of the twenty-six you've met, you've shagged two. Presumably the pick of the bunch?"

"They were the ones I had a second date with, yes."

"Isn't that a bit, you know… too soon?"

"Not for me. Sex is important to me, so if that's no good I want to know sooner not later. I'm hardly prolific."

Paula gave her a disapproving look. "I'm not sure about that."

"Well that's a personal choice. Thing is, Paula, mostly if I really like someone they're not interested in me, and if they really like me I'm not interested in them. The two so far are the ones where there was some mutual ground. One I never heard from again, so obviously just a player."

"And the other?"

"Couldn't keep it up for more than a few minutes."

Paula grinned. "Perhaps he was nervous."

"I don't care what the problem was. He failed the interview."

"Oh dear."

"So what do you suggest then... where am I going wrong? Come on Paula, put me straight."

"I don't know. The more you tell me the more I'm wondering if Mister Perfect might be in the ones you reject."

"What, amongst the poor, the married and the ugly?" She whistled a fragment of Ennio Morricone.

"I was thinking more of the topless and the anglers. You're not giving them a chance. They might be really nice guys. Or the ones that live more than ten miles away. That's no distance at all, doesn't even take you to Swindon or Basingstoke."

"You've got to cull them somehow. I can't go on twenty dates a week."

"Oh I don't know! Drink up, this one's on me."

"I think I've had enough, Paula. I'm pretty pissed."

"No you're not. We're gonna drink wine until we've sorted this dating malarky out and you've got a proper, structured plan of campaign."

"Knowing you, that will involve a mathematical formula."

"Stranger things have happened. Same again?"

★ ★ ★

Ordinarily, a text message arriving on Elaine's phone gave out a benign, gentle *Ping*.

This morning, however, was not ordinary. This morning, to Elaine, it sounded like a recording of the Great Gate of Kiev slamming shut, tape looped with added reverb. It was truly horrendous, the trauma multiplied by the fact that her iPhone was lying on the pillow right next to her ear.

She sat bolt upright, her bloodshot eyes staring wildly at the wall on the far side of the bedroom. A chair stood in front of it and her PJs were lying neatly over the back. The duvet lay in a crumpled heap beside her. She looked down at herself. She was still wearing her dress from the night before, but curiously no knickers. The urge to pee was strong so she staggered into the bathroom and sat on the loo, rocking backwards and forwards as her sense of balance played tricks on her. As she did so, she noticed her knickers on the floor, presumably where she'd shed them the night before.

Back in the bedroom she lay down, pulled the duvet around her lower body and picked up her mobile. 9:30am. The text was from Paula: *U get home OK?*

Elaine tapped out a reply: *Must have. U?*

The *Ping* from hell again. *Same. In my own bed so must have lol. Gr8 evening.*

Yeh gr8.

U alone?

Of course.

Didn't pull the cab driver then?

Lol. Cheeky mare.

I'm holding you to your pledge.

Uh?

The pledge you made.

248

Wot pledge?

About getting married.

Elaine's fuzzy brain struggled to absorb this last message. *Wot u talking about?*

OMG you don't remember!

Elaine thought back to their after-dinner conversation in the pub. She remembered talking about dating, and totting up how many she'd had recently, and Paula trying to give her advice. But nothing about a pledge to get married. She selected Paula's number and pressed *Call*. The voice that answered mirrored how Elaine felt. Rough.

"Now what!"

"Charming. Have you woken up grumpy?"

"No he's still asleep."

Elaine sniggered. "What's this about a pledge?"

"Do you honestly not remember? You must have been pisster than me."

"There's no such word."

"I made it up. English is an evolving language."

"Come on, tell me about the pledge."

"Okay, so we were talking about how many dates you've had off *Plenty of Fish*, and how you whittle down your messages by distance from Reading, whether they fish or can string a sentence together."

"I remember that."

"So, we ascertained that you've had twenty-six dates and shagged two of them – giving an average of thirteen before you drop your drawers."

"I can think of more subtle ways of putting it, but I kind of remember that too. Go on."

249

"Well, after some lively discussion and agreement that this sort of thing can't go on forever, plus my influence that you could be missing out on the man of your dreams by undervaluing some of these guys…"

"Yeh yeh, spit it out."

"We agreed that you would pledge, which you did…"

"Tell me for Christ sake!"

"That you will have no more than thirteen more dates… and that you will marry one of them."

"I never did!"

"You did."

"I don't believe you."

"You don't have to, I've got it recorded on my iPhone. I think it's called a *Voice Memo*."

"Let me hear."

"Hang on, I'm hauling my ass out of bed so as not to disturb Duncan. He's making grumbling noises… dressing gown on… and… in the kitchen." Elaine heard water pouring into a kettle and the flick of a switch. "Right, are you ready?"

"Ready."

"Here goes."

Elaine cringed with embarrassment as the recording played back and she listened to herself making the pledge, just as Paula had described. Her voice was very slurred and there was a good deal of background noise, but the words were unambiguous. The voice stated clearly that she, Elaine Kirby, pledged she would have thirteen more dates, and not a single date more, and one of them would be the man she would marry.

When it came to the end, Paula said: "There you go,

250

so you can't deny it and, what's more, I'm going to hold you to it."

"You can't, I was hammered!"

"Makes no difference, it was a pledge. And a pledge is a pledge."

"But thirteen... of all numbers to choose."

"It chose you. Unlucky for some, but not for you."

"Oh God I think I'm going to throw up."

"And no cheating! To make sure you don't, I'm going to insist you keep me posted about every single date, with feedback, and if you try and squeeze in extra dates without telling me there will be a forfeit."

"What?"

"To be decided."

"Paula, I have to go now."

"What's up?"

"I really am going to throw up..."

★ ★ ★

By early afternoon, having slept some more and downed several glasses of water, two strong black coffees and munched on a piece of dry toast, Elaine was beginning to feel half human again. She sat on the tiny balcony of her tiny flat with its view of the distant river and Caversham beyond, and mulled over her predicament.

How was she going to get out of this one!

It was crazy, a piece of drunken foolishness. She had no intention of sticking to it. She would carry on dating, but the pledge was nonsense. Nor would Paula make her stick to it; although she had sounded pretty adamant on the phone earlier. She'd been winding her up, of course, and it didn't really matter what Paula thought, it was her life and she'd not be pressured into such a huge decision based on a boozy speech recorded on a mobile phone. Her first marriage had been a brief and total disaster; she'd only been eighteen… still a kid. It had lasted under a year. Number two would last forever, so he had to be perfect.

It was bright and sunny, and becoming very warm, a pleasant change for a Mayday bank holiday; nice also that the first day of May actually fell on a Monday. The balcony caught the afternoon sun. It was on the top storey of the block, so private and not overlooked. She nipped inside, exchanged t-shirt and tracky bottoms for a snakeskin string bikini and returned to settle back on her chair with her feet up on the wall and her aptly named laptop on her lap. Almost immediately she undid her bikini top and let it drop onto the floor next to her.

Resisting the temptation to log on to *Plenty of Fish*, she chose instead to check for emails. Her inbox contained about thirty messages; half were alerts from *Plenty of Fish* that she had new messages, others offered vouchers for discounts at *Café Rouge* and *Pizza Express*, and there were a handful from friends and family. Towards the top was one from Paula Gilbert. In the subject box she saw a single word: *PLEDGE*. There was an attachment – an Excel spreadsheet.

Elaine clicked to open the message: *Hi Lainey, attached is something to help you keep track of your last ever thirteen dates. I want you to update it every week and send over for me to monitor. If you think this is intrusive and excessive, you're right lol. Love Paula xx*

The spreadsheet consisted of thirteen sets of rows each with columns and headers:

1. Name:	Date of Date:	Duration:	Shaggable?	2nd Date?	Marriable?
Feedback:					

Having studied it for a while, Elaine clicked on *Reply*: *Thanks, Paula, but I think I'll pass. If I stick to this I'll end up marrying someone for the sake of it, make a massive mistake and be miserable and shackled to someone totally unsuitable… bit like you honey ha ha!"*

A few minutes later Paula sent a text in response: *Mrs Doyle would say… give it a try anyway… go on go on. Besides, you made a pledge and pledges are binding.*

Elaine shook her head in disbelief. *Ur mental, do u honestly expect me 2 stick to this? We were just mucking about surely.*

Try it. I don't want an old maid for a friend.

Elaine switched off her phone and all but threw it onto the little round table by her side. Ridiculous! Not worth spending any more time over. She focused on her laptop and logged on to *Plenty of Fish*. There were twenty messages in her inbox. Six had no photo so she deleted them immediately. Then she sat back, sipped some water, and began ploughing her way through the rest. An hour later she had whittled them down to three and by the end of the afternoon had arranged a date for Wednesday and another for the weekend. The third candidate had fallen by the wayside having been too curious too soon about the size of her breasts.

★ ★ ★

The following Sunday afternoon, having washed up and tidied away after lunch, and observed Duncan slump into a doze on the sofa, Paula sat down at the computer in the spare bedroom and tapped in her email address and password. To her surprise, and delight, there was a message from *LaineyLou* timed half an hour earlier. The email contained no message, but it had an attachment. Paula opened the Excel spreadsheet. Two sets had been populated. She gazed in fascination at the entries:

Name. 1:	Date of Date:	Duration:	Shaggable?	2nd Date?	Marriable?
HUGH	Wed 3.5.17	2 hours	Yes	Hope so	Yes
Feedback:	Good start, really nice guy, enjoyed his company, made me laugh. Smelt really nice. Loads in common. 2 hours flew by. Goodnight kiss made me tingle. Probably the nicest man I've met since I started dating again. Reckon he's minted, drives a BMW. Hey Paula maybe this wasn't a bad idea after all. Not sure how he felt about me. See if he asks me out again. Bloody well hope so. If not 12 more chances left!				

A good start indeed, agreed Paula. Maybe thirteen dates wouldn't be necessary after all! She scrolled down.

Name. 2:	Date of Date:	Duration:	Shaggable?	2nd Date?	Marriable?
FRANK	Sat 6.5.17	40 mins	No	No way	No!
Feedback:	All the things Hugh was… this guy wasn't. Arrogant, rude, condescending. A knob. End of.				

Oh dear! Paula couldn't help giggling. You win some you lose some I suppose. She tapped out a text to Elaine: *Hugh is hot, Frank is not? LOL*

Too right! came the instant reply.

Have you heard from him – Hugh I mean?

Yeh sent me a text saying he enjoyed meeting and let's do it again, nothing since.

Do I get to see a photo?

Maybe when this is all over, you can see all 13.

Meany.

The following Sunday was a repeat. After lunch, Paula disappeared upstairs with a coffee and logged on. An email from Elaine was waiting for her with an updated spreadsheet attached.

Name. 3:	Date of Date:	Duration:	Shaggable?	2nd Date?	Marriable?
DAVE	Tue 9.5.17	30 mins	No	No	No
Feedback:	*Frank's twin brother! 30 mins of my life I resent having wasted forever being talked at by a beer bellied twat as he stared round the pub at every other female with a pulse. Know any good convents?*				

Yikes! A couple of bad ones on the trot. What next!

Name. 4:	Date of Date:	Duration:	Shaggable?	2nd Date?	Marriable?
JON	Fri 12.5.17	1 hr 10 mins	If desperate	If desperate	Not even if desperate
Feedback:	*Decent enough guy, quite enjoyed his company, he was very nervous and unsure of himself, saw his hand shaking at one stage, lacks confidence and charisma. A friend maybe? Maybe not. Have met a dozen like him before. Miss Perfect is out there somewhere for him but I'm not her. Shame coz he writes really well and sends lovely messages.*				

She turned to her phone and sent a text: *I feel sorry for Jon. Any news from Hugh?*

No!

The next weekly update arrived early this time. On Friday evening Paula checked her emails and found a new one which had been there since the night before.

Name. 5:	Date of Date:	Duration:	Shaggable?	2nd Date?	Marriable?
GLYNN	Sun 14.5.17	40 mins	No	No	No
Feedback:	Married! Could tell as soon as we met. Didn't look anything like his photo, probably a mate's or stolen off Facebook. Preoccupied with his phone, kept nipping off to the loo, to text her indoors I reckon. I saw a line of paler skin round the fourth finger on his left hand, where his ring sits. In his pocket probably. I tested him by asking for his home number, some bullshit answer about it being out of order. Not to worry, I said, let's have a second date in the week, I'll come and pick you up, what's your address? More bullshit. Been there done that before. Must think I'm stupid. Hate sodding time wasters!				

A thought popped in to Paula's head. She wondered if Duncan was playing around like this; on *Plenty of Fish* with no photo (or a false one), seeing if he could catch a bit on the side. Would explain why their sex life was non-existent if he was getting it elsewhere. Perhaps he didn't always go to darts twice a week. The thought vanished. He wouldn't, not Duncan. Didn't have it in him. He loved his darts.

Name. 6:	Date of Date:	Duration:	Shaggable?	2nd Date?	Marriable?
SIMON	Wed 17.5.17	2 hours	Yes then No	Never	No
Feedback:	Was going really well, attractive, fun dinner together, lots of chat, made me laugh, and I was thinking this guy I could really go for, all good UNTIL… saying goodnight in the car park. Hands everywhere, on my tits, up my skirt, over my arse and his tongue so far down my throat I thought I was gonna gag. When he realised he wasn't getting any he just walked over to his car and drove off.				

Lucky cow, thought Paula, imagining how good it would feel to have hands all over *her* tits and arse. Then

256

as an afterthought: *If he'd hung on until the second date he could have had the lot!*

On Sunday they exchanged emails.

ELAINE: *Hi, Paula. Well I heard from Hugh again, phoned me in the week and arranged to go out for dinner last night. Took me to a lovely restaurant – the French Horn at Sonning. Expensive! Told you he was minted, he paid thank god! Then back to my place, definitely passed the nookie test, he's quite a stud... feel like I've been well and truly rogered this morning LOL. Sorry, I know, too much information. Really like him but not sure about his motives, reckon he could be a player. And if he's seriously looking for someone he could easily go up market from me. Got a feeling that's it, probably won't hear from him again now he's had his end away, but who knows, if this whole 13 dates thing doesn't find me a husband I'd be happy to meet up with him once in a while to be wined and dined and the rest.*

PAULA: *Lainey, don't put yourself down. You may have wowed him too for all you know. Hope so, he sounds like a bit of a catch. The French Horn is really posh! Never been but would love to. The best Duncan can do for a treat is a Harvester or Wetherspoons. By the way that Simon sounds a nasty piece of work. I hope you fought him off bravely in that car park. How horrible to be mauled like that, although as a frustrated wife I wouldn't mind the attention. Only kidding. Disgusting behaviour. So, six dates – nearly halfway. How you feeling about it all, or are you quietly setting your hopes on Hugh?*

ELAINE: *Hugh's not gonna come to anything, I'm pretty*

certain, so I'll plod on, besides you told me a pledge is a pledge and I've got no choice. Can't let you down! I'm chatting to several blokes at the moment, a Peter, an Aaron and another Peter, though he likes to be called Pete.

A week later came the next instalment. Paula had been dying to hear the latest and had emailed Elaine on the Friday evening begging for news. She got short shrift: *You'll have to wait!*

As it turned out the update arrived on Saturday afternoon.

Name. 7:	Date of Date:	Duration:	Shaggable?	2nd Date?	Marriable?
AARON	Tue 23.5.17	1 hr 50 mins	Yes	Yes	Quite poss!
Feedback:	*Lovely guy, older than me (and older than he said he was in his profile!), late 40s I guess, but that's fine, young at heart so numbers don't always matter. Good looking, with a wicked sense of humour and made me feel very relaxed. Didn't want to say goodnight. A gentleman too, just a peck on the cheek and a hug when we said goodnight. Nicer than Hugh? Maybe not but a very close second, seems very keen, things are looking up again! 2nd date already arranged.*				

Wow, thought Paula – competition for Hugh! A good thing to take her mind off him. This one sounded promising. Please God, let him be Mister Right. Next was one of the Peters.

Name. 8:	Date of Date:	Duration:	Shaggable?	2nd Date?	Marriable?
PETER	Fri 26.5.17	45 mins	Maybe	Maybe	Maybe
Feedback:	*Nice enough guy but not sure what I thought about him, the quiet enigmatic type. Curious, not sure if I fancied him or not and what I thought of him. No oil painting but there's something about him… there's like an inner flame burning in there, a tad sinister even. Tempted to try and get to the bottom of it if he asks me out again. Probably an axe murderer or something LOL.*				

This had Paula beginning to text but she changed her mind and emailed instead: *Lainey, I'm really worried. Stay away from Peter if you get that vibe off him. A potential axe murderer – Jesus! Don't you take any chances. Aaron sounds great, the best yet in my opinion. And you sound very keen on him. Stick with him pleeeeeeese?*

ELAINE: *Aw thanks honey, I appreciate your concern, but don't worry, I forgot to say that Peter's much too old for me, like fifty, dated him out of curiosity mostly. And way too long in the tooth to be a serial killer LOL. I'll definitely heed your advice. I've got another Peter tomorrow, or Pete.*

Paula felt reassured by Elaine's reply. She clearly knew what she was doing and there'd be nothing happening with Peter.

Unusually, on Monday evening came a single update, presumably because Elaine wanted to get it off her chest and couldn't wait until the weekend.

Name. 9:	Date of Date:	Duration:	Shaggable?	2nd Date?	Marriable?
PETE	Sun 28.5.17	25 mins	Puke!	NOOO!	No brainer
Feedback:	AARRGGHH! Horror story! 15 years older than his pic at least, 10 stone heavier, no eye contact, no personality, no conversation, no brain. No way! Reckon someone else wrote his profile for him coz he could hardly speak English. Couldn't get away fast enough. Went to the loo after 10 mins and was tempted to try and squeeze out of the window. He just sent me a text saying: gr8 date wens the next 1… to which the answer is NEVER!				

Paula winced. She pinged off a text: *God he sounds awful. My money's on Aaron.*

Later that evening, as Paula lay in bed reading, came a reply. *U could be right, just had 2nd date, went well, he's crazy about me.*

Did you…?

I wanted to but he's a bit backward at coming forward. Had a good snog though.

Who's number ten then?

Reginald, on Wednesday. Sounds stuffy with a name like that but his messages are actually very funny. Seems familiar, might have dated him before in a previous life. AND… guess who's been in touch…?

Hugh?

Hugh! Wants to take me out again.

Wow, u pleased?

You bet.

Still reckon Aaron's the man.

I'm reserving judgment til I know if he can ring my bell.

RIGHT that's enuf, I'm off. Nite Lainey xx

On Thursday came another single update.

Name. 10:	Date of Date:	Duration:	Shaggable?	2nd Date?	Marriable?
REGINALD	Wed 31.5.17	3 hours	No	(see below)	(see below)
Feedback:	OMG Reggie the Wedgie – we went to school together! Great to see him, such a fabulous evening catching up and reminiscing. Thought he sounded familiar but didn't recognise him from his photo and profile but he says he thought it was me. Was the class clown, still makes me laugh. Lost his wife to cancer last year… v. sad. Talking about organising a reunion. Don't fancy him or anything but great to be back in touch, would love to see him again.				

Then it was back to a Sunday afternoon message, again just a single entry and the longest yet. Paula's eyes opened wider and wider with ever line.

Name. 11:	Date of Date:	Duration:	Shaggable?	2nd Date?	Marriable?
WES	Sat 3.6.17	4 hours	OH YES!	No	No

Feedback:	Don't be cross with me Paula, pleeese! I couldn't help myself, he was just so fit! 30, Ex-army, muscles everywhere, honest to god, sitting in the pub I must have been drooling and I could tell so were women at other tables. He oozed sex, like at some kind of animal level, bit like Daniel Craig only way sexier, I kid you not. His hand touched my arm when he handed me my drink and it was like an electric shock. Sooo, after a couple of drinks he suggests we take a drive somewhere quiet and I just went along with it, followed him like I'm in a trance, allowing it to happen. We drove out Riseley way and parked down a track somewhere near the country park, he'd obviously been there before, often I reckon. I got in the back of his car with him, and without a word being spoken, we stripped each other naked and... well, we fucked, and we fucked... and we fucked. It was outrageous! He was like a machine. I came four times. I've NEVER come four times before in my life, ever! I say naked, I forgot to take my heels off. They dug into the fabric in the roof of his car and ripped it, he didn't notice so I said nothing. He flipped me about like a ragdoll, we were outside over the bonnet at one stage, then when he'd eventually finished with me (and he took forever!!!) we put our clothes back on, said goodnight and I drove home. Paula, that man sorted my head out more in two hours than therapy has in two years. I feel fantastic.

Paula read it through several times. She felt shocked and aroused in equal measures, and, it had to be said, plain envious. "I've never come four times either," she said out loud. "Ever."

"What was that?" said Duncan who had come upstairs to use the loo.

"Nothing," she replied, getting up to close the door. She was sorely tempted to lock herself in and put her pocket rocket to good use. *God, reading this was better than watching porn*, she thought, which she sometimes did when the urge was strong, and it was a darts night, and Ross had gone to bed. As she sat gazing at the screen, a text pinged in.

U still want to know me?

U still breathing?

LOL yeh but I've been walking like John Wayne all day.

Not surprised! My god woman what r u like?

It just happened, couldn't help myself.

Risky. He obviously does that a lot.

Yeh I know. Honest to god though, Paula, it was worth it.

Did u use protection?

Always, sweetie. Always.

Phew! 2nd date?

Never to be repeated. Nothing in common, apart from the obvious.

So who's next?

No idea! Wes scrambled my brains. He'll be a hard act to follow – hard being the key word LOL.

Better than therapy u said.

You bet. I feel so clear headed, like I've got something completely out of my system. I thought Hugh was good but this guy fair filleted me.

ENOUGH! I'm off for a cold shower. Two more dates to go then it's decision time, Lainey. I'm still betting on Aaron.

Yep, back in the real world he's a contender. 3rd date tomorrow night. Hope my fanny's got some feeling back by then.

GOOD BYE!!! X

That evening, Elaine sent Paula a text asking if they could chat. Glad for an excuse to escape the telly, Paula wandered upstairs and lay on the bed with her phone in one hand and a glass of wine in the other. She scrolled down her list of recent calls and touched *LaineyLou*. Elaine answered immediately.

"What's up chicken?"

"Oh Paula, I'm all mixed up."

"Your brains still scrambled?"

Elaine chuckled. "Sort of."

"That Wes sounds quite a guy."

"God yeh, I've never known anything like it. But that's not why I'm mixed up… that's actually cleared things up for me. It was pure lust – you know, rutting sex. No basis for a relationship. I'm getting confused with this whole thirteen thing. I don't know where it's all leading. I've got two dates left, that's all… which is nothing. I'm running out of options."

"Do you need any more?"

"Do I? That's the problem, I don't know. There's Hugh and Aaron, I really like them both. I think I'd be happy settling down with either of them."

"Well, Lainey, if that's the case then our objective has been achieved already, wouldn't you say? Of course Aaron hasn't passed the nookie test yet. That might whittle it down to just a one-horse race."

"True. I'll find out tomorrow night. Thing is, I really like them both and can see either of them as a long-term partner… but they may not see it the same way. This isn't about finding a boyfriend, Paula, it's about marrying someone… that's the pledge. So if Aaron doesn't work out, that leaves Hugh. Either way, it's very early days. I'm not convinced Hugh isn't a player, we haven't spent more than a few hours together. I really like him, but a potential husband? I have no idea how he's feeling about me."

"Hmm, you're right of course. Maybe we're being a bit prescriptive with the pledge. Last thing I would want to do is push you into something that's potentially a huge mistake."

"I wouldn't allow you to."

"That's fair enough. Sorry, Lainey… if I've put you under pressure doing this. I thought I was helping. Maybe I'm not. Maybe I'm raising your expectations."

"It's fine. Actually it's been a good thing. You've made me focus more on the men I'm dating. When I look back on the twenty-six dates I had before, I was going through the motions. You were right, I could have met up with Mister Perfect and not even realised. At least this time I've been looking beyond the façade and seeing the person behind it. Forget the time wasters like the married one and the groper…"

"And the one with no brain."

"Him too. I've learned something from this, and that's to try and get to know them better. Not to be too superficial."

"Like it was with Wes?"

"Aw come on, Paula, he was an exception. You know what I'm saying. Would you like his number?"

"Yes please."

"You're kidding me!"

"I'm kidding you, I think. What shall we do then, forget the whole thing? Call a halt?"

"I don't know… I'm confused and feeling all dated out to be honest. I'm not really fussed about meeting anyone else at the moment. I just want to spend time with Hugh, or Aaron, and see how it goes."

"Fair enough. Mission accomplished I would say."

"Only if wedding bells result, and that's far from likely."

"I suppose the whole idea was a bit ambitious. I've enjoyed the journey though, better than a TV soap reading your feedback every week. Especially Wes – I reckon I got as much pleasure out of him as you did, reading what you got up to!"

"Did you... you know?"

"I did."

"Good for you. So where do we go from here?"

"You tell me."

"I don't know!"

"Okay," said Paula, "here's a plan. How about, see how it goes with Aaron tomorrow. If he doesn't match up in the y-front department you know that Hugh is the successful candidate. Have you got another date with him in the diary?"

"Tuesday."

"Great. You could be wrong about him being a player. Let's face it, he's doing the running. Meanwhile, for the sake of the pledge, why not go on the last two dates as well? You never know, there might be a late contender. Have you got any lined up?"

"Thursday, and possibly next Saturday but either will get bumped if Hugh or Aaron want to do something."

"Keep me posted as always. How does that sound, you still confused?"

"Thanks, Paula, I think I'm clearer in the head now. After number thirteen let's meet up and eat and drink and talk."

"You bet – can't wait. Good luck tomorrow with Aaron."

"Thanks. He's taken his details off *Plenty of Fish* already. Says he doesn't want to talk to anyone else now until he sees how it pans out with me."

"Aw that's a good sign, he sounds really sweet. How about Hugh, is he still on there?"

"Yes," said Elaine sullenly. "Logged on twenty-four/ seven it seems."

"Not so good. Like I said before, I reckon Aaron's the one."

"I think you could be right."

"Me too."

"Night Paula."

Apart from a few texts à propos nothing in particular, Paula heard no further news about dating until the following weekend. She made her Sunday afternoon pilgrimage to the spare bedroom in the hope that the final update in the *thirteen data saga* would be waiting for her. She was not disappointed.

Name. 12:	Date of Date:	Duration:	Shaggable?	2ⁿᵈ Date?	Marriable?
ROWAN	Thu 8.6.17	1 hour	No	No	No
Feedback:	A difficult one, my heart wasn't in it after a romantic evening with Aaron on Tuesday which was lovely. With a name like Rowan I kept thinking of Mr Bean, he was a bit like that, nerdy, works for a software company in Bracknell. A nice guy, polite, charming, smart, I liked him, but the timing was all wrong. When we left the pub I told him I didn't think we were suited and he looked gutted, said he'd really like to see me again. I felt bad driving home. Bollocks to all this dating. By the way, Aaron passed the test... worth waiting for LOL.				

Almost inevitable, thought Paula. Rowan didn't stand a chance. Didn't sound like Lainey's type anyway. And so to the thirteenth and last. Probably the same again, an *also ran*, especially after Aaron had succeeded in keeping in the running. My God, that woman was getting so much sex! Paula's envy was turning into outright jealousy and she felt strongly now that she was missing out. Maybe she should ask for Wes's number; get something well and truly out of her system too. Duncan need never know. But Wes probably wouldn't be interested in an overweight older bird like her. From what Elaine said, women were dropping at his feet – he could pick and choose. Perhaps he had an older brother. Paula pulled herself out of a developing daydream and focused on the last entry on the spreadsheet.

Name, 13:	Date of Date:	Duration:	Shaggable?	2ⁿᵈ Date?	Marriable?
TIM	Sun 10.6.17	3 hours	Maybe	Maybe	Maybe
Feedback:	*A very pleasant surprise. Another nice guy, felt like I'd known him for years, easy to talk to and we talked a lot. Was only meant to be a drink but we ended up having dinner and then walking along the river. We even held hands! Not what I was expecting and a lovely way to end this little pledge idea. Thanks Paula, you're a top mate. Looking forward to meeting up and tying this all up with you. Xxx*				

Paula smiled. Ah that was nice. At least the last one hadn't been a total waste of time and a chore. It sounded as if Elaine liked him. But the feedback was not all glowing like it had been with Hugh and Aaron, so presumably still a two-man race.

★ ★ ★

"Come on then," said Paula eagerly. "I've heard all about them, now let's see what they look like." Elaine moved her chair closer to her friend and fired up her iPad.

It was a fortnight later. They were sitting in the same pub near the Oracle where the pledge had been made two months earlier. It was midsummer now and just past the longest day, so even though nine in the evening it was still light. They had talked about the dating over dinner, at length; Paula asking question upon question, Elaine trying her best to answer. Yes, she had seen both Hugh and Aaron; no, she didn't have a favourite; yes, they both were still keen; yes, she could see what they looked like.

Elaine opened up a folder on her desktop titled *Dates Pledge*. Inside, as well as an Excel spreadsheet icon, were two rows of sub-folders, each bearing a man's name. Paula recognised them all: *Hugh, Frank, Dave, Jon, Glynn, Simon, Aaron, Peter, Pete, Reginald, Wes, Rowan, Tim*. Inside every folder was a single photo, cut and pasted off *Plenty of Fish*.

"Who would you like to see first?" said Elaine.

The reply was instantaneous. "Wes."

Elaine guffawed. "I should have guessed. Okay let's get it over with." Elaine clicked on Wes's folder then the photo file inside it. An image appeared, filling the screen; a man wearing tight jeans and a white t-shirt with biceps bulging beneath the short sleeves, a tanned face, perfect features and light-brown hair cropped short. He had one of those smiles that emanates from eyes as well as mouth.

Paula gazed at the photo. "Oh my God," she gasped. "He's absolutely totally drop dead gorgeous!" She squirmed a little in her seat.

"Isn't he?"

"Now I understand. I think I'd probably have done the same as you."

"What, ripped his car roof with your heels?"

"And the rest! Oh lord, can you email me that photo? I'd like to study it in my own time."

"You dirty old bird – alright, if you like."

"I like."

"Now please concentrate, this is not about you wetting your knickers over Wes. Look, this is Hugh."

An image appeared of a well-dressed man leaning against an expensive looking car, smiling warmly towards the camera. He was rather stocky in build and had dark, wavy hair.

"Hmm," said Paula. "Looks a bit of a smoothy."

"He is. Lovely personality though, and fun to be with."

"I think I prefer Wes."

"Well start thinking with your brain and not your fanny then!"

"Sorry." Paula sipped some wine. "He looks very nice. Now what about Aaron?"

Elaine clicked some more and soon they were looking at a very different man; older, slimmer, with a receding hairline. He was more casually dressed than Hugh and although not smiling, he had a distinct twinkle in his eye and an expression that suggested he was somehow flirting with the camera.

"Ooh I like Aaron,' said Paula. "He looks nice… a bit cheeky, and warmer, more empathic than Hugh."

"You could be right. He's very romantic, says lovely things about me. So what do you think?"

"I think you know what I think."

"Aaron."

"He's the one."

Elaine looked across at her friend, gazing into her eyes as if trying to weigh her up in some way… making an assessment. She said nothing. The look went on longer than was comfortable for Paula.

"What's up, Lainey? Why are you staring at me like that?" The gaze continued to the point that it became unsettling. "Lainey, you're spooking me here, what's going on?"

Elaine picked her handbag up off the floor. "Will you do me a favour?"

"Depends what it is."

"Will you turn away for a minute?"

"What for?"

"Please, will you just do it… for me?"

"No, I don't trust you."

"Well shut your eyes then."

Paula gave Elaine a deeply suspicious look, picked up her wine glass, turned sideways on her chair and clammed her eyelids together. "Whatever you're doing, be quick." She heard some rustling, then the handbag being plonked back onto the floor.

"Okay you can look now."

Paula opened her eyes and turned back round, looking at Elaine sitting opposite her. She appeared exactly the same as she had before, looking elegant as always in a white trouser suit, elbows on the table, hands curled around the stem of her wine glass. "What?"

Elaine picked up her glass with her left hand and raised it in the air. "A toast," she announced. "To my fab friend." Puzzled but happy to oblige, Paula lifted up her glass. "Thank you for being the best mate in the world and for everything you've done for me. Paula, I cannot thank you enough."

"But I haven't done anything. What have I done?"

As the glasses clinked together, Paula's attention moved from Elaine's face to the hand around her glass. Something was glistening. On her fourth finger was a ring that had not been there two minutes earlier. It looked like white gold with a single diamond held in place by four claws. A large diamond.

Paula gasped. "Lainey! What the…!"

"I'm engaged."

In her excitement, Elaine had spoken louder than she intended. The group of women at the next table overheard and started cheering and clapping. They shouted "Congratulations!' and "Go girl!" A wit amongst them said: "Keep wearing those trousers, darling, you'll need to."

Paula leaned forward and kissed her on the cheek and gave her a huge hug. They both had tears in their eyes. "You old sly boots, I don't know what to say. I am so happy for you." She sat down again, pulled a tissue out of her bag and dried her eyes. "Congratulations."

"Thanks Paula. Seriously, without you and the pledge this wouldn't have happened."

From behind her tissue Paula said: "Actually, I do have something to say – something rather important. Who the bloody hell are you engaged to? No, don't tell me, let me guess. It's Aaron isn't it? You took my advice. It's Aaron."

Elaine shook her head. "Not Aaron."

"What! Oh my God… so it's Hugh! Well I never,

that's a surprise. I know you really like him, and he's clearly a lovely guy. Huge congratulations, you'll be so so happy together, Lainey. Aw this is such exciting news!"

"Not Hugh."

Paula froze, statue-like, then slumped back in her chair. "But... but... if not Hugh or Aaron, who the hell else?" In her head she skimmed through the thirteen dates. "Is it Peter, the enigmatic one?" Elaine shook her head. "Reggie the Wedgie?" Elaine shook again. "Not Mister Bean surely!"

"Don't be daft, of course not."

Paula leaned forward and clutched Elaine's arm. "Wes! Please don't tell me it's Wes?"

"No, not Wes either. I'd be dead from exhaustion in six months." Elaine touched her iPad and it came to life again. She scrolled along the rows of folders until she came to the one at the very end; the thirteenth.

"Tim?" said Paula incredulously.

"That's right."

"But I didn't think he'd wowed you. Nice guy, you said and you felt like you'd known him for years, but that was all."

"Actually, Paula, I *have* known him for years." She opened up the photo in the folder. The imagine was very familiar to them both.

"Tom!"

Elaine took her friend's hand. "I played a bit of a trick on you, I'm afraid, telling you he was Tim not Tom. Sorry."

Paula took a huge slug of wine and slammed her glass

down on the table. "You'd better buy me a drink and tell me what the hell is going on. I am totally confused!"

With wine glasses replenished, Elaine explained.

"It's actually quite simple. I came across Tom on *Plenty of Fish* soon after we started the pledge. Or rather he came across me. I'm lazy and don't do searches, don't go looking, I wait for men to contact me. Tom had done a search and I'd come up top on matching his criteria. You can see who's looked at your profile, and so when I checked who'd looked at mine, there he was. When I looked at his profile in return, he would have known that too. Turns out he'd only just joined and I was about the first person he came across. He didn't contact me immediately, not until I was well into the pledge. A chatty message, asking how I was, that sort of stuff. I replied saying *all good*, keeping it very brief. We swapped a few more, all light and fluffy. Then one morning I get a text from him saying: *I miss u xxx*.

"How did you feel?" asked Paula.

"Confused, mixed up. I was enjoying the pledge and by then I'd met Hugh and Aaron and was seriously moving forward. Tom was in the past. I'd also just had my brains banged out by Wes, so when you and I spoke the day after and I was mixed up, it was as much about Tom as all else that was going on."

"What did you do?"

"I texted back: *Miss u 2 xxx*."

"Why didn't you tell me?"

"It was nothing to do with the pledge. I didn't want to talk about it."

"So then what?"

273

"We arranged to meet. He then became date number thirteen. I called him Tim to stop you putting two and two together. We were just going to have a drink, for old time sake. That was all. Honest."

"And?"

"And… it was just so wonderful to see him. I knew straight away I still loved him and it all came flooding back. He told me he'd been miserable, and splitting up from me had been the biggest mistake of his life… and he wanted me back."

"Did you believe him?"

"When we walked by the river after dinner, he was crying his eyes out. So emotional. Yes I believed him. But I had very mixed feelings, as you can imagine, having been dumped unceremoniously. He told me he did it to test himself, to see how he would feel without me in his life any longer, and that it hurt like hell. *Bit of an extreme way of finding out*, I told him. He just nodded and cried. Anyway, we agreed to meet a couple of days later. We both threw a sickie and drove over to Windsor and walked in the Great Park – one of our old haunts. We held hands for three solid hours. Then, when we were halfway round Virginia Water lake, he suddenly went down on one knee and proposed!"

"What did you say?"

"I told him I'd think about it. Then two seconds later I said I'd thought long enough and the answer was yes! It's what I always wanted."

"What about Hugh and Aaron?"

"They simply went out of my head. I forgot about them. I've seen them of course, I haven't lied about that, but only to tell them that I won't be taking it any further."

"How did they take it?"

"Hugh got angry, said *screw you* and stormed off. Aaron was very upset, wished me the very best and said if I changed my mind he'd have me back tomorrow."

"I was right about those two then."

"I don't think you're very often wrong, Paula."

"Well, well, well. So, Operation Pledge has turned up trumps... though not at all how I expected."

"You and me alike."

"Let's have another look at that ring? It's beautiful. Lainey, I am genuinely thrilled for you. You deserve this and all the happiness that lies ahead for you... and Tim."

"Tom!"

"Oh yeh, sorry, Tom. When's the big day?"

"To be decided."

"Can I be your maid of honour?"

"I wouldn't have anyone else!" Elaine fumbled in her bag, pulled out a Post-it note folded in half and handed it across to Paula. "Here, a prezzie for you. A thank you gift from me."

Paula looked down at the yellow rectangle of paper and unfolded it. It contained a mobile phone number. "What's this?"

"Wes." Elaine leaned forward so as not to be overheard. "Use it once, and once only. Get him to rearrange your brains like he did mine then start seriously considering your future life." She drained her glass. "When you've done that, we'll have one of these boozy evenings together and work out another pledge... only this time for *you*."